Now We Are Ten

Celebrating the First Ten Years of NewCon Press

Now We Are Ten

Celebrating the First Ten Years of NewCon Press

Edited by Ian Whates

NEWCON PRESS

NewCon Press
England

First edition, published in the UK July 2016
by NewCon Press

NCP 100 (hardback)
NCP 101 (softback)

10 9 8 7 6 5 4 3 2 1

ISBN: 978-1-910935-18-7 (hardback)
978-1-910935-19-4 (softback)

Text layout by Storm Constantine

Contents

Introduction by Ian Whates 7
The Final Path – Genevieve Cogman 9
Women's Christmas – Ian McDonald 19
Pyramid – Nancy Kress 27
Liberty Bird – Jaine Fenn 33
Zanzara Island – Rachel Armstrong 53
Ten Sisters – Eric Brown 65
Licorice – Jack Skillingstead 81
How to Grow Silence from Seed – Tricia Sullivan 95
The Time Travellers' Ball (A Story in Ten Words) – Rose Biggin 117
Dress Rehearsal – Adrian Tchaikovsky 119
The Tenth Man – Bryony Pearce 137
Rare as a Harpy's Tear – Neil Williamson 156
Utopia +10 – J. A. Christy 159
Ten Love Songs to Change the World– Peter F. Hamilton 171
Ten Days – Nina Allan 193
Front Row Seat to the End of the World – E. J. Swift 235
About the Authors 259
NewCon Press: the First Ten Years 263

Introduction

Ian Whates

I still have to pinch myself at the realisation that NewCon Press has been around for ten years. You see, the imprint was only supposed to exist for one single book, produced as a fund raiser. In October 2005 I helped organise a convention, Newcon 3 ('new convention 3'), which proved a spectacular success in every way but one: attendance. We were naïve, focussing on attracting local interest and failing to sufficiently engage the SF community.

Faced with a debt (being carried by others), I determined to edit and publish an anthology to raise funds. What should I call the 'publisher' of this book? Why, name it after the convention, obviously; it didn't much matter, this was only going to be one book, after all…

Even when I first held the finished copies of *Time Pieces* in my hands and thought, "I did this! I could do it again…" NewCon was only ever intended as a side-project, a hobby I could indulge in between writing. One book in the first year, one in the second, that should be fine. The signs were there in the third year, however, when we published a whole *three* books, but even then I didn't imagine that by the end of year ten NewCon would have getting on for eighty titles to its credit.

I owe a debt of gratitude to many people, notably Ian Watson, who was my partner in crime in those early days, offering advice and carrying out a second edit on the stories for each book, to Storm Constantine, who performs final layout on the content of virtually all NewCon titles, to Andy Bigwood, who lays out the vast majority of the covers, and to Helen Sansum, for constant support and unflagging belief even when I falter.

I am especially indebted to all the talented writers and artists who have contributed to the books. I've been privileged to work with some of the biggest names in genre fiction and also to showcase exciting new and emerging talent. That's what NewCon is all about, really. At the time we launched, there was a lot of talk about the short story being dead, of shrinking markets and the major publishers shying away from anthologies and collections. I've always loved short stories – anthologies borrowed from the library as a kid were my route into the work of so many authors who became integral to my reading thereafter. It occurred to me that a small specialist imprint might be able to make anthologies work where the big boys couldn't, which is why the anthology became the backbone of NewCon's output.

Now, of course, multiple-author volumes have enjoyed a resurgence, with many medium-sized and small imprints producing them, which is fantastic news for everyone who enjoys a good story, or even *several* good stories under one cover.

Over the years, NewCon has branched out, producing many acclaimed novels, novellas, and single author collections, but the anthology is still there, the beating heart of what we do. To mark our tenth birthday, how could I not turn to the anthology once again?

This book is intended as a celebration, one of several produced to commemorate our first ten years, and I'm thrilled by the cast of contributors and the quality of story they've produced. All of which brings me to one final group of people to whom I owe a considerable debt: you, the readers. Thank you for supporting NewCon; thank you for sticking with us and showing such faith in what we're attempting to do. I hope you have as much fun reading this book as I've had putting it together.

Happy reading! Here's to the next ten years.

Ian Whates
Cambridgeshire
May 2016

The Final Path

Genevieve Cogman

The rain splattering against the window pane was audible even over the game soundtrack on the computer. Annie considered turning the music up another notch, but that might have made it loud enough for Mum to hear it in her bedroom. Instead she got out her headphones and plugged them into the computer, blocking out the noises from outside.

These days Mum was actually glad to have her staying inside and playing on the computer. Sure, she had to spend some of the time on homework and research for school, but otherwise it was okay. Inside was a safe place to be.

Outside wasn't. There were the gangs, and the fires, and the murders. And then there were things which weren't in the newspapers or the online news, which Annie only knew about through shared gossip at school, and through official warnings which didn't actually say *what* you were being warned about, just that it was bad.

She'd done her homework for the night, French and maths and biology, and now she could get back to the game. It was one of those with a multi-path story, about being one of a group of pupils trapped on a deserted island after a shipwreck. The fun part was finding the right set of choices to get other characters to talk to you and tell you about their secrets and maybe end up as your boyfriend, and there were nine different endings you could get. Some of the online guides said there were ten endings, but the talk on the forums said that was just because some of the content had been removed before the game was published. But she wasn't that interest in reading the online guides. Well, not unless she really got stuck. It was more fun to work things out by herself. It gave her something to do at night.

Stopped her thinking about what was outside.

Annie sat at supper with Mum and Mum's guests and daydreamed while they talked. She'd rather be up in her room with a tray of food, but Mum had said that was *not an option.* She ran through alternative game routes in her head. She imagined Gaudenz, the Swiss boy on the island, doing the cooking for supper. He'd make Swiss cheese fondue. He'd do it over the stove, since they don't have a fireplace. What would he do when the island ran out of cheese? Had the game considered this?

"I heard there was an incident up on Yew Tree Street last night, with the Ellis family," Dr Andrews said. He was one of the guests whom Mum had round to supper most often. His hair had gone grey and thin, but his beard was still ginger-ish. If Annie's hair ever went partway grey like that, she'd colour it. Dr Andrews always tried to talk around things, as if he thought Annie was still only ten and wouldn't understand when he said *an incident*, but she was fourteen now and she knew very well what those words meant.

Mum gave him a frown. "I heard so too," she said, her voice very clipped. She clearly wanted the topic to stop right there.

But Dr Andrews wouldn't let it go. "I understand Vanessa Ellis was at your school, Agnes? I don't suppose you talked with her much –"

Annie could feel herself frowning, lowering her head like the little bull her mum sometimes called her. "I guess," she interrupted, knowing that would get her a *look* from Mum, though nothing like the look Mum was giving Dr Andrews. "We never talked much."

She added another reason of *why I don't like Dr Andrews* to the existing stack. He kept on calling her *Agnes* rather than *Annie* like everyone else did, even Mum these days.

"And what did you talk about?" he prodded.

"Stuff," Annie said. If this was a conversation in the island game, she'd have a list of answers to give him and she could make a reasonable guess at what each answer would do to their relationship. "She wasn't in my year, anyhow."

"Dr Andrews, really –" another of the guests butted in. She was Mrs Hawkins, and she and her husband both worked at the university. Normally Annie tried to avoid them because they wanted her to *read better books*, which meant anything other than what she usually wanted to read, but right now she was grateful for the interruption. "Annie's just a child."

"She's quite capable of answering a few simple questions," Dr Andrews snapped. "The Ellis girl wasn't among the bodies and–"

It was at that point that Annie threw her plate in his face and ran upstairs.

"I'm sorry, love," her mum said. "I won't invite him again. It was really disgusting of him to ask you all those questions. I'm not saying that you were right to throw your food at him," she added quickly, "but I understand it. I nearly threw my food at him too."

Annie twisted the remains of damp tissues between her fingers. Her eyes ached with crying. It was stupid. It was so stupid. She was a teenager now, she could handle this shit, she didn't have to act like a silly little *child*, having her mum sit on her bed with her and hug her and everything. All the guests had gone home now, and it was just the two of them.

"I did know Van a bit," she said reluctantly. "Vanessa. She was okay. They said at school that her house had been burned down because of..." It was so hard not to start crying again. "Because of the gangs. But is she alive? Dr Andrews said they hadn't found her –"

Mum hushed her before she could finish the sentence, and that was probably a good thing, because Annie couldn't quite shape the word *body*, couldn't connect it to the girl she knew.

"Dr Andrews doesn't know what he's talking about," Mum said. "Dr Andrews, if you will excuse the language, doesn't know his arse from his elbow. Don't you worry about Dr Andrews, love." She looked around the room for a distraction. "Tell me about your game. You've been playing it all these nights, you must have got somewhere with it by now."

"It's called *Island of Loneliness*," Annie said. She got up to start it on the computer and show her mum the loading screen. "It's by Jeweltree Publishing. It's really good. You're stuck on this island, you see, and there are these boys who were shipwrecked with you, and..."

"Oh, right, one of those," her mum said, grinning a bit. "Yeah, I've heard about those ones. I thought they were made in Japan, though?"

"I think they're made all over these days," Annie volunteered. She watched her mum trace one boy's face with her finger. "That one's Heinrich and he's from Germany, and you have to answer all his questions by saying you're really into sport and stuff if you want him to be interested in you."

"Programming," Mum muttered to herself. "Get them while they're young. Training to give the right responses."

Annie nodded. "It's really good programming. But it's not, you know, adult stuff. You just get happy endings with being rescued from the island and going off together towards the future and things. And the music's really great. And I'm doing the route with Ken at the moment, he's the American one who's into spirituality and wild animals, and that'll make all nine of them!"

Mum laughed. "All right, I get the message. They all sound like much better company than Dr Andrews."

"They are," Annie insisted. "They really are."

The new ending theme played happily in Annie's headphones as she watched the girl who was supposed to be her sailing off with Ken on their handmade raft. They'd reach the mainland and bring back help for the other survivors. Of course, it was too late for Louis (snakebite), Achmed (wolf attack), and Heinrich (cliff accident), but there were always casualties, whichever boy you were trying to end up with.

Van had said that maybe there *was* a special final route that you could achieve once you'd got all the separate ones, and that it meant keeping all the boys alive. She'd been one of the other people at the school who played the game. Her favourite ending had been the Louis one, where you found an airplane that had crashed there previously, and got it mended and managed to take off. But if you wanted that ending then you had to be mean to Jean-Paul, who was Louis' older half-brother and bullied him, and Annie rather liked Jean-Paul. She'd written fanfic about how he was only bullying Louis because they didn't understand each other and because Louis was a brat. People had given the piece good reviews.

She saved the ending next to the other eight, and restarted the game.

Sometimes Annie felt as if nothing was ever going to change. There was school, and then there was home in the evenings, and the game on the computer, and there was nothing else. Nothing. Else. Ever. She and Mum didn't go on trips any more because petrol cost so much, and because nobody wanted to go by train due to the gangs. School didn't do trips anywhere. The school windows were all shuttered these days, and the sports grounds were walled so you couldn't even see outside. When the school bus took them home, you could see bits of the streets out of the bus windows, but they weren't generally worth looking at. Grey walls, grey streets, black burn sites. Everywhere felt cold and hungry.

When Annie was older and she'd finished school, she was going to go to University somewhere else, somewhere away from here. Maybe London.

Thomas on the bus said that London was worse than here. She wouldn't listen.

Thomas said that he was going to run away, but where was there to run to?

Thomas said that Van had run away to join the gangs. That was so far beyond stupid it went straight into utter crap. Van had been Annie's *friend.*

That night, when Annie was doing the bit at the start of the game where you wander round the island and see all the locations, there was something new in the graphics. She almost missed it. The game didn't signpost: you were left to spot the new thing on your own. It was a pathway into the forest near the beach, curving into the background of the game art as if it had always been there.

Acting on a hunch, she picked the *avoid all the boys and go off on your own* route. Previously that had always been the shortcut to an early game over, either because your character had an accident (who'd have thought that spraining your ankle could be so fatal?) or because you didn't build up any emotional bonds and everyone died of starvation.

But this time there was a new option.

[X] Follow the path into the forest

"Annie!" her mother called through the closed door. "Are you ready for bed?"

Annie saved the game, and went to sleep grinning.

It was another dinner-with-guests, but this time Annie wasn't quite as bored. Mrs Hawkins was talking about what she called 'the selfish meme', which was interesting even in its gruesomeness, or more likely *because* it was so gruesome; so icky that it wasn't actually *real.* She was talking about sorts of evil character who kept on coming up in fiction again and again without any real link between the books or films or whatever, and then people doing the same thing (which Mrs Hawkins called *imitative behaviour* showed up in the real world too. Like in the gangs.

Annie was torn between wanting to ask questions and keeping her mouth shut so that Mum wouldn't start worrying about

Annie listening to all this. Though it wasn't really any worse than some of the stuff on television.

"Of course, the Jekyll/Hyde dichotomy goes back to werewolf legends," Mrs Hawkins said. "And the Dracula issue – well, vampires. It's the more human sort of evil that I'm putting forward as the subject here."

"Dracula was originally human," one of the other guests said. "Vlad Drakul, wasn't it? Or however you're supposed to pronounce it? Voivode of Transylvania, whatever. The Impaler, you know. The whole nailing hats to the heads of envoys and brutal punishment and all that. If we're talking about human evil, do you really need to go sourcing in fiction when you've got that for an origin?"

"Is this about the Bean cults?" the quiet man at the far end of the table – Annie couldn't remember his name – said, and the whole table went silent.

"It is," Mrs Hawkins answered. Her face was pinched and thin. (Everyone looked thin these days. Even Mum looked thin.) "No linking factor that we've been able to discover, no common ground, but they've been springing up across Britain and we keep on finding the same common imagery. And it all goes back to Bean by way of Sweeney Todd. The cave, the hanging tree, the –" she looked at Annie, and cut herself off, mouth closing like a trap.

"But you have the Wendigo myth before that," the quiet man said, filling in the hole in the conversation. "That's a clear mythological source for the cannibalism concept."

"But you can trace the Wendigo myth back to human action," Mrs Hawkins counter-argued. "In the stories it's the action of eating which opens the victims up to possession. If you –"

"I'll just clear the dishes so we can have dessert," Mum announced, stopping the conversation before it could get really interesting. Even if it was probably about to also get really gross.

Annie did some Googling that night. Yup. Really gross.

Cannibalism wasn't sexy or cute, and she stopped half the searches before she could even finish loading the pages; seeing the description text was enough.

Besides, the game was much more interesting. There was a tenth boy on the island. He lived in a hideout down the forest path, and Annie had to keep on rejecting all the dialogue options with the other boys in order to get him to talk with her.

The character was very secretive. She wondered what his background was. Hidden spy? Lifelong outcast? Grown up on the island after being left there as a baby? He wouldn't even tell her his name. Maybe that was the end point of his character quest?

The other characters were having difficulty finding food in the game, but she was refusing all interactions with them, so it didn't really matter. They just stood around at the campsite saying things like *we're all going to starve*, with their character models looking prettily gaunt and haggard. Maybe the tenth boy knew where there was a food store? Then the endgame might be her getting together with him and saving everyone, and them all leaving the island together. That'd be neat.

Nicola wasn't on the bus the next morning.

Thomas wanted to talk about it, but Annie turned her back on him and put her earbuds in, and listened to the game's soundtrack, and thought about endings.

There was nothing worth looking at outside the bus windows.

"Do we have to have rice again for supper?" Annie asked.

"Yes," Mum said. "It's supposed to be good for you, and I'm sure I could do with losing some weight." Her smile looked pinned on to her face, and if there had been background music, it would have been ominous.

Annie decided to pick the best possible option. She just hugged her Mum, and stopped arguing. Sometimes there wasn't a really good game route, there was just a least bad choice.

Mum was so thin these days.

Options:
[X] Talk to Ken about hunting
[X] Talk to Louis about picking vegetables and fruit
[X] Talk to Jean-Paul about setting traps
[X] Ask how people are
[X] Go and see the boy in the forest

Annie clicked on *Go and see the boy in the forest.*

"They're going to put us all in mass boarding schools," Thomas said. He wouldn't stop going on at her, even though she made it absolutely clear that she *did not want to talk*. "My dad says that it's because of the gangs and the food supplies. And they're talking about conscription."

"Wasn't that what they did during the Second World War?" Annie regretted saying that a moment later, because it meant that Thomas thought she was actually interested in the conversation.

Thomas nodded. "They had a food shortage then too. But they didn't have such bad pollution. And the police are already armed..."

"What's that got to do with anything?" Annie said. "They've been armed since before we were born. It's only our mums and dads who go round being weird about that. And why put us into boarding schools?"

"Because then they can centralise the food supply. And then they'll have us all in one place. No more families going missing..."

Annie tuned him out. It didn't stop him talking, but at least if she wasn't listening she didn't have to think about what he was saying.

The game music played in her head as the boy in the forest talked to her about ethics and religion and reality, and she tried to guess the right answers to progress the game.

She had to go back to previous saves more than once, but each time she remembered more of what he wanted to hear, and she got a little further.

She was tired of rice for supper. She was still hungry.

The woman across the table looked at her with weary eyes. "I'm sorry, love," she said. "There's nothing in the shops these days. Tell you what, why don't you go and play on your game for a bit? You look too tired for homework."

Annie heard the word *game*. It cut through the music in her head. She nodded, and bared her teeth in a smile.

The other boys on the island had been vanishing. She was the only one left. She fled to her boyfriend in the forest for comfort and safety, and this time he gave her meat from his stewpot.

"You're one of us now," he said.

"But you still haven't told me who you are," she complained.

"I'm Sunny," he whispered. His voice was in the headphones and it was in her head and she nodded along with it, listening to the music. "I'll be waiting for you. We all will."

Annie went down the stairs on silent feet, as quiet as a mouse. The carving knife was in its block in the kitchen.

Later, after she had eaten, she set fire to the house, and went away to find the island, and to find Sunny and all the others.

Women's Christmas

Ian McDonald

Eleven days of rain and on the twelfth, on Women's Christmas, it broke. I took Rosh down to the hotel in sharp low winter sun. We were half-blinded and sun-dizzy by the time we arrived at the Slieve Donard. It was a good thing the car was doing the driving. We left early to get as much spa time as possible in before dinner but Sara had beaten us. She waved to us from the whirlpool. She was the only one in it. Women's Christmas was an odd lull between New Year and the Christmas present discount voucher weekend breaks. We had the old Victorian pile almost to ourselves and we liked it.

We sat neck-deep on the long tiled bench and let the spritzed water play with us. The big picture window looked out over the beach and the mountains. The low sun was setting. The sea was a deep indigo and the lights were coming on along the curve of the bay. The rain had washed the air clean, the twilight was huge and clear and we could almost smell the day ending. Those eleven days of rain had been eleven days of snow, up at the height of mountain tops. They glowed cold blue in the gloaming, paler blue on dark.

"It'll be up soon," Rosh said. Then Dervla appeared in her swimmers and we turned away from the window and waved and whooped.

"Did someone remember to bring them?" Dervla asked, as one of us asks every year.

"They're in the back of the car," I said. Every year someone asks, every year Rosh picks them up from the airport, every year I sling them in the back of the car.

We soaked in the pool and steamed in the sauna and tried the new spa devices in the pool, which pummelled you and tormented you and beat you down with powerful jets of water.

"I'm not sure about those," Dervla said. This was our tenth Women's Christmas in the Slieve Donard.

It's not a northern thing, Women's Christmas. It's a thing from Cork and Kerry, where the feast is still strongly observed. January 6th is the day: the Feast of the Epiphany, Twelfth Night, the night you have to have your decorations down or face bad luck the whole year. It's sometimes called Little Christmas, or Old Christmas Day, a name I find spooky, like something sleeping deep and long that you don't want to wake. It's to do with different calendars, I believe. If Christmas is turkey and sprouts and meaty, wintry stuff, Women's Christmas is about wine and cake and sweet things. Eat sweet and talk sweet, Alia in work says. She's Syrian – well, her family came from Syria. And we talk. Five sisters scattered all over the island have a lot to talk about. Afternoon tea and cakes and cocktail help, but the talk's not always sweet.

Men traditionally look after the house and make a fuss of the women at Women's Christmas, but luck with that from the men in our lives. The hotel provides reliable pampering and it has the spa and decent cocktails. We didn't even have a name for this little family gathering until Sinead mentioned our Epiphany sojourns to a five star hotel to a neighbour down in Cork and she said that sounds like Women's Christmas. We took the name but it was our own thing: *these* women's Christmas. The Corcoran sisters.

Sinead came cursing in from Cork. The good weather had stalled somewhere in Kildare; she had driven through one hundred and fifty kilometres of rain and flood, maintenance was overrunning and road speeds were down to sixty. She was pissed off at having missed the spa. It part of the ritual.

"Tell me I'm in time for the cocktails."

"You're in time for cocktails."

Sinead would always be in time for cocktails.

There was a new thing, from up there: a cocktail everyone was drinking. Blue Moon. I liked the sound of that, so Rosh told us what was in it: gin and blue Curacao. We asked the barman to show us blue Curacao and Sinead screwed up her face and said, Oh I don't fancy that very much. We stuck what we knew and liked. Fruit and straws. Non-alcoholic for Dervla. She's been three years off the drink and looking better for it.

"First thing," Dervla said. She was the oldest – twelve years older than me, the baby, and assumed she was the natural leader of the Corcoran sisters. We raised our glasses and drank to Laine.

I forget that not every family has an aunt who went to the moon. I was twelve when Laine left. I told everyone at school that an aunt of mine was going to work on the moon. They weren't as impressed as I wanted them to be. When Laine launched, I imagined it would be on every screen in the country. I still thought space and the moon were big, unusual things. We got private feed from the launch company and had to pay for it. Dervla brought prosecco to cheer Laine up into space. Dervla would have celebrated the opening of a letter with prosecco back then. We had hardly a glass down us before the smoke was blowing away on the wind. The thing I remember most was that I was allowed a glass of fizz. My excitement had become embarrassing and when I went to look at the Moon, trying to imagine anyone up there, let alone Aunt Laine, I made sure no one saw me. It's easier now there are lights, and the big dick they stamped out on the surface, but twelve years on, at the new moon I can see the lights but I can't remember clearly what Aunt Laine looks like. She wasn't that much older than Sara, a good sight younger than Dervla. More a cousin than an aunt. Ma never really approved of Da's side of the family. That's not really her name, she said on those rare times when Laine came to stay. Her name's really Elaine. I tried playing with her, but she was into outdoor stuff like bikes and building dams in streams and getting muddy. That's ironic seeing as she's permanently indoors now.

Then the money came.

The food really isn't so great here but we had the old dining room almost entirely to ourselves. In keeping with the traditions of Women's Christmas, we took a late afternoon tea. Sandwiches with the crusts cut off and mushroom vol au vents, sausage rolls, cake and fruit loaf. Fondant fancies. Tea, or light German wines, not too dry. We ate while the staff took down the decorations. We were glowing from the spa and the cocktails.

Dervla's oldest was in a show in Las Vegas, middle Jake was rolling along in his middling way and the only thing Eoin would have was GAA all day every day. The laundry was ferocious, but, in these days when qualifications count for nothing, football was as valid a career path as any.

Sinead's Donal was settled in San Francisco now. The company had moved him into the materials development section already. *He'll be the next one off to the moon*, Rosh said and we all looked at her. Three Cosmopolitans or no, a Corcoran woman is expected to follow the rules. *He's found himself a nice girl*, Sinead said and the mood lifted like the Christmas weather.

Sara would have gone on all night about the divorce but Women's Christmas was about eating sweet and talking sweet and no matter the settlement it was better than Bry.

Rosh's news was old news to me because I saw her every other day it seemed. New house new man. Again. New job maybe. It was new and exciting to the others. Dervla gave the company report. Corcoran Construction was in better shape. The losses from the previous two years had been reversed. Her talk was of finance I didn't understand. I never had a head for business, and I mistrusted Michael around all that money so I asked the rest of them to buy me out. Wisely as it transpired with that gobshite Michael. Sinead was a silent partner but Sara positively revelled in the boardroom battles and corporate politics. I put the money in safe investments, let the rest of them run the empire and saw them once a year, at Women's Christmas.

Aunt Laine sent us money from the moon. She was making a fortune, something in mining. That was what she had studied. The idea had always been to get to the Moon; that was where the work was, that was where the opportunities were. Make your fortune, send it back. The streets of the moon were paved with gold, except I heard once that gold has no value up there. Send home the money; buy the slates for the cottage and a decent headstone. The Irish way. Laine set up her brother and her parents, and then looked around for others whose lives she could transform with her money: her cousins, the five Corcoran sisters. She wanted us to use it to encourage women in science and engineering. We did: we set up Corcoran Construction.

The money still came down from the moon, quarterly. We hadn't needed it in years. Corcoran Construction had made us safe. Aunt Laine was our indulgence fund: West End musicals, weekend breaks, shopping sprees, family holidays and every year we blew a whack of it on our Women's Christmas.

The Baileys was on the second bottle, and Sara had an audience now. I didn't want to hear about the bastardry and the fuckery. Michael was five years back but certain times, certain places bring him close. Like angels, he stooped close to Earth at Christmas.

I went out for a smoke. The sudden cold took my breath away; the air was so clean and clear it seemed as brittle and sharp as glass. I lit up and sat on one of the smoker's benches, listening to the night. Sound carried huge distances on the still air. The sea was a murmur in the dead calm. Car engines, someone revving. Shouts from down on the promenade. I tracked the course of an ambulance siren through the town and up the main road behind the hotel. I heard a fox shriek, a sound that spooked and excited me in equal parts. The wild things were out and closer than I had thought. I shivered hard and deep; the alcohol heat was evaporating and I was in party frock and shoes. There would be frost on the lawns in the morning and ice where yesterday's rain lingered. I was glad the car would be driving us back up north.

The air was so clear I could see lawns, car park, beach lit by a pale glow, the light of the three-quarter moon. There were artificial lights up there, machinery and trains and stuff, but the moonlight outshone them. Half a million people lived on the moon, building a new world. Laine went there. Someone I know went there, and was there, and would remain there for the rest of her life. Everyone knows the rule. If you don't come back after two years you don't come back at all. She'll be back, we said, before even the smoke from the launch had cleared. She didn't come back. Maybe that was where the damage was done.

I opened the car. The gifts were in an Ikea bag. The money was not Laine's only largess: every year for ten years she sent gifts from the moon. We held Women's Christmas because that was how long it took her gifts to arrive. It was complex process; tethers and orbiters and shuttles. Names I didn't understand. Every year we would pick up the gifts from the airport and bring them down to the hotel.

We never open them. They are stowed, nine bags, in Rosh's storage unit.

The gifts were small but exquisitely packaged. They looked like kittens in the bottom of the big blue bag. The labels were handwritten. I sat in the back seat of the car and ripped open the one addressed to me.

Laine Corcoran's gift to me was a small, plastic figure, the size of my thumb. It was a big-arsed, big-titted girl with the head and skin of a leopard. She wore hot pants, a crop top, pointy ears and big hair, and she carried a ball in her right hand. I thought at first it was one of the action figures Conrad used to fill his room with, before he went to his dad, then I saw a tiny logo on the back. It was a mascot for a sports team. I couldn't recognise the sport.

I never thought of sport on the moon.

A 3-D printer had made it. 3-D printers made everything on

the moon. Corcoran Construction was experimenting with them in the building trade.

It had cost Laine a fortune to send this from the moon to me. I put it back in the box, refolded the packaging as best I could, and hid the gift under the others. No one would ever look. I was cold to the bone now and shivering hard. I went back into the hotel. Sara was opening the third bottle of Baileys.

Pyramid

Nancy Kress

One & Two

The first two floors are mostly filled with parties. People move excitedly in and out of various rooms, laughing and talking, showing off what got them in the door. Many of them are young. Drink flows freely. In private rooms, a lot of inventive sex occurs. There are dozens of rooms, corridors, indoor gardens. The din is enormous, happy, and unceasing.

Many of these young people don't realize that the structure is a pyramid. When they were outside, the slopes of the pyramid were shrouded in clouds. Or else the young people were too busy with their own affairs, as young people often are, to look up.

Not everyone is euphoric. In a few of the rooms, discussions are earnest rather than celebratory. Theories are debated, or fine points of execution, or history. These discussions can become quite heated. Names are called, efforts disparaged. Sometimes people fling up their hands and walk out of the room, scowling. Two or three times there have been fistfights.

In other of the rooms, mostly at the back of the structure, an older group sits sombrely, looking as if they are holding a funeral. These people seldom make trips to the refreshment table or the cash bar. The people here would be better off if they left the pyramid entirely, and a few of them do.

Most of the furniture on these two floors is worn, a little seedy. Sofas bear the imprint of generations of butts. The carpet is threadbare, the art on the walls a mixture of sentimental kitsch and proletariat paintings decades out of date.

A staircase, broad and well-worn, rises from the middle of the first floor up to the third. The partiers glance at it frequently. The steps are worn in the centre, the risers scuffed from being kicked by eager shoes. The staircase is made of sturdy wood reinforced with steel. It will outlast the pyramid itself.

Someone ascends the staircase, and there is a momentary pause as people watch her go.

Three & Four

Floors three and four are almost as noisy as the ones below, but the food and wine are better, although not that much better. Most of the people look and behave much the same as those below. However, everyone here has succeeded not just once, but at least twice. A few people stand out: there a man so straight and confident that people wonder audibly if he is a military officer. Here a woman that causes whispers when she passes. A few people on Floor Three look frankly crazy. The din is just as loud as below.

It has an undertone, however, of anxiety. The number of earnest groups in back rooms has increased. The arguments are less theoretical, more personal. There is less sex.

This time the staircase going up is off-centre. It is narrower than the staircase below, and carpeted. The carpet looks a little dingy, beige tending toward brown.

A man goes toward the staircase and ascends it. He goes straight from the third floor to the fifth. Everybody on both floors notices him. After a second of silence, the chatter and arguments resume.

Five

This is the first floor with furniture in good condition. It looks as if it is replaced often. The crowd here is noticeably smaller, although all ages are represented. For the first time, liquor and food are passed by white-clad waiters rather than having to be queued for at the bar or buffet table. The waiters' coats could use laundering. All the bad art has disappeared, replaced by colourful, unframed posters that are changed often.

The amount of sex has dropped off noticeably, but the amount of drinking has increased. Still, the parties on this floor are happier than the ones on Three and Four, nearly as happy as those on One. People laugh and toast each other and compare efforts.

The staircase rising to the floor above again sits in the centre of the room, rising gracefully in iron spirals. The treads are narrow and the risers high; it takes more sustained effort to ascend. A spotlight shines on the staircase. Occasionally, the spotlight brightens, as if searching.

Six

This is the most anxious floor of all. Everyone here has completed more than one successful effort, or they would have stayed on Five. Multiple successful efforts are, in fact, the hallmark of Six. But people here talk very little about efforts. They circulate, chattering lightly, flirting and telling stories, but all the time their eyes appraise each other. Who is next – *you? Her? Not him, surely – I never thought much of anything he did.*

It is not a happy floor. Yet, there are pockets of contentment, people sitting on brightly coloured pillows on the floor, talking among themselves or to outsiders.

This is the first floor to contain outsiders, people who did not enter through the door on One. Perhaps they came over bridges spanning the cloud-filled spaces between buildings. There aren't many outsiders, but everyone wishes to talk to those who have come. Some circle the outsiders tentatively, waiting to be noticed; some crash right to their sides and start talking; some seek others to introduce them. About half the outsiders carry small cameras.

The waiters who carry around food and drink wear clean jackets. They offer decent wines, canapes that have been freshly made in a kitchen somewhere.

The posters on the wall are printed on better quality paper, but they change just as often.

The staircase is solid cherry, carpeted in green, and very few people ascend it.

Seven

The outsiders on the seventh floor outnumber the people who have come up the staircase. There are only a dozen or so of the latter at any time. The outsiders cluster around the others, eagerly talking and asking questions about the singular, unusual efforts that have carried people to Seven.

This floor is furnished well. The sofas are all new – somehow, they are *always* new – deep and cushiony. The posters are printed on high-quality stock and framed in rich woods: ebony, teak, mahogany. The wine is excellent. Waiters, like outsiders, outnumber those coming from below. Many of the waiters cast jealous eyes on the guests, usually but not always when no one is looking.

So do some of the outsiders.

There is no carpet here. The floor is marble, luxurious but highly slippery. The staircase floats around the room, sometimes nearly invisible. You have to squint to see it.

The people who have come up from Six are flushed, happy, expansive. Most of them converse eagerly, although a few stake out a corner of a deep sofa or club chair and shake their heads when anyone approaches. Both types, talkers and non-, glance at the next staircase. A few boast that the outsiders should visit them when they are on Eight. The desire to see what lies on Eight is palpable, like a too-rich perfume.

Most people do not stay on Seven very long. Their visits are measured in weeks, sometimes only one week. They descend the staircase back to Six, or, more rarely, make it to Eight.

Eight

Eight is, oddly, more full than Seven. Nearly everyone who mounts the floating staircase to this floor, stays. This creates a sense of security that lets muscles relax, stomachs unclench, eyes shine with the certainty that nothing will be taken away from them. Outsiders besiege them, many of whom are pretty girls. The food is exquisite, the wines superb, the waiters and other attendants obsequious. Money permeates the air – *is* the air. Efforts lie piled around the room to be admired. On Seven, each party-goer had only one, but here some people have four, nine, even twelve. The posters have been replaced with original paintings. People talk about their boats, planes, theatres.

The party – for it is a party – is pretty much non-stop.

Yet there are two more floors in the pyramid. The staircase to Nine is conspicuous, made of pure gold. Most people ignore it. This is an older crowd, and they know this is as high as they will go. It is high enough. From the windows, they can see that they are well above the clouds.

Nine

Yet, a few do mount the ninth staircase – maybe one a year. Two, in a great year. At any given time, Nine holds no more than half a dozen people. They, too, can look out the window at the clouds, or wave down at the crowds outside. To the people on the sidewalk, they glitter. More than a few consider them gods.

Yet, curiously, Nine is less opulently furnished than eight. Perhaps no one feels they need to try so hard. The sofas and tables are good without being ostentatious. The carpet is a natural Berber. Tables are long and polished. Each person has his or her own table, piled with both their efforts and with offerings from the crowd below. How do the offerings arrive on the tables? No one really knows, but every morning they are there.

On the wall hang not posters nor colourful paintings, but portraits of the people who live here. They are identified by their first names alone: Neil. Ursula. George. The walls between portraits are really only narrow strips of stone, slanting sharply upward as the pyramid reaches its apex. Between the stone are vast windows with panoramic views. The people on Nine see everything.

In one corner stands the last staircase. Wood again, narrow, a little rickety. The people on nine don't look at it, except for the outsiders. The outsiders speculate about it all the time.

Ten

Everyone on Ten is dead.

They lay stacked in coffins, and yet the stacking seems respectful rather than careless. The room has a high, pointed ceiling; the walls slant inward sharply and are all made of glass. There are no visitors here; the dead people are known only by the efforts they have thrown from the windows when they entered. Those efforts fluttered in the breeze and then descended slowly through the clouds to the land below – more slowly, it sometimes seemed, than the laws of physics permitted.

The sun shines through the wide windows during the day, the moon and stars at night.

There is no higher to go, and no more time to go there. No chatter or party. Yet everyone below would do anything, anything at all, to lie up here one day. Even – as was once said by someone on the tenth floor of a different pyramid – rob his mother, if that's what it took.

There are cobwebs in the dusty corners of this room, and some of the coffins are Victorian, decorated with scrolls and hair brooches hundreds of years old. Yet the names on the coffin, due to some perpetual angle of sunlight or starlight, shine brightly. Jules. Mary. Isaac, Arthur, Philip, Robert. Octavia. Alice.

In another contradiction of normal physics, when the pyramid falls – and they always do, always – this top floor will fall last. Or maybe it will not fall at all, just detach and sail higher, higher, toward some unforeseeable space, far beyond time.

We can hope.

Liberty Bird

Jaine Fenn

This is the moment. That first glimpse of space, coyly revealed by the widening doors. Kheo gives his instruments the attention they require, but his eye is drawn downwards, to the banded glory of Yssim, the cold and distant light of the stars beyond.

His exit is faultless. The Clan insisted he pre-program it, rather than take even the miniscule risk of their favoured son screwing up and dinging his yacht on the hangar doors. That would never do, not with the whole world watching.

Some impulse had made Kheo visit the engineering hangar three days before the race. He should either have been preparing himself mentally with relaxation and centring exercises – as his family would prefer – or drinking, gambling and womanising in the lowtown rings – as the media would expect – but he had a sudden desire to be alone with his yacht, without the tech crew fussing around.

The hangar was the largest open space on the liner and the ship's spin provided near-normal gravity here. After two months away from Homeworld, the echoey open space and illusion of full weight were disconcerting. In the low lighting *Liberty Bird* was a point of colour, although her red and blue hull was muted by the oily shadows.

Kheo reached up, tracing the fusion yacht's perfect lines, his hand passing just below the Clan crest emblazoned on her side. Someone had left the steps in place; it was only logical he use them to climb into the cockpit. He sighed as he sealed the canopy. *Liberty Bird* was the only birthright he wanted. Yet the race she had been built for might not be held many more times and if his family had their way this would the last time he would be permitted to compete. That made claimimg his third win even more important.

He started at movement glimpsed out the corner of his eye. Someone out there, down on the hangar floor. A thief? A saboteur from a rival clan who had somehow got onto the Reuthani liner? His heart raced. The net was buzzing with stupid gossip: with no one to keep them in check any more, ancient clan rivalries were getting out of hand.

No, just Chief Mechanic Sovat. Kheo liked Sovat, respected him. Yes, that was what he felt: *respect*. Sovat often worked late, went above and beyond.

Except Sovat didn't appear to be working. More like waiting. Another of the tech team walked in, a younger man whose name only came to Kheo after a moment's thought. Greal: junior propulsion specialist, university educated, rather effete for the rough-diamond world of the yacht-techs. Why were this mismatched pair meeting here so late? Not for something nefarious, he hoped. They appeared to just be talking, standing close.

Oh. Had he really seen –? Did they really just –?

Sovat stepped back, then looked around. Kheo shrank down in the seat, holding his breath. The Chief Mechanic's gaze passed over him, and he turned back to his companion. More brief words, then the two men left, Greal following close to Sovat. Kheo had no doubt they were headed somewhere more private.

Kheo clears the great wheel of the hangar-deck at a pace the watching cameras will no doubt find pedestrian. Of course, speed is relative: the liner is in a high, fast orbit around the gas giant far below. The first thrust of acceleration as he brings the main engines online is deceptive; he actually needs to lose orbital velocity before the start of the race.

He rotates *Liberty Bird* and peels away from the Reuthani Clan liner; the huge blunt needle is strung with spoked rings, their sizes and positions determining their place in this microcosm of clan life: engineering, living suites, gardens, entertainments and accommodation for the few thousand citizens permitted to accompany their betters off-world for this annual jamboree. In a touching if tacky gesture, a block of portholes in the central midtown ring have been selectively lit to spell out the words *Good Luck Kheo.*

All around Yssim, other Pilots are leaving their liners. Most clans, including his own, only field one Pilot these days. Some clans no longer participate in the Flamestar Challenge. Other clans no longer exist.

The yachts head for the Royal Barge, a smaller vessel in a lower orbit around the gas giant. Though the Barge now lacks any royalty, tradition still dictates that the race starts from there. It will take several hours to reach the Barge, and the formal start of the race. The approach is critical to a good start. In his five previous races, Kheo has tuned his coms into the razzmatazz that surrounds the biggest event in high society's calendar. All across the system, pundits are discussing the latest form reports released by the clans for their teams and mulling over the detailed ion-stream data. Every other year, Kheo has revelled in the sense of being at the heart of it all yet free, out in the vastness of space.

Not this time. He selects some roots-rock – not his usual sort of music, but it should blast his head clear – and stares out into the beauty of the void, urging his mind to remain blank.

Kheo was expected to show his face at the hangar the next day, both as a courtesy to the techs working on his behalf and to attend a briefing on the current configuration of the ion-streams. He had been looking forward to the tactical discussion of routes and fuel management, to sharing the respectful camaraderie of the men. Instead he was uneasy, almost nervous. He made himself chat to the usual people; act normal.

And everything *was* normal. In the daytime bustle, Kheo wondered if he had been mistaken; perhaps he even dreamt the encounter he had witnessed the previous evening. He spent enough time imagining such things.

Sovat was as brusquely efficient as ever when he took Kheo over the latest engine test results. There was no sign of Greal.

Sovat was the last to leave the briefing room, and he paused, as though waiting for Kheo to say something. When Kheo failed to speak, the Mechanic turned to follow his fellow techs out.

Kheo took a different route back to the suite-decks, choosing rarely used corridors and secondary float-tubes, doing his best to avoid the crew, minor family and hangers-on with their ready smiles. He spent the journey trying to work out whether the look Mechanic Sovat had given him had been an invitation.

By the time he has the Royal Barge on visual, Yssim itself is too large for his mind to interpret as spherical. The gas giant is a sky-spanning backdrop of mauve and azure, lavender and turquoise. He is close enough to spot details in the roiling turbulence between the coloured bands. Thanks to the false-colour projections enhancing his view through the canopy, he can see the ion-streams: ethereal threads and skeins, twisting and curling out from the massive world, curved lines of force linking it to Estin, the pus-yellow moon constantly pummelled by Yssim's tidal forces.

Now comes the first test. The intricacies of orbital mechanics make an actual start line impossible. Instead Kheo, and every other Pilot, must interpret detailed positional readings then use them to apply delta-V, at the same time keeping track of the movements of the other yachts.

The exact moment the race starts is determined by the AI-enhanced stewards on the Barge, who are monitoring every one of the twenty-three yachts to determine when all of them are present in the prescribed volume of space. Just being in position isn't enough: you need to be on the right heading and, ideally, as near the front of the volume as possible.

Fifteen ships already lined up… another entering. And

another.

He makes a tiny adjustment; raising his orbit slightly. He's in a good position but he can't afford to leave the start volume before the last yacht enters. A false start not only annoys the watching billions, it means the culprit has to start in the secondary volume, behind everyone else.

The penultimate yacht enters the volume. Kheo's got less than five seconds before he leaves it…

The final yacht is in place.

His board lights green.

He keys the preset that maxes the drive. The gentle hand that has been pressing him into his seat becomes a grasping fist.

The Flamestar Challenge is on.

Two days before the race, Clan Reuthani held the pre-race banquet in the liner's Great Mess, a name which had made Kheo smile when he was growing up.

Kheo's first banquet had been seven year ago, shortly after his sixteenth birthday. Uncle Harrik had been First Pilot then, and Kheo had joined in with the drunken and enthusiastic chorus of the Reuthani Clan anthem which serenaded him to his rest. Harrik had won the Flamestar that year, a victory made more special because that had been the first staging of the race since the Empress had been ousted; their Clan yacht had even been renamed in recognition of the coup. In all, his uncle had won twice in eight races. Impressive, but not as good as three out of six.

This year, as the diners picked over the second course of the third remove – sweet jellied consommé upon which floated spun sugar confections in the shape of fusion yachts – a lull in the quiet murmur allowed an overloud stray comment to surface.

"Liberation's become a dirty word!"

The speaker was Kheo's father, the Honourable Earl Reuthani. At his words silence fell across high table. Several people on nearby tables glanced at the chair between Kheo and his mother. Next to him, Prinbal sighed. His younger brother currently greeted most parental comments with sighs but for once Kheo could have joined in.

"Surely you aren't suggesting we were better off under the Empress!" That was Harrik: no else would dare speak up, but the combination of being an ex-Pilot and having fought in the Liberation gave him the right to question the Earl.

"Course not, she wasn't even human." His father was drunk, as usual. "What I mean is, the commoners forget that most of us rose up when they did, an' fought beside 'em. And now they're angling for this 'New Liberation' – from us!"

At least Clan Reuthani still exists, thought Kheo grimly.

His brother was watching their father, absorbing the adult interactions even as he pretended to disdain them.

His Mother said, "But I doubt the malcontents will get far. We need *some* continuity. Most people realise that. What we should be worrying about is all those other systems out there."

"Surely contact could be to our advantage," said Kheo, thinking of the new technologies he had heard about via the recently instituted 'beamed virtual' connection. After centuries of imposed isolation they were finally part of the universe at large.

A cousin chirped, "Yes, who knows what outsider technology could mean for the Flamestar Challenge?"

Assuming it continued. Now that the massive extravagance of moving everyone of note out from Homeworld to run a race around the largest body in the system was no longer maintained by the Empress's brutal taxes, the race was becoming unsustainable. Which just made it more important that he won it again this year. But as discussion returned to the upcoming race, Kheo found his taste for the festivities dulled. He was glad when he was sung to his rest.

Alone in his room, his mood darkened further. He had spent much of his adult life being secretly grateful that he had been too young to fight in the War, that his elder sister had volunteered instead, although he doubted Father would have let an older son join the fight. Now, facing a life of responsibilities he never wanted and knew he was not up to – not to mention the frustration and hypocrisy – he almost envied his dead, heroic sister.

The first stretch is a long straight burn.

Kheo's initial gamble paid off: he has a solid starting position. But so have half a dozen others, including Umbrel Narven. She's one of two female Pilots, vanguard of the kind of changes the Earl hates; she has a reputation for recklessness and her clan has some of the best techs, inherited from now-defunct clans. With two close seconds and a third but no win to her name, Narven's the one to watch.

A couple of competitors are already lagging behind, possibly because their yachts aren't as well tuned as his, or possibly because their starts didn't give them the trajectory they wanted for their chosen path through the ion-streams. Everyone else is still a threat.

Thirty minutes in and the field is spreading out. Now the tactics start to show, as each Pilot plots the precise course they'll be taking through the near-invisible energy maze formed by the ion-streams. Kheo has assimilated all available data on the current disposition of the streams but now, close up, he can get more detailed readings and make final adjustments. It looks good: the provisional trajectory he agreed with his team won't need significant adjustment.

The projection of the streams overlays the view ahead, a shifting, sparkling curtain coloured every shade of the rainbow. The colours are a code imposed by his comp. He is heading for the golden-orange area, nearer Yssim than Estin. Running close to the gas giant has inherent risks, being liable to fluxes and gravitational effects that could affect his instruments and put stress on his yacht, but he has the skill to navigate it and *Liberty Bird* is up to the task. And the crowd will love it.

But he is not the only one risking a close skim. By the time they are fifty minutes into the race, his sensors show two other yachts lining up for similar courses. One of them is close enough that he thinks he can actually see the tiny black speck against the looming ion fields. His instruments ID it as the *Aurora Dream.* Clan Narven; he might have known.

The sense of emptiness lingered. He woke with a ridiculous urge to cry, but saw it off with a cold shower, along with all the other unwanted desires and unsafe emotions.

He was nervous at the prospect of going to the workshop but, in the end, what else would he do the day before the race? His heart tripped when he saw Mechanic Sovat, and he looked away.

After the daily briefing he lingered, and was unsurprised when the Chief Mechanic did the same. Kheo searched for the right thing to say. Finally, as Sovat raised an eyebrow and turned to go, Kheo managed, 'Do you really think Clan Narven's directional thrust innovations pose a threat to us?'

If the mechanic had any idea that this wasn't what Kheo wanted to say he gave no sign. "They might well, sirrah. You'd best take the lead from the start; they have the advantage in hi-gee manoeuvring. Make Narven's yacht work hard to catch you, and stick the course. Just like I said."

Which he had, in the meeting, only a few minutes earlier. "Right. Yes." Kheo looked at the man's hands, because they were safe. Except they weren't. They were fascinating.

"You're a good pilot, sirrah."

Kheo tried not to be over-pleased by the praise. Before he could stop himself he looked up and said, "I believe you worked late two days ago."

Rather than answer immediately Sovat bent forward a little, leaning on his fists; those perfect, sinewy hands. Kheo got a heady whiff of oil and sweat. "What makes you think that?" said Sovat quietly, then added, "sirrah."

"Never mind my reasons, Mechanic," Kheo was glad of the

table, which was high enough to hide his body's response to the encounter. "Were you in the hangar the night before last?"

"I was." Sovat's gaze never wavered.

Kheo found his own eyes drawn, once again, to those hands. "And were you alone?"

"No, sirrah. I had Apprentice Greal with me."

Kheo must have imagined the small hesitation between 'Greal' and 'with'. "And did anything happen?"

"Happen, sirrah?" Kheo would swear the man was *enjoying* this. "What sort of thing were you thinking of, sirrah?"

"I… I could check the camera feeds, you know."

"So you could, sirrah." The mechanic smiled laconically. "But I doubt you'd find anything to alarm you."

Because Sovat had edited them. The Mechanic was careful, thorough: he must have lived with what he was for years. Kheo wanted to hate such forward planning, such contrivance, but found himself admiring it. This man could not only face the truth, but live with it. "If," he managed, "I did see anything some people might find alarming…" he swallowed, half expecting an interruption, but the other man remained silent, "I'm not sure I'd be alarmed, myself," he finished in a rush. His face felt like it had caught fire.

Sovat's voice was soft. "Perhaps you wouldn't, at that," he said.

"And if, if I was not alarmed when, when most people would be. Normally, that is. Would that be … something of interest? To you."

Sovat remained silent.

Kheo swallowed. "I was asking you a question."

"Were you now, sirrah?" Was that caution or knowing acceptance in Sovat's voice?

Acceptance, Kheo decided. They understood each other. No damning words, no absolute confirmation, but there was that connection, that shared experience. Except Kheo's experiences had been confined to fantasy, until now. "What if I had been here, with you, instead of Apprentice Greal? Would something have happened? Something the cameras wouldn't see, and that no one," he felt his breath growing short, "no one ever needed to know about."

Sovat paused before answering, then said, his voice regretful, "No."

"No? Why not?"

"A matter of taste, sirrah. Personal taste."

"What are you saying? I'm not your *type*? But you're… and I'm…" *And no one else is. Except Greal, apparently.* "I could report you, you know. What about that, eh?"

"You're free to do as you will, sirrah." Sovat sounded calm; Kheo had no idea if he was concerned about the threat. "Your word carries far more weight than mine."

But with doctored cameras, it would just be his word. And he could never betray the only man he had ever spoken to in this way. Not even if that man rejected him. "Well, just… remember that."

"I always do, sirrah. Was there anything else?"

"No. Nothing else."

After Sovat left Kheo sat alone in the briefing room. Then he locked himself in the nearest restroom alone, and privately explored the possibility that Sovat would walk in, and find Kheo was his type after all. Then he showered, thoroughly.

Having been both vindicated and rejected in one short conversation, he returned to the family suite, heading straight for his rooms. Here he checked the publically available information on Mechanic Sovat. The man's first name was Appis, and Kheo spent a few moments saying the name, *Appis Sovat*, before chiding himself and looking deeper.

There was nothing incriminating to be found. Had there been the technician would not be in the position he was in today. Kheo uncovered only one item of note, from before the War: when Sovat was twenty-six two of his male friends had been charged with gross indecency. One had opted for surgical readjustment; the other had not relented of his perversion and had been exiled 'at the Empress's service'. Further research revealed that the man had died two years later, at a mine in the bleak high plains of South Arnisland. The verdict was death by natural causes. It generally was, in the mines.

Kheo hisses in triumph as one of the two yachts peels away, slowing as it does. *Too rich for you, eh?* He has taken the shorter, riskier path twice before. The first time, he won. The second time overdriving the engines damaged his yacht, and ended his race. Who would have thought two other pilots were also willing to take the skim? Or rather, one now. Umbrel Narven is still in the race. And her yacht is going to enter the streams ahead of him. He'll be hard pressed to catch her.

No, that's defeatist talk: he is still the best Pilot, in the best ship.

Umbrel Narven no doubt thinks the same about her own skills and vessel.

"Ah, there you are!"

Kheo looked up from his desk and forced a smile for his mother. "I thought I'd get an early night…" He waved the display clear.

"Very sensible. But first, I have news."

Kheo knew that tone. "You'd better come in."

She swept into his room and perched on the more upright of the two chaises. "I didn't want to distract you until we were sure, not with the race coming up –"

"It's tomorrow, Ma, and I don't want to be distracted, you're so right." Kheo ignored his mother's wince at being spoken back to.

"Ah, but this will give you something to race for."

"Have you… finalised arrangements? You have, haven't you?" Making the right match was as much the duty of an oldest son as racing in the Flamestar Challenge. More, really: the

Empress had dictated that Clan scions must prove themselves before marrying, but she was gone. Given the dangers of yacht-racing, many Clans, already depleted by the War, forbad their heirs from taking part. And whether or not the race endured, it was no activity for a family man, as his mother had reminded him on his last birthday.

"I have!"

"With Leilian Fermelai?"

"Well, you two used to play together so well when you were children. And the poor thing lost both her parents in all the nastiness." Meaning: unlike Clan Reuthani, Clan Fermelai had not acted against the Empress. "We'll announce the engagement en route back to Homeworld, and hold the formal party at the Manse."

"This isn't what I want." His voice sounded dead in his ears.

"Kheo, I know this is hard for you. It's hard for all of us. But you have to settle down. Leilian is technically the head of her clan but she's only a woman, and with most of her family gone… this is better for everyone. She will be a good wife."

He wanted to protest further, to say he did not want a wife, good or otherwise, but it would be futile.

More gently his mother added, "This marriage is a necessary thing. I hope you can find happiness in it, Kheo, I truly do. But if you cannot… provided you do your duty, a blind eye can be turned."

Does she know? But he had done nothing to act on his feelings; on the contrary he had made every effort to live up to the image of the yacht-racing noble rake. "What do you mean?" he asked as evenly as he could.

"The unsuitable women," said his mother, in the verbal equivalent of scraping excrement from a shoe.

Ah yes, those women, the entertainers and hostesses; eager to please, and notorious enough that his rumoured liaisons with them maintained his reputation, yet low enough that his failures and foibles would never reach the wrong ears. He had been careful in his choices. He wouldn't miss the embarrassment and guilty revulsion; nor the fear that they saw him for what he really was.

"You won't have to worry about them," he said.

"Good." His mother's smile told him that she, like everyone else, believed the carefully cultivated image. "That's settled then."

The *Aurora Dream* is pulling ahead, Narven's lead opening up second by second.

So, no win. No glory. No final chance to shine before subsiding under the weight of duty and acceptable behaviour. The best he can hope for is second place.

Why can't I just be happy with the privileged life I was born into? He knows the answer: because he can't be himself.

Am I being selfish? Perhaps; there were choices, plenty of them. He could have fought in the War, despite being young. He could admit what he really wants in a lover, although where would he find that in the world he lives in, where such things are never spoken of, even if they are no longer punished with more than a fine? He could stand up to his father, although the old man is quite capable of disinheriting him; an unthinkable prospect.

Plenty of choices there. Shame he has been too much of a coward to take them.

He blinks away stupid self-pitying tears and focuses on *Liberty Bird*'s instrument panel. Here is the one thing that is good and simple and right about his life, directly in front of him. And he is about to come in second, in his final race. It's all downhill from here. Winning isn't just desirable any more: it's the only option, whatever the cost.

There isn't much time: he scans his readouts, their meaning as comforting and familiar as the drapes above his bed, or the face of his childhood nurse. It would be a minor adjustment to his trajectory.

He makes the change.

An alarm sounds.

He ignores it.

Kheo never slept well the night before a race. He doubted any Pilot did. He ended up resorting to the chemical remedies offered by the Clan doctor.

Perhaps that was why, when he was escorted through the halls and corridors of the liner the next morning amid cheers and thrown petals, he felt as though he was watching the festivities from afar, rather than being the reason for them.

Sovat – Appis – was in the hangar, amongst the honour guard of techs who stood respectfully silent while their Pilot crossed the floor to his yacht. Kheo gave him no more regard than was normal, including him in the faint nod of gratitude to his crew as he passed.

Only when he took his seat in *Liberty Bird* did he fully wake up. He performed the usual pre-flight checks with a combination of the utmost care and little conscious thought. By the time the hoist had inched him into the hangar's massive airlock, he was as ready for his fate as he had ever been.

The trajectory alteration is subtle; a matter of a few degrees in one plane. The difference between passing through a volume of space with no appreciable matter in it, and the lower path, where the number of molecules in the vacuum might constitute the start of an atmosphere. Enough of an atmosphere to cause drag and test *Liberty Bird*'s engines, certainly. But the ultimate shortcut – if it works.

He is deep in the ion-streams now, their flickering representations dancing around his yacht. Every other racer is above him; some still appear to be ahead, but they have further to go. It is too early yet to know if his crazy ploy will bring victory.

His com flashes: the support team requesting emergency contact. No mean feat given the ionic interference; they must be juicing up the signal with everything they've got. If he answers, will it be Appis Sovat on the com? He is Chief Tech, after all. The prospect of hearing Sovat's voice again makes Kheo hesitate. Then he catches himself and turns his attention to his console. The drive readout is already edging out of the safe zone, and there's a constellation of amber warnings. Suddenly one of them spikes red: a jolt thrums through his yacht. What was that? Ah, navigational thrusters. Even this is too much atmosphere for them. Well, he's stuck on this course now. As for what happens once he's on the far side, whether they'll blow clear … first make it to the far side, then worry about that.

The ship feels wrong. It's a subtle sensation, a faint vibration, but if he carries on, it's only a matter of time before structural integrity begins to fail.

His life is so complicated. The tension of duty and desire. His inability to be himself. And always he has taken what seemed like the easiest path, only to find complications besetting him. Not now though. Now everything truly is simple. He will either win this race, or die trying.

Another red light: radiation warning. There is only so much energy his suit and canopy can protect him from. The view outside is more spectacular than ever, like a great forest of energy, the psychedelic ion-streams like twisted trunks of impossible trees.

This in itself is the easy way out, of course. Yes, even as he defies death, he's still a coward.

The vibration becomes a shudder. Suddenly Kheo is scared. At least his body is: racing heart, dry mouth, dizzy head.

What am I doing? This insane stunt isn't bravery: it's avoidance, the ultimate avoidance.

The ship begins to shake. The drive readout spikes into the red. He reaches for the console but everything's moving, wild forces pulling at him. And even if he could get his hands on the controls, what could he do? The course is set. Too late to change it now.

I'm a fool. A coward and a fool.

A great concussion hits, throwing him in every direction at

once. He is going to die, here, now. Die without facing himself.

Massive constriction – *but I was expecting an explosion!* – and he is wrapped in chilly gel. As the sedatives kick in he realises two things: he has lost the race and he is still alive. When, seconds later, the drugs ease his stressed system into therapeutic unconsciousness, his last thought is that the former doesn't matter, only the latter.

The media love it. Kheo Reuthani's miraculous escape after his death-or-glory bid for victory eclipses Umbrel Narven's win. Kheo feels sorry for her.

The rescue clipper barely arrived in time to stop *Liberty Bird* drifting into the nearest ion-stream, an experience he would not have survived even encased in crash-gel. By the time his yacht was hauled in, he had received enough radiation to increase his risk of long-term health problems – and to destroy any chance of him giving Clan Reuthani an heir.

Mother visits him in hospital. "I've seen your results."

She could be talking about an exam he failed. "I guess the wedding's off then." He tries not to sound triumphant. He feels sorry for Leilian Fermelai too. He does not, for once, feel sorry for himself.

"Not necessarily. There may be a medical work-around to the, ah, fertility issue. Perhaps even some advance from out-of-system."

"Ah, so you'd accept outsider medicine to solve the Clan's problems, then?"

"One must adapt."

A shame, then, that she had not pressed his father to adapt to the proactive approach many Clans had instituted after the Liberation, of taking sperm or egg samples from their Pilots in case of such accidents. "Yes, one must. I'm sorry, Mother. I won't marry that poor girl just to save face. Let Prinbal have his chance. He wants to lead the clan more than I do anyway."

He is treated to the rare spectacle of his mother lost for

words.

The general consensus is that he had a lucky escape. If his drive had not cut out when it did, *Liberty Bird* would either have shaken itself to bits, blown up or been crushed by Yssim's atmosphere. Kheo keeps his opinion on the matter to himself.

He is still welcome in the hangar, where work is underway to ensure that *Liberty Bird* will race again. He might even be the one to fly her, when and if his father forgives him for declaring Prinbal the Reuthani heir. Assuming the Flamestar is still going then.

It is only natural that Sovat leads the repair work. And it is only natural that Kheo and he should take the chance to talk about the state of *Liberty Bird.*

Their conversation, held in the meeting room while the techs work outside, begins with an assessment of the damage, and what is being done to fix it. Kheo looks at Appis Sovat's hands twice, and his face once. He realises that the Chief Mechanic loves the yacht as much as he himself does, perhaps more.

"She was lucky, wasn't she?" asks Kheo. "Well, we both were. *Liberty Bird*, and me. Losing power at exactly the right moment to bounce us off Yssim's atmosphere." He hopes his words don't sound too disingenuous.

"So they say."

Kheo seizes his chance. "You don't think it was luck then?"

"It was *fortunate* the engine shut down soon as the rads and outside density reached critical. But not luck, sirrah, no."

"Ah." There had been a move, immediately after the Liberation, to install overrides to stop Pilots overdriving their engines but it had been deemed unnecessary, and insulting to the Pilots. "I… see." Kheo picks his next words carefully. "Having such a *fortunate* shutdown wouldn't be hard to arrange for someone with the right skills."

"I imagine not, sirrah." The tech's tone is careful.

Kheo ploughs on. "But one would have to ask why anyone

might arrange for such a thing."

"I've seen it before, sirrah." Sovat is looking at him directly now; he can feel it. "More than once."

"Seen what?" says Kheo slowly. He manages to raise his gaze as high as the tech's chest.

"The boys who can't live with themselves."

"Wait, you think I made the choices I did just because I… because you... You know nothing about me, Technician!" Except the one thing Kheo wished the man didn't know. His embarrassed anger lets Kheo meet Sovat's eyes.

"True enough, sirrah." The tech's voice and gaze are gentle. "And I'm not saying there's just the one cause. But that's part of it: us being what we are. It's not worth dying for, you know."

"It's pretty damn hard to live with."

"Hard for others to live with, yes."

"What do you mean?"

"Just that, sirrah: we're what we are. It's those around us that make it a problem."

"Unless we get caught."

The tech shrugs, though it is a considered gesture. "That's still true, for now. But not every change is for the worst."

"No, it isn't. Listen, I know I'm not, er, your type… but if I did want some advice about, well, safe places, where people like me, like us…?"

"I'd be happy to give it."

"Thank you." Kheo hesitates. "And thank you for knowing what I needed even if I didn't. Had anyone found out what you did –"

"I'm better at my job than that, sirrah."

"Even so, you risked your career for me."

"A career don't matter a s–spit compared to a life, sirrah."

Kheo nods. "Quite so. Good night, Engineer Sovat."

Alone in the briefing room, Kheo exhales. He calls up the plans for his yacht. The thought that he might never pilot *Liberty Bird* again is hard to face, but face it he will. Who knows, perhaps when contact with the rest of the universe strengthens he might fly something more amazing, perhaps even travel between the stars? Now that is a good dream to hold onto.

After a while he shuts down the display and goes to find his mother. There is something he needs to tell her.

Zanzara Island

Rachel Armstrong

"They vow to amend their lives, and yet they don't;
Because if drown'd, they can't — if spared, they won't."
Byron, Canto 5, Don Juan

The blood-gorged mosquito splattered on Ines' leg. Being hypersensitive to everything, the pregnant woman felt the tiny feet and stylets steal a bead of blood. Now the exploded body, too full to avoid her crushing blow, smeared her skin around a swelling punctum. She rubbed her belly. This was no time to contract any mosquito-borne disease with the baby girl growing inside her. Yet she was fortunate that the genetically modified mosquitoes of Zanzara Island bred few females. Chances were, she would not be bitten again for a while as the lothario, hairy-nosed, pollen-feasting males were woefully short of mates. Now, there was one less female on which the desperate suitors could lavish their long-legged attentions.

Pedro sighed, his attention on Gabriella. "There she goes again. That kid's definitely not all there."

"Leave her alone. She's just playing."

Gabriella's lips were moving but, being downwind, her father could not make out what she was saying. She appeared to be giving a running commentary while pushing a clump of plastic and debris away from the Venice shoreline with a stick. For the first few seconds it appeared to be reluctant to move and got repeatedly sucked back into the shore but soon, with persistent coaxing, it found a favourable current and sailed outwards into the lagoon.

Ines tried to silence Pedro's further commentary, but he

objected.

"At thirteen you're supposed to have outgrown imaginary friends."

The neat little clump of matter bobbed on the waves and sparkled momentarily under a shard of sunlight.

"But why ten? You have no fingers or toes?"

Foamy bubbles split and dissolved into the waves. Gabriella had read that these were the souls of mermaids that, not being human, would not go to heaven. They would silently dance on the surface of the sea for all eternity, without having experienced any kind of real feelings at all.

"Is consciousness a feeling?"

The morning was already melting into afternoon but it was too hot to be properly hungry. Tempers were starting to fray with the rising heat of the city. Even on the waterways where it was possible to bathe in the lagoon breeze, the traffic choked with rage. A gondolier nonchalantly tipped his ribboned hat at the backed-up string of river traffic he'd created when making an illegal broadside turn. Voices, fists and tempers rose above the engines and Pedro shook his head. Canal rage was endemic in the waterways.

"Gelato time."

Ines, who in Gabriella's opinion was the very embodiment of 'third time lucky', taught English and French at the Liceo Foscarini, the oldest high school in Venice. She had a no-nonsense approach to life and sympathetically linked arms when talking about important things. In fact, the child and her stepmother shared many things in common, including a common ancestry that had been established through DNA samples they'd donated to the Genographic Project, which was a research programme that used genetics and ancient documents to trace the origins of the first inhabitants of Venice. Their forefathers had migrated to the Veneto from modern-day northern Turkey even before many Italians sought refuge in the lagoons from the invasion of Italy by Attila the Hun and the Germanic Lombards in the 5th Century. Although very little was still known about their forefathers, their ancestral line had actually built the very fabric of the city. They sunk poles, drained the earth with canals and put bricks around the aqueous foundations of a fledgling settlement where none should have been possible.

"When your mother died, your father's new girlfriend was not ready for a family," Ines explained. "She left him with little more than broken kitchenware and a shopping list of complaints neatly laid out on the kitchen table."

"Oh."

"But you have me and your father now. We're a team. I want to be there for you and your new little sister. We'll be a family together."

"Okay."

Gabriella could not remember her own mother, who had apparently been so sad after childbirth that even electrical shock treatment applied directly across her head, could not help reunite her with the miracle of life.

"Limone prego."

Pedro watched his daughter sweep the dripping ice with her tongue. She pulled it into a point and demolished the softening crystals while scouring the water's edge. Without so much as a backwards glance, she was on her belly again at the waterside in animated conversation with a small pile of bobbing flotsam. This sun-fractured fragment of plastic swung like a magnetic compass between two tangles of algae. One was green and surface dwelling, while the other was brown and lurked several inches below the waves like a shadow, feeding on longer wavelengths. None of the entangled bodies appeared to be able to agree on where they should be along the shoreline.

"But how do you know you're *you*?"

Pedro shook his head. Why did she always wear that same turquoise shirt? Why could his daughter not be more feminine? Or at least show more of an interest in her appearance, like other girls her age? Was Gabriella punishing him?

Ines gently threaded her fingers through his hand, with a reassuring squeeze. Having waited patiently for his daughter to show some kind of reaction to her inevitable abandonment issues, Pedro was devastated that they never arrived. Each day Gabriella's eyes stayed dry, he feared that the delayed grief would manifest in other, potentially catastrophic, ways.

"What do you mean that thinking and feeling are the same?"

Being part of the Venice *Polizia di Stato*, Pedro and his colleagues patrolled the waterways in pursuit of smugglers, illegal immigrants, gangs, and traders. He'd seen his share of catastrophe. Yet, amidst the chaos caused by thefts, attacks and disputes, waterways congestion was the main issue that urgently needed confronting. Not only was the gondolier service thriving but new vaporetto lines had also entered service along with private hotel boats and city tours. The volume of boats and frayed tempers severely clogged the official routes to the islands. Yet, while collisions between vessels were recorded, drownings were not.

The day was sweltering and Pedro and Ines took refuge in the shade. He flicked through the news articles on his smart phone, while Ines spread a tatty book on her lap and began to read *Don Juan.* Around the reclining couple's feet, tiny lizards threaded through cracks in the paving stones, licking male mosquitoes from the air like dew. Gabriella found shelter from the sun under a bridge where plastics, algae, limpets, barnacles, engine oil and bacterial biofilms had secured tenuous attachments to the brickwork and formed a complex micro-reef where the water met the air. Shellfish tightly clenched the brickwork and barnacles grew into briccole like a second skin. Once these anchors had taken hold, the assorted assemblages found it much easier to loiter along the shoreline, like hair around a sink plughole. Apparently discussing a new configuration between the various shoreline bodies, Gabriella did not notice that the gargantuan shadow cast by a 12-deck cruise liner had eclipsed the sun. As she launched her little seedling island, the excited tourists glided past like gods on clouds, cheering and pointing at St. Mark's Square, the Doge's Palace and the Bridge of Sighs. While children waved up at the smiling crowds from the shoreline, canal water was backed-up into local toilets.

A plastic water bottle jerked its way down from one of the towering balconies arriving in the water several seconds after the cruise ship had gone.

"What do you mean 'food'? Ines says plastic never, ever goes away."

Pedro felt the sudden chill of the passing liner and instinctively drew his knees to his chest. He didn't want to think of work. Yet the imposing shadow reminded him of the twenty-five strong team of captains and a pair of tug boats which were assigned to board cruise ships outside the lagoon to protectively guide them through the city. The luxury liner boom contributed significantly to air and water pollution in the city and sucked out sediment from the lagoon. Now, there was less than one-third of the original salt marsh left. Adding insult to injury, these beasts also injected over two million tourists each year into the streets, which were already under constant siege from the side-effects of mass tourism. Venice's very fabric was buckling under the products of its own success.

"What's a quorum?"

"Like a family of ten then?"

"But that means you never get to do anything by yourself."

Gabriella's little clump of matter ducked and dived in the colossus' wake, disappearing from view as she fashioned more impromptu sculptural collages. The carefully sculpted flotsam migrated with other debris like seedling cells, compelled by the umbilical draw of the setting sun. Each of these tiny bodies struggled like weak swimmers to join in eddies that skirted the briccole and made their way towards a barely perceptible vortex situated around a hundred metres south of San Michele. Napoleon had forged this island cemetery, to deal with the unsanitary issue of burying bodies after he'd invaded the city. San

Michele itself was formerly two islands and become one when the canal between it and san Cristoforo della Pace was filled in during the early 19th century. Now, Gabriella had inherited the responsibilities of her forefathers in producing a new kind of settlement within the Venice bioregion. Together, child and Ecolevithan were thought-linked through the assembly of a strange, distributed, organically fashioned embryogenesis. As in the Venice of the ancients this fledgling settlement was an unnatural construction – a synthesis between humans and ecosystem. Instead of a city fashioned in inert materials, a whole new kind of entity began to take shape.

"That's six. Just four more for a quorum."

Locals already fondly referred to this debris as Zanzara Island – a continually differentiating synthetic body of plastic, algae and biofilms. Owing to the density of stagnant pools, the civic authorities had already granted permission for a research laboratory to test a new strain of genetically modified mosquitoes on the pleats, rolls and folds of matter that shaped its warty back. With climate change pushing tropical diseases ever further northwards, Venetians were at risk of malaria, dengue and yellow fever. The stagnant puddles that scarred Zanzara's surface had become hatcheries for mutant mosquitoes. Bundles of pointed eggs and tiny breathing tubes punctuated the menisci of these worlds. Yet, most of the creatures metamorphosing inside the egg sacs had been genetically modified. They were not destined to produce new populations of egg-layers but selected to shred the female X chromosome and leave only those that bore the Y hallmark of the male sex alive. In these tiny Byronesque swimming pools the sexual orgy that once guaranteed mosquitoes their dominion over the land never arrived. On sunny days the puddles hummed as newly metamorphosed flies broke from their membranous, eggshells and spread their wings under soft gusts of air. These tiny specs of life were carried like dandelion seeds towards the main island mass of the city. So, season after season, male progeny relentlessly hatched and stumbled on flotsam over the choppy waves to the mainland in search of females. Zanzara's extraordinary ecology intermingled with Venice's island of the dead, in a strange dance of sterile ecological eroticism that fed a subversive fertility that deeply entangled life and death. Unlike the vigorous poet, however, the wooing flies were doomed to fail in their mission, leaving the future of their kind at the mercy of a new conspiracy between technology and the subversive forces of the natural realm. Yet, while the proto-island genesis gestured towards natural biological decline, the discarded plastics and the intercellular matrix of algae and biological systems that polluted the lagoon strengthened its subversive epic embryology. These side effects of the Anthropocene even potentiated other ecosystems sheltering fish fry from the gaze of predators and buffering their tiny bodies against the unpredictable and sometimes sudden currents. Gabriella pushed another carefully fabricated island of debris into the lagoon.

"Seven."

Ines paused, and put the book down for a while as a cloud of male mosquitoes drunkenly raided pollen and plant juices from a scrawny, bright yellow weed that had shattered a paving stone on the walkway. She was amused by how Byron portrayed Don Juan as a victim of his sex. In contrast, the poet's own libido guaranteed he habitually completed the four-and-a-half mile journey from his residence at the Palazzo Mocenigo to the Lido beach across the Lagoon where beautiful courtesans held naked swimming parties. Such an endeavour was quite a commitment to love, particularly at the turn of the 19th century, as the canals were little better than open sewers. Yet such filth did not deter him until he was in a state of utter sexual exhaustion. She glanced over at Gabriella as she floated yet another raft of rubbish into the water, like a tiny boat.

"Eight."

The mutant mosquitos quietly arrived amidst small-scale protest. "No zanzara geneticamente modificate" was spray-painted onto old brickwork on walls and alleyways. In truth, there was never anything to resist. Tiger mosquitos were an uncontrollable plague that filled the strained hospital casualty with antibiotic resistant secondary infection lesions by the score. Malaria warnings were periodically issued despite environmental controls that targeted natural breeding grounds. Just as there was no great ceremony when the engineered eggs were inoculated into the stagnant Zanzara pools at dusk, the moral arguments against the technology were muted. The mutants were actually regarded as a kind of artisan practice, like the glass blowers of Murano. Oxitech scientists based in a laboratory in Marghera skillfully injected very small amounts of DNA into each 1mm long egg. The expensive handcrafted survivors of true-breeding mutants were carefully pipetted up and lovingly incubated in suspension. They were hand-reared to adulthood and guided with soft paintbrushes into compounds to mate with wild type mosquitoes. Those strains that were breeding mutant flies could be detected under dark light with glow-in-the-dark genetic markers. Once a stable line had been engineered, the Oxitech boat was sailed out to the shallow pools of the embryonic island and inoculated with tiny transformed eggs. Although environmental protesters periodically sabotaged the breeding ground, breaking up large areas of the biofilm, lagoon debris and plastic assemblage by driving motor boats through the flotsam, its sheer will to exist and relentless accumulation of debris around San Michele overwhelmed the vandalism. The developing Eco Leviathan continued to thrive.

"Nine."

A fresh gust of wind brought another revelling crowd of male mosquitoes hovering over the raft of an empty plastic bottle to the mainland sniffing the air for signs of females. Crowds of children suddenly appeared with their families, looking for a place to hang out for the evening following a clown over the bridge that drooled a long sausage-shaped bubble from a bucket and makeshift wireframe. They stood bewitched under the soapy rain as the undulating globes fizzed and popped into nothingness with the fading light – like mermaid foam. There never seemed to be time to properly finish anything.

Gabriella woke excitedly. Pedro had already gone to work and Ines had only just risen, having spent most of the night fighting off abdominal tightness.

"Zanzara has a new family. Please take me! Please!"

"We should bring a chain for the child, then".

"Don't be silly. It's not for people."

"Gabriella, whom are you talking to?"

"It's not really talking, Ines. It's a think-thing. Like knowing and feeling all at the same time."

"So why do you make words then?"

"Just habit. I guess."

Although the discomfort in her abdomen was growing, Ines gave in to Gabriella's relentless pleading and sent Pedro their plans by SMS.

"Going to Zanzara. Won't be long. Ix."

They took the 42 circular vaporetto from the Fondamente Nuove. The child was getting impatient. Ines swayed through the barriers. A tourist couple shuffled along a bench to make room for the pregnant woman. She was already regretting her decision as prolonged pains radiated across her back and lower abdomen. Gabriella clung impatiently to the rails and looked for San Michele on the horizon. Along the busy maritime highway gondoliers cheekily crossed the vaporetto routes. They threaded their way between the moving vessels to boast far better views of the scenery than the cheaper public transport.

Pedro was wasting his time arguing with the trader. His focus was elsewhere checking his phone for messages from Ines. She'd barely slept and was almost due. He wished Gabriella hadn't been so insistent in going to San Michele. Ines should have been tougher with her. The conman was gesticulating wildly, his face fracturing into defiant slithers of smiles, which told Pedro that he was very comfortable telling lies.

Gabriella turned around to Ines and waved joyfully. She could see Zanzara's puckered back, with its stagnant mosquito pools and newly formed family of biofilms. The light was scattering prettily over their surface, like a swarm of fallen stars.

A gargantuan wave from a monstrous liner crashed into the ferry, steering it directly into the path of a returning vaporetto. A gondola with a cargo of shrieking tourists nose-dived into the mud. Glass, metal and shards of wood crashed around Gabriella and Ines, as the vaporetto deck split and instantly jettisoned them into the murky water.

Gabriella did not feel the intrusive cold or wetness of the lagoon. She instinctively scrambled for the surface but the rolling vaporetto mercilessly sucked her back into the muddy waters and held her down.

Ines felt the contractions strengthen but failed to draw breath. She succumbed to the terrible calm of airlessness as a tiny bloody head began its head-down journey into the murky fluids that now swathed them both.

Stricken by the dreadful sight of her little sister being born to oblivion and the sensation that something was forcing itself into her airways, Gabriella began to count.

"Ten."

She mouthed the numbers with her lips.

"Ten."

Somewhere between peace and another place, Gabriella compelled the Venetian soils forged by her ancestral line to count along with her.

"Ten."

The tradesman's derisive smirk lingered as Pedro's attention focused on the police radio announcement, which urgently hissed details and its disgust at the unfolding vaporetto disaster. Those that had not been thrown into the water were already being herded on to other smaller boats and they were already recovering bodies with horribly faded faces. With ashen countenance he sped with his colleagues towards San Michele and began a desperate search among the wreckage for signs of life.

Ines was not responding to his calls. Her phone was dead.

"Ines? Gabriella?"

Pedro caught sight of a shroud-like object. He tugged at the turquoise cloth and recognized it as Gabriella's favourite shirt. There appeared to be altered blood in the water. As it started to come loose he could make out a child's figure encased in a strangely translucent film, like bubble wrap. He urgently motioned for assistance and several of his colleagues reached into the murky water.

"You may not want to see this, mate."

The object was offering an extraordinary amount of resistance. Welders were summoned. As the rescue team finally released the strange membranous substance, Pedro could just make out Gabriella's body. The seaweed like material appeared to be occluding her airways, as if it had suffocated her.

Another figure wrapped in this substance bobbed suddenly to the surface. It was Ines, shockingly waxen.

Pedro vomited over the side of the rescue boat.

"Oxygen, quickly someone! The newborn has not yet drawn breath!"

The tiny bloody body was still attached to a cling-wrapped umbilical cord.

"Sit down for God's sake if you're going to stay."

Gabriella was immediately tipped into the recovery position having been dissected from the biofilm and an attendant medic placed a finger on her neck, shaking her head.

Blood continued to leak from Ines' abdomen as she too was released from the dreadful tangle. She fell limp and grey, like a dead fish, onto the deck.

Defeated, Pedro sunk to his knees and sobbed.

As he did so, the tiny bundle within the warming blanket began to bawl and as the life-giving breaths restored her, as if she'd been in a deep sleep.

"Over here! Over here!"

"Quick! The child! These membranes seem to have stopped water from entering the lungs. Despite the prolonged submersion, she might just have a chance of life."

Pedro could not recall just for how long he cried. Or how much was joy – or pain. Yet, the shock and the extraordinary survival of the baby was infectious, as the rescuers too wept in solidarity at the strangeness of the situation.

As warming blankets were wrapped around the tiny baby, Pedro hugged her tightly as they were shepherded into water ambulances and the midday sun shone joy into the waters.

The networks of embryonic thought-actions that formed the evolving body-consciousness of the Zanzara Leviathan did not cease but remained vigilant to danger. It flicked water into some of the shallow pools on its puckered surface to top up the quickly evaporating fluid. The artisan mosquitoes were now intrinsic to the nascent creature and would be taken care of as its own.

Ten Sisters

Eric Brown

One

Revenge is the greatest motivator.

I escaped from the asylum after months of planning. For eight weeks I had bled myself, little by little, of three litres of blood. That morning at dawn I squeezed through a bathroom window, doused the blood across the cobbles of the alleyway next to the asylum, then fled across London and laid low for a month. There was no press coverage of my 'death', of course, but I was confident that the medics at the asylum – and more importantly Anna de Birkenstock – would assume that I was dead. No one could survive losing so much blood, after all. I immersed myself in holo-dramas, dreamed of revenge, and in between times fantasized about taking a colony ship to the stars.

Then I began my surveillance of Anna de Birkenstock, the millionaire business tycoon, patron of the arts, and the person I most reviled in all the world. She opened hospitals and galleries, appeared in online political debates championing a strict libertarian agenda, and propped up corrupt regimes in far-flung countries to further her business. And all the while, unbeknownst to all but her most intimate aides and clinicians, she planned to live forever.

A month after my 'death', I outfitted myself in the style of body-hugging two-piece Anna favoured, bought jewellery identical to that which she wore, and hired a limousine. On a morning when I knew she was sleeping in after a late-night party, I took the limousine across London to a small, exclusive clinic.

The security guard took one look at me, smiled obsequiously, and waved me through the swing door. The chief clinician, flustered at the unscheduled arrival, ushered me up to the penthouse suite where the patient slept.

I told him that for the next thirty minutes I was under no circumstances to be disturbed. Locking the door behind me, I turned and faced the bed.

The girl pushed herself up on to her elbows and stared at me.

Her gaze comprised disbelief and fear. I smiled; it was as if I were looking into a mirror, seeing there the tremulous dread I too had experienced when in the presence of Anna de Birkenstock.

I took her hand; her instinct was to pull away, but I held tight. "I'm not who you think I am," I murmured.

Her eyes widened.

I said, "I am not Anna de Birkenstock."

"Then who...?"

I squeezed her hand. I stared into her face, pale and oval, her hair drawn tightly back like that of a ballerina; she was perfection, and gazing at her it was all I could do not to weep.

"I escaped," I said, and told her the truth about herself. "And now I'm taking you away from here..."

"But the operation?"

"They lied to you," I said. "You're not undergoing it for your own good, but Anna's... I'll explain later. Now get dressed."

I opened the valise I had brought with me and pulled out a two-piece identical to the one I was wearing, along with an array of jewellery. Dazed, she dressed; I applied lipstick and make-up to her face, and minutes later she was ready.

"Now listen carefully," I said. "Take the valise and leave the building by the front exit. Don't worry. You'll be fine. They won't suspect a thing. There will be a taxi waiting outside. Give the driver this."

I passed her a card on which was printed the address of an apartment in Chelsea. I gave her a twenty euro note, a key to the apartment, and told her to smile. "I said don't worry. I'll see you at the apartment later this evening. You'll find food in the fridge."

She shook her head. "But how will you...?"

"There's a rear exit. I'll slip out minutes after you've left. Now go."

I hugged her, watched her step from the room, and a minute later checked that the way was clear before making for the access stairway.

Two

I hurried from the clinic, changed in a nearby hotel room booked especially for the occasion, and emerged wearing a bright summer dress and high heels. I wore a blonde wig, designer glasses, and a poncho in the latest fashion.

I took a flier north to Hampstead and rendezvoused with Richard – the junior medic who, six months earlier, had risked his life by telling me the truth. Soon after that I'd made my plans, enlisting Richard's aid in stealing de Birkenstock's credit pin for just one hour. That was all the time I'd needed to transfer the funds from her account, the funds which would – in time – subsidize my revenge.

This was our first meeting since my 'death', in case Anna's people had become suspicious and arranged to have him followed.

We had to act fast. In the morning, with Anna^{2}'s disappearance, Anna de Birkenstock would lose no time in getting her people to prepare Anna^{3}.

Richard piloted a flier from the rooftop pad and headed north-east to Suffolk. "Where is she?" I asked.

"Allenby Hall, just outside Newmarket." He inserted the flier into the stream of air-traffic heading out of the capital.

I told him how we would succeed in liberating Anna^{3}, and he listened attentively, his head to one side and his lips pursed. He smiled and reached out to take my hand.

I changed again when Richard landed in the lane outside the walls of Allenby Hall. By the time he converted the flier to a roadster and approached the imposing iron gates, I was Anna de Birkenstock in person, suited and bejewelled; I had her arrogant demeanour down pat.

Richard wore a chauffeur's peaked cap and waited in the drive while I breezed up the steps to the front door and demanded to see Dr Franklin, Anna de Birkenstock's chief physician.

He was flustered by my unannounced arrival, but of course acceded to my wishes.

I recalled the times, growing up in the asylum, when Anna de Birkenstock had visited me. A woman identical to myself, though older: how much older had been hard to fathom, as anti-aging procedures, as well as surgery, had worked their wonders. I recall her kindness, the compassion in her eyes – a solipsism I mistook for altruism, back then.

Dr Franklin escorted me into Anna^3's room, announced me and withdrew.

She was standing by the window, staring out, and turned as I crossed to meet her.

She was, of course, identical to the girl I had liberated from the clinic just hours ago.

She smiled. "Ms de Birkenstock... a pleasure."

"Would you care for a walk around the grounds?" I said. "I'd like to hear how you are enjoying life here at the hall."

She acceded – no request of Anna de Birkenstock's was ever refused – and we left the room and descended the wide staircase. I told a hovering Dr Franklin of my desire to enjoy the sunset. He smiled uneasily, discommoded at the lack of precedence, but simpered and gestured us across the hallway.

We emerged into the warm early evening and walked away from the house. Despite my confidence that nothing could go wrong, I felt as if a target were pinned between my shoulder blades.

We strolled across the vast lawns towards a stand of elm.

In a soft voice she told me of her studies, how she was

looking forward to university in three months. She was eighteen, like me, with all her life ahead of her.

I made the occasional comment, but my thoughts were far away. I recalled my reaction when Richard had told me the truth of my existence – when he had, in just a few words, laid bare the lie of my life. I had not believed him, of course – how can you believe that everything you held as true was no more than a sham, and what is more an evil sham perpetrated by people who you had not only trusted but, in some cases, even loved?

I had refused to believe him, six months ago, until he had produced medical records to back up his claims, and promised that he would help me to escape.

I would not tell Anna^3 now, for fear of provoking a hysterical reaction. Richard would explain everything later, and I'd introduce her to Anna^2 once we were back at the apartment.

We walked through the elms, rounded the house, and came to Richard's flier stationed beyond the wall of the kitchen garden.

He opened the rear door and I gestured Anna^3 to climb inside. With an uncertain glance at me, she did so.

I slipped in beside the girl and Richard powered up the turbos. We rose, turned and banked away from the hall.

Anna^3 sat forward, alarmed, and stared at the rapidly diminishing shape of the stately home. "Where are we–?"

She said no more, as I directed a sedative spray at her face and she slumped back in the seat.

The flier swung south and accelerated towards London.

Three

Richard emerged from the bedroom we had allocated to Anna^3.

"How is she?"

"Very much as you were, all those months ago when I broke it to you. Shell-shocked, in a word."

I brushed past him. "I'll talk to her."

Anna^3 sat on the bed, her knees drawn up to her face, her head bowed.

She looked up as I approached. She had been crying.

"I know exactly how you feel," I said, sitting beside her. "I know exactly what you're going through."

She nodded, dumbly. "It's... hard to believe. Everything I thought... My life..." She broke down.

I held her hand and murmured platitudes.

"We're identical," she said, "you and I."

"Identical on the outside," I said, "and on the inside, too, right down to the chromosomal level. Which is why Anna..."

"Don't!" she cried, pressing her forehead against her knees and sobbing.

A little while later she looked up. "So... Why have you saved me?"

"How could I leave you there?" I asked. "And also... You can help us."

"Help you do what?"

"Eventually, to kill Anna de Birkenstock." I smiled. "In the meantime, I'll introduce you toAnna^2."

I led her from the room, through the apartment, and knocked on a bedroom door. A small voice said, "Yes?"

I opened the door and ushered Anna^{3}inside. She stopped on the threshold, staring at the identical girl sitting on the bed, hugging her shins.

"I'll leave you two to talk," I murmured, and withdrew.

Richard was waiting in the lounge. He crossed to me, took my shoulders and pulled me to him. I stiffened, as always.

"Anna..." He gestured to the spare room.

"No, please... I can't."

"You can trust me, you know?"

"It isn't that," I said. "Give me time."

"You're so cold."

"And wouldn't you be cold, if you'd gone through what I've gone through, been brought up to believe...?"

"I told you, you can trust me."

I honestly didn't know whether or not I could trust him. But my reluctance to give myself to Richard, physically and emotionally, was more fundamental than any notion of trust. Quite simply, I felt nothing for Richard... *or for myself.* I was consumed by the desire for revenge, and felt nothing more.

Even a desire for life was beyond me, for I fully expected not to survive the forthcoming ordeal.

Four

We sedated the Annas' bedtime drinks and at ten that night set off in the flier.

We had little time to lose. By now the authorities would be aware that Anna^{2} was missing, and that an impostor had breached the security of Allenby Hall and abducted Anna^{3}. As we sped from London, heading for the South Downs and Kemp House, I knew that security surrounding the rest of the Annas would tighten considerably. Abducting Anna^{4} would be far more difficult than the taking of Anna^{2} and Anna^{3}.

Which was why, this time, I would not be presenting myself in the guise of Anna de Birkenstock.

We came down a mile from the house and proceeded the rest of the way on foot.

Security had, as I feared, been stepped up. We sedated three guards, one by one, in the grounds of the house, leaving them trussed and gagged. We broke into the house through a ground floor bathroom window and crept through the silent house to the second floor. A guard sat on a chair at the end of the corridor, leafing through a magazine. Richard breezed up to him, spraying sedative in the man's face when he looked up, startled.

"Where now?" I said.

He pointed along the corridor. "Third door on the left." He had worked with Anna^{4} for a month before being seconded to the asylum where I had been imprisoned.

We approached the door and I lasered the lock to slag.

Anna^{4} was still asleep as we crept into the room. We had decided that the best way to abduct the girl, this time, would be to sedate her; Richard would then carry her from the house, myself leading the way with the laser set to stun.

I applied the sedative spray and Richard eased the girl over his shoulder in a fireman's lift.

Cautiously we made our way down the stairs and out through the front door. Ten minutes later we were back at the flier and heading north to London with our unconscious cargo.

Five

Sunlight slanted through the kitchen window. The four of us sat around the table, nursing mugs of coffee. Anna^4 was wide awake now, and recovering from the shock of discovering exactly who and what she was.

We wore identical pyjamas which I'd bought in preparation. A stranger, peering in through the window, would have beheld four identical sisters.

"It's strange," Anna^3 said, smiling at us, "but I'd often wondered what it might be like to have a sister."

Anna^4 laughed. "The same."

I said, "Imagine how I felt when Richard told me that I had multiple sisters."

Anna^2 looked at me. "How many?" she asked.

"Nine," I said.

"Nine sisters..." Anna^4 said in wonder. "Ten in all. Ten sisters..."

We heard the front door open and Richard entered the kitchen. "Anna^5 is being held at a small cottage hospital in Carmarthen," he told me. "Security is lax."

I stared at him. "It is? Why on Earth...?"

"I'll tell you on the way."

Richard showed his pass at the reception desk, introducing me as his assistant. I wore an auburn wig and wire-framed glasses. The nurse hardly gave me a second glance.

We made our way through the tiny hospital to the private room, and Richard paused outside the door. I was not looking forward to meeting Anna^{5}, knowing what she had endured.

I entered after Richard and crossed to the figure in the bed.

Anna^{5}'s head moved in our direction. I tried not to gasp in despair.

The girl's eyelids were stitched shut after the operation to remove her eyes.

"Hello?" she said, tentatively.

Richard sat down beside the bed. "It's Dr Elliot," he said, taking her hand.

"Doctor!" Her face, it was no exaggeration to say, lit up. "Doctor, no one will tell me... But when will I be able to see again?"

He squeezed her hand, and my stomach turned as he lied, "Soon, Anna. Quite soon, now."

He eased past me and looked up and down the corridor, then tapped my shoulder to signal the all clear.

I moved to the bed, slipped the sedative from my bag and sprayed her in the face. Richard opened the window and, together, we carried her from the bed and eased her out.

Minutes later we lifted off and returned at speed to London.

Six

The following day we discovered from an orderly in our pay that Anna^{6} and Anna^{7} had been moved from the Manscombe Mere in Derbyshire and secreted in an unknown location. From another source we learned that Anna^{8} had been transferred from a hospital in Scotland to a secure psychiatric unit near Manchester, and we agreed that a raid on the unit would be too risky.

However, from the same source we found out that Anna^{9} and Anna^{10} were due to be transferred from a safe house near London to hospital in Kent. As promised, security was deliberately light to avoid drawing attention, but even so I was relieved when everything went to plan. We stopped the ambulance in a roadblock, stunned the guards and liberated the Annas.

We returned to London, and I revelled in the knowledge that by now Anna de Birkenstock would be well and truly rattled.

We sat around the kitchen table that evening, the seven of us. Richard had retired to bed, alone, despite his entreaties for me to join him.

We drank coffee and discussed the future.

"And the other Annas?" asked Anna^{4}. "Annas six, seven and eight?"

"We will liberate them, eventually – perhaps after we have eliminated de Birkenstock."

Anna^{5} leaned forward, eager. "And how will we do that?"

I counselled caution. "We can't rush into this," I said, "despite our wanting to get it over with."

"To exact revenge..." Anna^{10} said.

"There will be time enough," I said. "We must plan carefully, take everything into consideration. Security at the castle she calls her home will be tight, even though they can't know exactly what we're planning. They must know we're up to something, and they'll be prepared for every eventuality."

"And when she's dead?" Anna^{4} said. "What about our futures?"

I had looked no further than exacting sweet revenge. "Then our difficulties will be just beginning."

Anna^{5} murmured, "And will I ever see again?"

Seven

The following evening over dinner I noticed Richard and Anna^{10} exchanging glances. They were guarded, surreptitious, but I knew the look in Richard's eyes, and the corresponding willingness from Anna^{10}.

I had suspected, of course, that with other Annas from whom to take his pick, he would soon move his attentions away from me.

But did I suspect even more? Even then, my suspicion primed, did I expect an ultimate betrayal?

That night I waited behind my bedroom door and listened for the sound of Richard's door opening along the corridor. At a little after midnight I heard the quiet sound of footsteps. I cracked my door open half an inch and watched as he crept along the corridor and slipped into Anna[10]'s room.

I moved along the corridor and pressed my ear to the door.

Their voices were indistinct, but discernible.

"She doesn't suspect?" she said.

"I'm pretty sure she doesn't."

"She's a clever one," said Anna[10]. "When does she plan to...?"

Richard replied. "She thinks you're still at the castle. She said it's best to bide our time, let the furore of the abductions die down."

I hardly believed what I was hearing. *She thinks you're still at the castle...*

Their conversation ceased and they made love.

My heart hammering, I hurried back to my room. I found my laser and crouched down against the wall beside the door, listening for the sound of Richard leaving Anna's room.

In the early hours I heard a door open and footsteps passing along the corridor. I allowed five minutes to elapse.

Enraged and yet exultant, I slipped from my room and approached Anna[10]'s... Except, of course, the woman behind the door was not Anna[10].

I had waited months for this moment, envisaged the look on Anna de Birkenstock's face when I raised the laser and told her that, far from living for ever, she was about to die.

I turned the handle and hurried into the room, switched on the light and approached the bed, gripping the laser in my outstretched hands.

Anna sat up, sleep-confused and blinking. "What...?"

I stood over her, the laser aimed at her perfect head.

I tried to discern in the lineaments of her oval face some indication that she was older than me and all the other Annas. But it was as if I were staring into a mirror, seeing only a reflection of the face I knew so well.

"Very clever," I said.

She smiled at me. "What are you talking about?"

"Infiltrating the Annas," I said. "Very clever. But why?"

She tried to bluff. "I don't know what you're talking about. I'm Anna[10]..."

"No, you're not," I said. "I heard you talking with Richard earlier. I heard everything. It was a set up," I went on. "You used Richard, paid him to tell me the truth." I shook my head. "But why?"

Perhaps to buy herself time, she said, "I thought I knew you all – all of you Annas. You are, after all, *me*. I thought I knew how you'd react to anything. But you'd each been brought up in slightly different environments, each susceptible to slightly varying stimuli. I selected the one I thought the strongest – you, Anna[1], and had Richard tell you the truth."

"To see how I'd react?"

She smiled, sadly. "No, Anna," she said. "I wanted you to know the truth so that I might explain myself."

I stared at her. "Explain?"

"To make you understand why–"

I interrupted. "I understand *why*..."

"No, you don't! That would be impossible. You're young, in perfect health. If you were like me, old and failing–"

"How old are you?"

"Would you believe that I am almost sixty?"

I swallowed, sickened. "No."

"Of course, I don't look that old. I have access to all the best anti-aging drugs... But drugs can only do so much. When my organs fail, one by one..."

"You bitch!"

"I don't want to die yet, Anna," she said, almost pleading with me, beseeching. "Don't you see?"

"So you had us cloned, to harvest..."

"If you were me, Anna..." she began. "Look into your heart, your soul, and admit that I am right. You would kill any of them, out there, for increased longevity."

"No!" I cried, backing up against the door.

She said, "I wanted to explain myself, to try to make you understand. To... to gain your absolution." She shook her head. "I never envisaged that you would be this strong, this resourceful. I didn't expect you to flee, and rescue the other Annas"

"You could have stopped me at any point," I said.

"Of course. But I was intrigued. I wanted to see what you were planning. Richard suggested stopping you, once he learned that you wanted to kill me – but I wanted to talk to you, face to face, to make you understand."

"Understand?" I laughed. "Oh, how I've dreamed of this moment! How I've dreamed of getting revenge. How does it feel to know that you're going to die, very soon – how does it feel to know that, despite your dreams, you won't be living forever?"

She maintained her poise, I'll give her that. She smiled at me as her left hand inched, little by little, beneath the pillow.

I raised the laser and aimed at her head. "I really should bring all the other Annas in here to watch you die."

I had meant to extend our dialogue, make her repent, perhaps admit the errors of her ways, but I knew that that would be impossible.

And, perhaps, I feared something that she had said: *that she wanted to make me understand.* I feared that I might sympathise with her.

As her hand moved towards whatever weapon she had concealed under the pillow, I pulled the trigger, once, and the laser drilled a neat hole through her forehead. She didn't even have time to look surprised.

In the silent aftermath, my heart thudding, I stared at the corpse and considered my actions, and what I should do then.

I checked that the corridor was clear, then lifted Anna de Birkenstock's body and dragged it across the corridor to my room. Having regained my breath, I arranged the corpse on the bed and slipped the laser into her hand.

Then I made my way back to her room, lay on the bed and tried to sleep.

Eight

I was awoken from a fitful doze by the sound of a rapid knocking at the door. As I lifted my head from the pillow, Richard hurried into the room. He sat in the side of the bed, reached out and cupped my cheek.

"Anna[1]," he said. "She's dead. She shot herself."

I shook my head, feigning shock. "She *must* have known about us..."

He looked confused. "But she was so driven, so single-minded in her need for revenge. This doesn't make sense."

I slipped out of bed and moved to the door. "Come with me."

I hurried along the corridor to my room and held the door open for Richard. We moved inside and I stared down at the corpse. I took the laser from her loose fingers and looked at Richard.

"What now?" he said.

"Sit down," I ordered.

He crossed to the chair beside the window and sat down. I moved to the door, leaned against it and stared at him.

"What?" he said. His expression became alarmed when I raised the laser and aimed at him.

"I know all about it," I said. "Your betrayal – your part in Anna's plan."

His eyes narrowed. "Who are you?" He sounded frightened.

"Anna[1]," I said, and had the pleasure of seeing the fear in his eyes as I shot him through the chest.

I woke the other Annas and I told them that Anna de Birkenstock was dead, then outlined Richard Elliot's betrayal.

A stunned silence greeted my words, then blind Anna^5 said, "Anticlimactic, but a relief. What now?"

"Now we move from here, immediately. There's no telling if her people are aware of our location. I have another place across the city."

We lost no time and, one by one, we took taxi-fliers across town to the safe-house in New Camden.

Nine

They came for us two days later.

We were seated around the kitchen table, bathed in sunlight – six identical young women exchanging details of our lives to date, our hopes for the future. I promised I'd supply them all with new identities via contacts I'd made in the capital. They would be forced to undergo plastic surgery to alter their appearances, and life would not be easy.

But at least now the future belonged to them; we were individuals, I told them; we were no longer *property*.

The security team entered without a sound, almost with reverence. Within seconds a dozen black-garbed armed men moved around the table, covering us with their snub-nosed weapons.

I hardly had time to register my shock.

Across the table, I watched with disbelief as Anna^5 stood up, smiling. "Take them away," she ordered.

A gentle hand fastened itself around my arm and eased me to my feet.

Ten

I sat on the bed in a room at Allenby Hall, looking up as Dr Franklin entered and smiled down at me.

Days had elapsed since my recapture, but I had not counted

them. I lived in an eternal present, the past a source of regret, the future too terrible to contemplate.

"Anna de Birkenstock will be arriving shortly," he said, "for the operation."

"Anna...?" I began. "But you know she's not Anna de Birkenstock! The original Anna is dead. I killed her, and Richard, back at the flat."

His gaze silenced me. "Of course we know all about that."

"So why...?"

"Think about it," he went on. "How could we go public with de Birkenstock's death? Think how that might have affected the success of the de Birkenstock Organisation."

I stared at him, appalled by his cynicism.

He laughed. "Oh, you little fool! Don't you realise – it wasn't Anna de Birkenstock you should have despised, but the tycoons and businessmen behind her: her backers, Anna, the people who put her where she was."

I shook my head, despairing.

"And now," he said, "we need to be seen to have a strong leader, a figurehead. You see, what matters is that the Organisation prospers, makes us all very, very rich." He smiled. "Now take your pill, there's a good girl."

He placed a pill and a glass of water on the bedside table.

"What...?"

"Your pre-op medicine," he said, and slipped from the room.

Later, alone, I stood by the window and stared down at the long gravelled drive as a limousine pulled up and a tall, elegant figure stepped out.

Anna^5, or Anna de Birkenstock – not that it mattered: we were all, of course, identical – paused, and, as if sensing my presence, raised her head to stare, blindly, at the window.

Compelled, I lifted my hand and waved.

Licorice

Jack Skillingstead

Becoming human hadn't really worked out. Just look at this place. Ethan lay on the trundle bed's thin mattress. The room enclosed him in dismal seediness. A bare light bulb stuttered and buzzed in the ceiling socket. Shadows twitched over the bed, the pressboard dresser, his clothes draped on the arms of the upholstered chair. The room smelled of sweat, toilet water, and deeply absorbed cigarette smoke. Ethan's shoes pointed at the door, black socks drooping out of them as if they'd decided to abandon Ethan but hadn't quite the animation to take the first step, let alone disengage the security bar and turn back the multiple bolts and latches.

Ethan held a black pill, no larger than a peppercorn, between thumb and first finger. Four out of ten pills remained – three if he swallowed this one now. He based consumption of the pills on a standard denary system. The whole universe was denary-based. Ethan himself was one of the original Ten Creators, so he should know. As such, he was, technically, all powerful. At least he would be if he hadn't chosen to become human. And becoming human *really* hadn't worked out.

Also, Ethan wasn't his name.

On the sidewalk under his window, a man and a woman began arguing. "Please," the man said, "I'm giving it to you."

"You can shove it up your ass," the woman said.

Ethan sat up on the trundle bed, making the springs squeak tiredly

"I don't want to lose you," the man on the sidewalk said, practically sobbing. "Take it. I won't hide anything from you again. Not ever."

Easy to say, Ethan thought, *after what you've already hidden and only revealed once she'd caught you.* And here it was again: Ethan inside another person's head. It happened all the time if he didn't take his pills. Was this why he had no firm identity of his own? Let the so-called doctors parse that one out. Ethan's ability to migrate through other minds had served him positively when he was writing stories for *Galactic Tales of Wonder* and *The Uncanny Zoo.* Other than that, it didn't help. He feared straining through the minds of everyone around him while his own body remained immobile forever. Also, no one ever bought his stories. He resorted to the computer at the public library where he posted his favorites for free download on Amazon. When after a week they achieved fewer than ten downloads each, even when added together the numbers for three separate stories, he panicked and pulled them all. He and the other Ten Creators had designed a denary Universe. It was bad luck to fuck with that.

Ethan got up, took ten shuffling steps to the kitchen nook, pressing his fingers to his temples. At the sink he held a dirty coffee mug under the faucet and turned on the cold water tap. Water trickled into the mug. Silently, he counted to ten then cranked the tap off. He pushed the pill between his lips and washed it down. The water slid oily over his tongue and tasted like tarnished copper.

He waited, leaning on the edge of the sink, head down, counting backward from ten. When he reached zero, the pill released its chemical power (or so he imagined) and knitted closed the leak in his mind. Self-contained once more, Ethan approached the window (ten steps in a modified stride). Under his bare feet, the loose, paper-thin carpet felt like the skin of a malnourished animal. At the window, he pulled the curtain aside. Iron bars fenced him off from Brooklyn. Below the windowsill, a man in a rumpled sport coat pressed something into a woman's reluctant grasp. The man was about Ethan's age, thirty or so, but heftier than Ethan, who at best presented as malnourished. The woman wore a black cocktail dress and too many rings. Her hair fell messily across her cheek. Was it deliberate, or had it come undone? "Take it," the man said. "Go look. It's all there. You'll see it's nothing. A lot of talk. Dumb talk."

The woman made a fist around whatever he had given her. Was she about to strike him? Having taken his pill, Ethan had no idea beyond his imagination. Perhaps it was always imagination; he didn't like to consider that. Though he knew he was one of the original Ten Creators of the Universe, in this human form he had so often been mistaken for an ordinary madman that Ethan sometimes believed this was indeed the case.

"Joe," the woman in the black dress said, and Ethan, though she was clearly speaking to the man in the rumpled sport coat, felt himself addressed. Ethan backed away from the window (two steps plus a silent count of five to serve the multiple equaling ten), confused. Outside, the man sobbed openly. "Wait –"

Footsteps retreated. The woman leaving him? After a sobbing interval, a second set moved off.

She had spoken his real name. It was Joe, not Ethan. Joe contained only three letters and so wasn't even a multiplier that could equal ten. No wonder he hadn't remembered earlier! His name was bad luck.

If she knew him did that mean she was one of the Ten Creators of The Universe? Perhaps he was not the only one who had decided to try exile in human form. Was he not alone after all? Alternatively, it might be nothing. Are there coincidences? He couldn't remember what he and the others had decided about that. Joe pulled on jeans, a t-shirt, and a shiny blue warm-up jacket. He plucked his traitor socks from his shoes and filled both socks and shoes with his feet. Outside, the air smelled of a recent rainfall. The wet sidewalk gleamed like seal skin under the street lamps. Joe felt disoriented. The air buzzed with nervous energy, like the failing light bulb in his room. People shouldered past him, their faces moving, emitting noise. Words. Joe was like them and not like them. He held his breath and counted down from ten, the denary calming him, centering him.

Joe.

At the end of the block, the woman in the black dress halted by a lamp post, staring at the object in her opened fist. After a moment, Joe understood she was weeping.

At his halting approach (his head was full of tens; moving down the sidewalk in ten-step sections while counting cracks in the pavement), she opened her hand and dropped the insubstantial thing, a tiny wad of paper. She glanced at Joe then turned and passed under a pink squiggle of neon. Joe stooped to pick up the wadded paper. He pried it open with his fingernail and read the word hand-printed across the wrinkles. BOOSTAR555. He counted letters and numbers. Ten again. Proof that coincidences were not part of the design.

The pink squiggle was a martini glass tilted festively (drunkenly?) over the doorway of the Moonlight Lounge. Joe stood under the neon sign listening for the code to unlock the secret mystery of BOOSTAR555. He imagined the code whispered intermittently from charged gas trapped inside the pink glass tubing. It was the key to releasing him from human bondage.

Go after her. She's one of you.

Joe entered the lounge, where answers waited. Recorded cabaret music failed to enliven the environment. Heavy wooden booths absorbed the already-dim light. A stuffed raccoon stared down from the back bar with black marble eyes. Two men together and the woman in the black dress sat at opposite ends the leather and oak bar, feet propped on the brass rail. The men stared blatantly at the woman, and the woman stared at her drink – something blue in a stem glass. Her fingers picked apart a cocktail napkin, like scavengers hunting for a morsel.

Joe looked at BOOSTAR555, then closed his fingers around it and approached the bar. He sat, leaving one stool open between himself and the woman, as if they were expecting a mutual friend, or the answer to an important question. Succumbing to the ambience, Joe ordered a scotch.

The woman ignored him, her cocktail napkin reduced to

confetti that failed miserably to suggest celebration. Joe watched from the corner of his eye, anticipating a pattern, a true coded message, something. When coherency didn't emerge (a theme in his blighted life), Joe opened his hand and placed it on the bar between them, BOOSTAR555 in his palm. "You dropped this," he said, "didn't you?" Adding the question reduced his advantage, and he wished he could take it back.

The woman looked sidelong at his hand. "Not mine," she said.

"It's a code, isn't it? From Joe."

She turned her head and looked directly at him. Her unevenly applied lipstick gave her mouth the appearance of a double meaning. She narrowed her eyes, or refocused them, and he realized she was already drunk, and must have been even during the argument under his window. "And you are?" she said.

"I'm –"

"Who do you *think* you are?"

His reply dissolved. Her question was so relevant. He closed his mouth to form a new answer. She was angry, indignant, perhaps righteously so. He found it difficult to interpret the signs. Joe rummaged through a store of expected responses – a box in a dingy corner of his mind which contained the sorts of things people might say in given circumstances. He found something and quickly adapted it, first trying the words in the privacy behind his eyes. *You seemed upset.* "I'm nobody," he said aloud. "You seemed upset." The addition of *I'm nobody*, though technically accurate, may have been a mistake. She drew back. *Don't improvise*, he told himself.

"I'm upset," she said. "Why shouldn't I be?" She picked up her drink and finished it. "Blue Jasmine."

He frowned, not understanding.

"You want to buy me a drink, don't you?" she said, clarifying things. "That's the point, correct?"

"Yes?"

The bartender removed the woman's empty glass and

shredded napkin. He mixed a new drink, strained it into a clean glass, and set it before her on a fresh napkin. "Cheers," she said, tilting her glass toward Joe. He stared at her. She rolled her eyes. and drank. Joe sipped his house scotch. It was awful. He put the glass down and pushed it away.

"About the code," he said.

"What code?"

"Here." Joe tapped the wrinkled paper with BOOSTAR555 written on it. She swept her hand at it and the scrap of paper fluttered to the floor. Joe grabbed for it and almost fell off his stool. Holding onto the edge of the bar, he reached down and came up with the paper.

"It's just his password." the woman said. "Are you going to drink that?" She pointed at his drink.

"What? No."

She pulled his glass over.

"Whose password?" he asked.

"Joe's."

"I'm Joe."

She held his glass of scotch to her lips, eyeing him owlishly over the rim. "Huh?"

"My name. It's Joe. Are you saying this is my password. And by password do you mean code? I need something to unlock my powers."

"You're fucked up." She threw her head back and finished his scotch. It pulled her face into a knot which loosened after a moment, her eyes blinking rapidly to catch up. "I'm out of here. Call me a cab or, what is it, Uber. Now you're supposed to say you're a cab. You're an Uber doesn't sound right."

"You're one of the Ten, aren't you?"

The bartender loomed in. "You okay, Allison?"

Allison.

The bartender knew her. She came from the neighborhood. Had she been monitoring him? Was Joe the only one in the dark? The raccoon observed them beadily from its dusty perch on the back bar.

"I'm A-okay," Allison said and started to stand, then abruptly dropped back on her barstool, as if a faulty mechanism had given way, as if pins had slipped out of her knee joints. "Give me another drink, please." The bartender filled a glass with water, garnished it with a lemon rind, and set it before her. Allison regarded the water without comment. She turned to Joe. "Is Joe really your name?"

"I think so."

She laughed. "Don't you *know*?"

He smiled because her laugh suggested it was the appropriate response, even though he didn't grasp the humor. He supposed it was a thing missing in him; one of the things.

"You're pretty strange," Allison said.

"Am I? I think you're one of the Ten."

She squinted. "Listen. Don't get any bright ideas."

"I don't understand." Joe drew back a little, as if distance enhanced clarity.

"People *know* me in this place, all right?" She turned to the bartender. "How about another Blue Jasmine?"

"Drink your water, Allie," he said. "Then maybe."

Allison made a face and picked up the glass, held it a moment, then set it back down. She leaned towards Joe. "Sometimes it's a pain in the ass to know people."

"Yes. *Yes.*"

"Aw, what do you know about it."

"I –"

"Anybody ever cheated on you?"

"No."

"You're lucky." She grabbed the scrap of paper away from him. "This password, it's supposed to make me think Joe – my Joe – is sorry. But all it means is that he wants me to love him even if he goes online and talks to men. I'm supposed to log-in, okay? Go on his account and see it's all harmless. You know what I think?"

"Not yet."

She squinted. "I think *my* Joe has identity issues."

Joe's attention quickened. Perhaps too eagerly, he said, "I do, too."

"You don't even know him."

"I meant me, I have identity issues."

"Oh, God. Really?"

"That's why I said I think so when you asked if my name was really Joe. *Because I don't know.* Can I tell you something? Something in all seriousness?"

"In all seriousness?" She looked intently at him, swaying on her bar stool. "Only if you get me another drink."

Joe motioned for the bartender. "I want to try one of those blue things." When the new drink arrived Joe held onto it until the bartender turned his back, then he passed it to Allison, who drank half of it and quickly handed it back. She regarded him unsteadily. "Go ahead, Joe. If that's your name."

He sipped the Blue Jasmine. His disorganized thoughts floated and bumped into each other like cargo in a flooded hold. "That's the thing, I don't know if it's my real name or not. I guess it doesn't matter. The name is like the body. It's an identity marker, not the identity itself."

"Joe. Honey. What the *hell* are you talking about?" Then in a stage whisper, "Quick, give me that." She grabbed the almost-empty glass, finished it, and put the glass down just as the bartender turned and frowned suspiciously at them both. Had the raccoon whispered to him? "May I have another glass of water," Allison said. "This one's warm."

Looking unhappy, the bartender scooped ice into a glass, filled it with water, and set it before her. She gave him a sloppy lipstick smile and turned back to Joe. "Do go on."

"Never mind," Joe said. He felt defeated by the encounter, as he did by most encounters.

Allison grabbed his jacket sleeve. "No you don't. Tell me the rest of it."

Joe looked at her hand. "Remember – I don't actually *know* any of this."

"Go on."

"I don't belong here. I'm not one of you. One of them, I mean – if you're a Ten."

"You've got eyes. Do you think I'm a ten?"

"I want to think it. That code, if it could unlock me, then I would know everything."

"Who's 'them'?"

"Them. The human race. The natural humans."

Allison shook her head, like it was attached to a wobbly spring, making her hair flip across her cheek. "Sorry, but you pass. You might not be a shining example, but you definitely pass the human test."

Joe smiled weakly. "What it feels like is I just started, out of nowhere, in a dumpy apartment a couple of blocks from here. I didn't even have a name until I heard you say 'Joe,' and then I thought that sounded right. I thought, yeah, that's me. I'm Joe. For sure. Before that, I called myself Ethan, but that's just a name on a license I found in a drugstore. Look."

He dug his wallet out of his hip pocket. It wasn't really his wallet. He'd lost that on the subway a couple of weeks ago. He opened the wallet and showed Allison the driver's license, which had the face of a movie star on it and the name "Ethan Hunt."

Allison snorted. "Impossible Missions Agent. Are you even for real?"

"It was already in the wallet. Ethan's a good name, as good as any other. At least you get ten if you double it, unlike Joe. After I lost my real wallet, I started not remembering my name. The name I've been using as a human."

"I don't get it. You have amnesia or something?"

"No, not like that."

"Joe? You're making my head hurt."

"My head hurts all the time, too."

"If you don't remember who you are, that's amnesia."

"Except I do remember. It just isn't believable. So I don't. Believe it. I don't believe my own story, is what I'm saying. If you stop believing your story, the story stops working."

Allison blinked. "What story?"

"*My* story. My life story. Everything I've done, every decision, every external force that moved me – everything that led to that stinking apartment. I can't believe it."

"But is your name really Joe, or isn't it?"

"Like I said, when I heard you say it, that's when I realized it could be mine."

"I can't tell if you're making fun of me."

"I'm not making fun of you.'

Doubtfully, Allison said, "Okay."

Joe experimented with a smile. It felt false, which made him wonder if he meant it. No, it was a sincere but failed effort. You could say the same for the last thirty odd years. Except Allison smiled back at him, so maybe it wasn't a failure. How could he tell? How did anybody tell?

Allison picked up the empty glass. "I wish I had another drink."

"If we wait a few minutes maybe he will give you one. Or he'll let me order, probably, but I think he's on to us. I don't trust that raccoon."

"What?"

"I'm not saying it's alive, playing possum or whatever. But it could be a disguise for surveillance equipment with a direct link to the bartender."

She looked at him for a long moment, then seemed to come to a conclusion about something. The conclusion unhooked her attention from Joe, and she looked past him. "He's not going to give me any more drinks tonight. It's how it goes."

It took a minute for Joe to realize she was talking about the bartender. "We could go somewhere else."

"Out the door with you, alone? I'm not *that* drunk."

Joe deflated a little, probably not enough for anyone outside his head to notice. Maybe if he could act more normal for once, she would trust him. 'What time is it?"

Allison glanced at her phone, the screen a glowing playing card in her hand, briefly lamp-bright, then black again. "Almost midnight. You got an appointment?"

"No. I take these pills? One a day. I started with ten, but there's only three left. I took one a little while ago, but if it's past midnight then technically it's a new day."

"What kind of pills?"

"They keep me from... spreading out. You know how a wave rolls out on the beach and kind of absorbs into the sand? That's how I get, except the sand is people, all the people everywhere. Sometimes the animals, too. There's no more of me left at that point, because I'm everywhere else."

Joe reached in his pocket for the plastic pill container and set it on the bar. A few strips of paper, all that remained of the label Joe had scraped off, clung to the orange plastic.

Allison picked up the container. "Why'd you tear the label off?"

"I didn't believe it anymore. Besides, they were the wrong pills." Joe unscrewed the cap and shook a pill into his hand. "These are the right ones. They don't make me so sleepy."

Allison leaned in close. "It looks like some kind of candy."

"It isn't candy."

Allison picked the pill out of his palm before he could pull his hand away. She scraped it with her ruby-painted fingernail. She held it under her nose. "Smells like licorice." Allison touched the 'pill' with the tip of her tongue. "It *is* licorice."

Joe looked away. He watched his fingers drum nervously on the bar. "It doesn't matter what you think it is."

"It's not what I *think* it is – it's what it is."

Joe looked up. "The point is, it's what *I* think it is, not what anyone else thinks. That's how my powers work now, since I don't know how to unlock my true identity anymore. Which is why I thought you might be one of the Ten and BOOSTAR555 might be the code, only I don't know how to use it. So I'm locked."

Allison popped the bit of licorice into her mouth.

"Hey –"

"Candy," she said.

His frantic heart bumped against the bones of his chest. "I have to go." He stood awkwardly, as if his legs didn't belong to him.

"Have a nice day," Allison said. "By the way, do you even hear the words coming out of your mouth?"

"Of course I hear them."

"Maybe all you hear are the voices in your *head*." She laughed, which sounded like other people at other times in his life, all through his life, really. His human life. Allison covered her mouth with her hand. "Hey, I'm sorry. I'm a little drunk."

"It's not voices, in the sense you mean it."

"What?"

"It's all the voices. Every voice, everywhere. The whole world comes out of me. It comes right out of here." Joe tapped his forehead. "*Your* whole world, everybody's whole world." Allison stared at him like she was seeing something she wasn't supposed to see, which he hated but was used to it, generally.

"Take it easy," the bartender said.

"If I was unlocked, I could snap my fingers and *poof* the whole world would go away. Your whole world."

Now everybody in the bar was staring at him. It felt as it always felt, even when he wasn't in a bar, even when he was alone in his room, which is where he mostly stayed. He'd lost his last crappy job, washing dishes at The Burrito Barn. The money was mostly gone. Pretty soon he would be on the street. That's why it was so important to unlock his powers.

He backed up toward the door, moving his lips, counting. Everybody watched him, even the raccoon. As he turned and pushed the door open, Allison said, "Hey, mister, try saying the code backward."

One of the guys sitting at the end of the bar laughed. "Yeah, dude," he said, "Make the big bad world go away, starting with yourself."

Out on the sidewalk, Joe or whoever he was supposed to be, quietly said, "555RATSOOB" then snapped his fingers at the door under the pink neon martini glass, like he was snapping them at everybody everywhere, all of them. "Poof. *Poof.*"

The bar didn't go anywhere. Allison wasn't one of the Ten. BOOSTAR555, frontwards or backwards, was not the code. And his little black pills were nothing but licorice bits.

Poof.

The world didn't vanish, but Joe did, leaving himself standing on the sidewalk. What surprised him, while there was still a 'him' that could be surprised, was that the raccoon really was playing possum, perched up there so quiet and still, watching over the humans in the Moonlight Lounge.

How to Grow Silence from Seed

Tricia Sullivan

Rob has never been so happy. As he runs up the stairs of the community lab on Romford Road his boots make the metal steps resound like gongs. He is fresh from a finance meeting. Even though it's after eleven pm and most of the crew will be in the pub, he knows Injala will still be working.

Except that Injala isn't there. At her station a child crouches on the floor, covered in emergents. They look like worms. He recoils. He stares for some seconds before he realises that this is Injala herself. She is shrunken and distressed out of all proportion to the problems Rob knows how to deal with. When he bends over her she grabs hold of his forearms with a bitter strength, her young eyes nightshade with fear.

"The walls are trying to kill me," she says in a tear-guttered voice. "The walls have a mind and it's trying to shrink me to a point and then bang me to a negative dimension. Look!"

She points. Up in the high industrial windows curl Injala's augmented vines, their leaves gilded by streetlights. All around, the pock-marked walls of her workspace are the same as ever, their paint spewing a cycle of news and entertainment feeds because she has been working on the ambient effects of mainstream media culture.

Her friends also spill bright and unreal from the walls, expressing increasingly concerned enquiries for her well-being.

"Injala? Do you need someone to sit with you until it passes?"

"Quit running your cogs, baby. Take a break."

"Remember, it's only information. It's not real, Injala. You can pull out any time."

The friends' distant panic makes Rob feel oppressed. He

shuts them down. In a thin film over every other data layer, Injala's work pops and fizzes along the walls with what looks and sounds like noise: the activity of the plants she has been training. No one but Injala understands them: she has laid her cogs open to them.

"There's your trouble right there," he mutters. He should have seen this coming.

He glances around the loft as if expecting to find a helpful fairy godmother to take over from here. At the far end of the deserted communal space, Abdul is doing some old-school recreational DNA hacking, oblivious. Rob looks back at his girlfriend. She used to be so wild. Her ideas used to take his breath away. Who knows what lives in her flesh now? Interfacing with plant AIs has turned her into an illegal mess of terror, irrationality and snot. She has become a phenomenon wholly beyond his scope.

"Come on, Inj. Snap out of it. I want to tell you about the meeting I had. About my visibility project. Our project."

He says "our" more in the hope that recalling her to the days when they worked together will cheer her up than because he means it (her only involvement was to suggest a modelling technique). Then he notices the crawling things slipping from her skin to the fabric of his shirt, melting into him with hallucinatory ease. He jerks away.

"Love is a predator," she said when they first hooked up at Imperial. She was like a maze, a series of narrowings of choices that led around corners that led to him losing himself in her. Her sensory appetites coupled with a seeming disinterest in him – her endless fascination with everything but him – made him believe there was something *to* her. He believed her a treasure vault of sorts, a person to be kept and encircled and unlocked over time.

Rob now realises he has unlocked a nutjob.

"Did your plants make these emergents?"

She shakes her head. "We only made them visible. These

influences have been here all this time, but I couldn't see them. Look, they're everywhere… they are in the waves. They've been attacking me and I didn't even know it. They are attacking all of us, all the time!"

"This has gone far enough," he says. "Look at yourself. It can't continue."

He drags a ladder from the corner of the loft and puts it up to the windows. He fancies that the plants are snarling at him even though they can't move. They are smart enough to make him nervous with their ability to receive information out of the air, interpret meaning. Injala has been developing this species for six years. Her thesis shows that plant filtration can reveal hitherto unrecognized structures in the bombardment of signals from commercial entertainment. *"Dangerous ideas,"* she wrote, *"fly stealth underneath ordinary signals. Some of these can be shown to be the product of adroit manipulation by advertisers, but others are emergent. The latter are more sophisticated than anything the designers can dream up, and they appear to act volitionally."*

Privately, she speaks of demons.

Perhaps because her tendency to self-experiment has resulted in a growing dossier of mental illness, Injala has failed to convince any universities that the results of her self-inflicted experiments are unbiased. "Maybe if she hadn't drunk the Kool-Aid she'd be taken seriously," one American department head bluntly remarked. When Rob hinted that Injala could go to work for one of the ad agencies who were keen to use emergents, everyone in the bootstrap lab rose up and came at him as if he'd suggested the murder of a thousand kittens. Never mind. Let the freelancers have their little part-time projects. Rob is going to be large and he only wants the same for Injala.

He tugs the nearest plant from its hook. "Inj, these influences are abstract. They can't hurt you if you can't see them. Just come out of augmentation and they won't bother you."

"No!" she screams, and even Abdul looks up in alarm. "Rob, don't!"

Gripping the pot in one hand, he opens the window with the other. Her hysteria is getting to him. He just wants to make it stop. He will throw them all out, smash the plants on the pavement below. He doesn't care if they are sentient.

She scrabbles up the ladder behind him and she seizes the trailing vines.

"Please. Don't hurt them."

He presses down on the urge to throw the fucking plant. In the same way you press down on a fresh wound. Stop the bleeding. He replaces the plant on its hook and climbs down. He has to be the better man.

"Everything okay, guys?" Abdul calls.

There is a mild struggle between the two of them, faintly sexual. Most of the crawling things stop at his clothes, but the ones that touch his skin make him shudder. Everything about her freaks him out, even the child-smell of her dirty hair.

"I'm getting you to hospital."

"No."

"Yes."

"No."

He puts his hands on her shoulders, determined to calm her down. That's when her head falls off.

He fumbles it like a basketball, startlingly heavy and bone-hard hot. The cushy softness of her face plops into his hands like a leaden sponge. He tries not to stick his fingers in her eyes, but one of them falls out nonetheless. It looks back at him from the floor.

He probably screams.

The rest of her body is clawing at him, snatching at the head as if it suspects him of trying to steal it. Rob notices that there is no arterial bleeding even though he can see the severed ends of the vessels and the stumps of neck tendons. He somehow puts the head back on her neck but then she sets up an unholy wailing. The sound of her drives him away. He runs out of the building and onto the street. There, he is sick.

"It's okay," he reminds himself. "That didn't happen. Did. Not. Happen."

It's obvious she somehow induced him to shift levels – or the plants did – and he feels like a tool. He is too experienced with augmentation to be tricked into dropping out the bottom of reality without notice. Still, the neural effect is convincing enough that his terrified body won't allow him to return to the lab.

He hangs around for a while. He can see Abdul's shadow moving back and forth past the lit windows. No ambulance comes. She's probably all right.

He pushes off.

Rob will write Injala a vague letter, apologising for the breakup because he knows she will blame him even though he hasn't done anything wrong. "I have backers," he'll write. "If you were yourself right now, I know you would want me to go for this. It's going to be large."

Rob doesn't actually know how she would feel about his project being funded while hers is not, but his cognitive dissonance containment capacity has already maxed out; he must take his former girlfriend's approval as given. As for the emergents that cling to his clothes, he will capture them and keep them sealed for months before finding the courage to investigate. Only when his own project fails and the investors drop his contract will he get curious enough to check out the apps that her plants have extracted from the maelstrom of information on the waves.

At which point fame and money will be his, like loyal dogs.

After Rob has gone, the little girl crawls into the emergency washdown and rinses the blood off with her chubby, competent young hands. Emergents generated by her own plants have rooted in her and sprout from the backs of her knuckles and behind her ears.

"They are protecting me," she tells Abdul, who hovers with a towel and a cup of tea.

"Why are you so small?" he asks. "I feel I should call your mother."

"Never mind that," she says in her high voice. "I need you to help me make something. Please."

Abdul works on Injala's project for several nights running. He wants to get it just right. When he is done, they carry her most important plants downstairs and put them in a stolen shopping trolley whose immobilisers have been snapped off. Injala hugs Abdul goodbye and pushes the loaded trolley little by little all the way to the Dartford Crossing. She gets older rapidly as she walks. By the time she encounters other castaways and riffraff in the dead zone between Dartford and Erith, she is a woman again, and the foetus in her belly is well-established. There are supple, shining leaves in her hair.

I find a butcher shop under the A206 bridge. The Butcher will cut out your cogs for you, no questions asked. It's necessary because the waves are unregulated out here in whackjob land. No price plans, no premium content. All you get is noise and ubiquitous advertising, and occasional illegal science experiments being carried out on the inhabitants without their knowledge. Waves bombard you mercilessly. People come here when they've fallen out the bottom of the economic shopping bag. If they stay, they invariably cut out their cogs.

There is plenty of empty ground. I move in beside the Butcher but politely decline his offer of a neighbour's discount. I set up my plants on nearby land, using the dead air under the bridge as protection from the waves when the demons start to get to me. I watch the Butcher remove people's cogs to be sold on or recycled. I watch people stumble away from this procedure damaged, bereft.

Back in the real world, the procedure we endure is written off as an information-age variant of self-harm. Many people aren't susceptible to the dangers on the waves; consequently, accepted logic says people like me must be imagining things. We are inherently off-kilter. The bombs that go off inside our heads aren't planted by anything malevolent; they're just self-destruct devices that originate within us.

The things that live in the walls attack you in the middle of the night, and in the morning when your injuries become visible people say, "What have you done to yourself?"

It's like when a little kid makes another little kid punch himself with his own hand and then says, "Why are you hitting yourself?"

It's like that.

"You think the world rejects you but that's not so," my mother said to me, when my work using plants as receivers first started making me paranoid. She said this as if it were some great insight, like she'd been up all night thinking about it and if she didn't say it, the whole idea would evaporate. "Really you're the one who rejects the world. You're like a transplant patient. You want to live, but when you get this foreign body inside you, you can't cope and you start to attack yourself. It's probably a new disease, something they'll find a name for and twenty years from now it will be a syndrome with a Latin name, and everybody will understand when I say you have it. But right now I don't know what to tell people."

She said this while putting lettuce in her salad-spinner, pulling the cord, inspecting the results. I sat on a stool at her kitchen counter and examined the scars on my knees. I'd gone over the handlebars of my bike so many times as a child. Never cried at that, but with the plants showing me what's really in the air I was weeping helplessly every other day. On the days I wasn't crying I was breaking up pieces of pavement with a sledgehammer in the empty lot behind the community lab.

"Madame Curie died because she was investigating a phenomenon no one could see," I told my mother. "She was killed by invisible things. Her notebooks are still too radioactive to touch."

My mother said, "But don't you be. Don't be too radioactive to touch."

Speaking of mothers. Mir is born seeing and hearing and sensing all I can sense and more. I am terrified for her. As best we can, Abdul and I have equipped her to fight off the things that live in the waves, but I want to do better than that.

I've already taught the plants to make dangerous influences visible. That was the hard part. Now that emergents are visible, I teach the plants to interfere with them, neutralise the dangerous constructs or transform them into something else.

And so the Silence creeps out from beneath the bridge. It spreads. The plants shelter us from the waves, and as they grow they begin to form a quiet zone on the bank by the bridge, above the brackish water and beneath the flight paths of the traffic helicopters. What was waste ground is becoming something new.

The Butcher and I and one of his customers cook noodles over a campfire while Mir squirms in my lap, fascinated by the flames.

"I'll have to branch out into insect farming for protein," he tells me. He complains that the Silence has lost him business, but he's fascinated by what I'm doing. I persuade him to go in with me growing more plants, investing in boosters for the existing trees; they are capable of so much more. We take a small rent from the people who want to shelter in the Silence. I feel good about this, because I know that thanks to the Silence the susceptible can function out here without losing their cogs, and this brings in a slow trickle of income for everybody. A tent community grows up within the Silence.

We are careful to keep it small, beneath notice.

Five-year-old Mir tells me she's finding souls in our marshland. They are runaways, she says. They are lost and dissolute. They seek refuge in the jumble of scrub and mud, drifting on the air until their fragments are trapped by the plants' information filters and reconstituted.

I think about this. I don't know if the souls are real before they come here, or if they accrue out of the processing that the plants do when they neutralise incoming waves. Lost souls roost in the treetops and among the catkins, a by-product of the Silence industry.

Some of them belong to famous people. Mir plants them in the earth to settle them. She seems to know what to do; maybe the plants tell her.

Mir is eight when Karranga shows up in a helicopter. I haven't seen Karranga since university. She is well-dressed and nervous. I can't imagine how she found us. She says she is a journalist and she's aware of my work. I'm not sure I believe this, but I fill a pot with water from a blue extension hose we've diverted from a housing estate. I make tea and we squat outside my yurt at sunset. In the soul garden the plants furl their leaves for darkness.

"Explain it to me," she says. "I want to understand."

I gesture at the flora around us.

"They are intelligent. They receive information out of the air and they can interface digitally. They connect to my cogs and extend my senses. They make the invisible visible. When we link them with the right data-combing software, the plants can identify causal apparati and feedback systems that result in what I call *presences.* Political movements and tactics and yearnings and arguments all have lives of their own even though we think of them as abstract. I can perceive these presences directly, and in the case of hostile presences, I can teach the plants to block their influence on my mind. But to find out what's hostile and damaging, you first have to experience it. That's the ugly part."

"What about Mir? She didn't ask for this life."

"Mir's a new generation. She doesn't need cogs. She can pick up on the waves directly just like a plant, and they protect her instinctively. She's safe here."

I expect Karranga to ask me how that's possible, and I decide

I won't mention Abdul's contribution to Mir's biology; but she doesn't seem interested in the *how* of Mir. Instead she says, "You remember Rob? From our Endologies class?"

She acts like she doesn't know I lived with him for three years. She smells of cloves and something more bitter. She stubs her ciggy out in the mud.

"He's large now. Offices in the Strand."

I say nothing.

"He told me he analysed your work. Said he wanted to find out what kind of thing came after you. You know. When you had that breakdown."

I snort. "And it ate him. Right?"

She swings her head from side to side in the way of people who deliver bad news. "He isolated it and made tweaks. Said it was highly intelligent and someone had to control it. Might as well be him, right? He's been leasing it out as a kind of intellectual precision-guided munition."

Smoke in my ears and nostrils. No pain at all in the lost eye, but my gorge rises. Wish I could breathe fire. My skeleton clatters inside my flesh.

"Leasing it to whom?"

"Does it matter? It's got some kind of corporate applications. How to fuck with the head of your enemy type of thing."

I want to say I'll crush him. I'll kill him. I'll unwrite him from history. But that's all nonsense. I can't even bring myself to say his name. I imagine myself 'confronting' him. How I'd slink around and hide, stalk him, wishing all the while I could bring him down with a death ray from my remaining eye. He'd finally catch me at it and I'd break down in tears and he'd take my hand, act all sympathetic and humanitarian. Maybe offer me some pity money before swinging off to lunch with a set of lawyers and a publicist. People would say how sad for her (meaning me).

"He sent you," I say, because it's obvious. Karranga has the grace to squirm.

We both look at Mir, who is squatting in the weeds, talking to them.

"I know," Mir whispers, nodding to her plant friends. *"I saw that, too. It was so funny."*

She places her palms over the seed-tips of the grass, tickling herself. Then she jumps up and runs off, laughing.

"He misses you," Kerranga tries. But you can't lie to me out here. The Silence is my place.

"How did you find us." It's not a question, it's a complaint, and she manages to make her reply sound like an apology.

"His DNA's in Mir. She came up on a routine scan."

I look at her with the eye I don't have anymore. Let her see the dead flesh.

"Fuck you, Karranga," I say. "If he picked up Mir's signal then Mir must have left the Silence. How could that happen? She is always with me."

Almost always.

"How you discipline your kid is not my problem."

Nearby in the mud, Mir has set about playing tug-of-war with a stray dog. I think the rope is actually one of my T-shirts.

I don't say anything for so long that Karranga reaches over and touches my wrist.

"I'm not on his side," she tells me. "I'm here for you, too."

"Tell him he can't have her," I say, dry-eyed. It feels as if Rob has shoved his boot into my teeth, even from afar. Mir and I struggle for every scrap we have. Socialise with broken people. Feels like we're hiding all the time. He has everything he wanted. Now he wants to take Mir? A surge of inchoate feeling rises. I want to puke, want to come, want to hit out. I shake.

"Where can I run? What will happen to my plants? They've started mixing with the local flora. I can't just pick up and go. The people who come here depend on the Silence."

"All he has to do is go to the council and get an order against you, and you'll have to leave," Karranga says. "But listen, Injala. You don't have to keep this quiet. What you're doing, it's rather amazing and people will want to know about it. Why not be proactive, come out of hiding? I'll help you find support for your work."

"I can't go back."

"Why?"

"I'm afraid."

"Of what."

Of what not? The sky, the air, the noises, the interstices of words, the unspoken, the gazes, the emptiness between saccades of my own eye. I know there are things that could slip into those empty spaces and steal my agency. The unwritten, the unsayable, the cracks in the sidewalk.

I don't say any of that. I shrug, but don't say:

The AIs in the air can dismember you pretty much anytime.

I finally manage to say, "It's one thing to make Silence in the middle of unintentional junk noise, because that's all that's out here. Filtering out deliberate attacks in the commercial airspace is another thing. You said it yourself. People like Rob are deliberately making predators and setting them against their enemies at will. I can't expose Mir to that. Look what happened to me."

My teeth are chattering, just thinking about it.

"Stop shaking, Injala," Karranga says fiercely. "Don't collapse. You cannot afford to flinch."

Is she kidding? My whole life is a series of flinches. And retreats. And not showing up. It's who I am.

I train my one eye on her.

"Tell Rob I said no. Just no."

My words are final. Karranga recoils from their force.

"Okay," she relents. "I'll tell him."

Then Mir says, "I want to see my dad."

Mir takes me down by the willows and shows me where to dig up Rob's soul. It's misshapen and lovely and it smells of the bottom of the tide and long afternoons with nothing to do, of the things we never prized when we had them, which retroactively gleam.

Mir squeezes it like a cantaloupe she's testing for ripeness at the market. Her hands on the boundaries of his soul remind me so much of Rob's hands that for a second I feel no gravity and I cannot move or think. Then I gently prise her fingers away.

"Did you go looking for him?" I ask her. As gentle as I can.

She shakes her head.

"His soul just came here," she says. "He didn't want it any more, and it left him."

She swings up into an alder tree, singing.

Kerranga takes us in the helicopter with her. Mir carries the soul in a Tesco bag, and I carry one of my oldest plants in a pot on my lap. For self-protection. This is my first time north of the river since I fled Hackney, and I'm not prepared for the greening of Covent Garden and Aldwych and Charing Cross Road. Buildings are covered in grasses, and walls are thick with moss. Mir presses her face against the cockpit window, foliage standing up stiffly from her shoulders and the backs of her wrists as her plants taste the waves.

"What are you picking up, Mir?" I ask her casually. Yellow-toothed mouths gnaw at my breasts and throat. A litany of hatred pours into my ears and nostrils like smoke, and there are winged monsters in the air around us, every glance from their multiple globular eyes an indirect attack. Already I feel faintly suicidal.

I do not yet see my old enemies, but I'm afraid. I tell Kerranga this and she shouts, "Oh, Rob's product is high-end. He doesn't let his work just roam the streets like any old headbug."

"The plants here are simple," Mir observes. The attacks roll off her unnoticed. "None of them can do what we can do. They could learn a lot from our plants."

Still I keep expecting Rob's agents to come out of somewhere. I still remember how the invisible, negating presence came at me that night in the lab. What did Rob do with the samples he took from me? How did he contain the influence of the emergent? How could he direct it when I did nothing more than cower before it?

Maybe he deserves to be large. It seems he did what I couldn't do.

Mir flows through the fragrant coffee shop, dark and gracefully declarative as calligraphy. She inhabits the room with such vivid surety that the milling adults seem attenuated, incomplete. Rob is camped at a table whose data-rich surface he swipes to darkness as we approach. Pleasantries are exchanged and Kerranga makes her excuses.

Rob's baritone voice carries tension like a military base on lockdown. "I have all my biological output tracked. You can't be too careful these days. I was worried about copying, assault. I never expected this. At least, I never expected that it could happen and you wouldn't tell me."

There is hostility in the tapping of his fingers on the counter; he paints me as the betrayer. His expression says, *How could you do this to me? See what a nice guy I am.*

He is a nice guy, as far as that goes. So?

He stares at Mir like she is water or starfire. What does he want from her? I try to find the answer as I always did when we were together, in his smell and the set of his movements, the between places that are only ever implied, never named.

"What are you doing?" I say. Mir begins to play a game in the interactive surface of the table.

"She could have so much more in this world," he whispers. "Please don't deprive her of what she could become."

I am not parsing this. There is no point in trying to pretend, and I start to twitch and laugh and roll my solitary eye and if I'm lucky I won't wet myself but you never know these days. I haven't had an easy life. He is uncomfortable that people are looking at us, and I let out a few barks to put the boot in.

Then I realise he's sincere.

He really thinks I would give her up.

"I know how talented you are, Inj. And I'm sure you've passed it on to her. I give you all credit. You found the emergents. I couldn't even see them. The thing that attacked you? I didn't know what it was, so it couldn't hurt me. But I knew it had to be *something*, because of what it did to you."

"Have you learned how to stop it?" I ask suddenly. There is always that hope.

He spreads his fingers, crunches his face. "I sort of took it in the other direction," he says. "I found out what this species of thing could do, and then I altered it. I derived the code and tweaked it so that I could do head trips on anyone I might name."

"So you turned it into a weapon."

"More like an agent than a weapon, but I guess you could –"

"And then you sold it?"

"I didn't need it for myself! I don't hate anybody that much. It really is a killer, Inj, and when it's done with someone it doesn't even leave a trace it's ever been there. I mean, I've got to hand it to you. You are pretty tough to have survived, considering how susceptible you are to that sort of thing."

"Someone has spilled juice on me!" squawks the table, and Mir breaks up laughing. I mop up Mir's spilt juice and remind her to sit quietly, but she isn't used to polite society.

Rob gives her a code for his system. "Here are the games," he says, pointing.

"Are you sure that's a good idea?" I ask. "She can't mess anything up, can she?"

He waves a hand. "It's fine. My stuff's bombproof. Let her play."

He looks me in the eye, then.

"I did what I said I would, Inj. I got the recognition. I'm large. I can't be touched. I can give Mir the same thing."

Mir leans into my hair, whispering. "There's a blobby thing eating his face, Mum."

I stroke her hair, hand her a piece of biscotti. I am secretly delighted about the blobby thing. It makes his authoritative air more bearable.

"So, Rob, you talked to Abdul?"

"He went to Australia. Won't return my messages. Why? What's Abdul got to do with anything?"

I lean in.

"We made some adjustments to Mir."

He stares.

"Like what?"

Now he is looking at her ears, her leaf-strewn locks, the pale green "hairs" on the backs of her arms. They are tiny spines that catch signals out of the air and alter them.

In broad terms, I explain Mir to him. She swings her legs and trawls through his apps hungrily. She is bound to mess up his stuff; but I did warn him. He is now too distracted, thinking about what is going on in her body, to give a moment's thought to what her eyes and fingers are doing to his system. He's getting angry, but clamping down on it.

"You haven't even taken her to a doctor, have you?" His eyes flash, proprietary. Accusing.

"Do you really want to do this, Rob?"

"No… Inj, you know I don't want this to get nasty at all, I don't want to make either of you uncomfortable. But I'm just… saying… *have* you taken her to a doctor? I can help. Let me do some things to help you. It doesn't have to be so hard."

Yes, it does.

"I have hung on out there a long time," I say in a grey voice. "I don't want to come back. Not any more. I don't need what you have. Can't you see that your work is feeding the emergents? You're enriching their environment, increasing their sophistication all the time. The emergents are eating you alive and you don't even care. They will use you up and move beyond you and by the time you realise what's happening it will be too late."

He chuckled. "I forgot what you were like, Inj."

I am on a roll now.

"But *I* didn't forget what *you're* like. You will give us away. We are sitting right on the underbelly of the system and it can't see us, but now you know. It's only a matter of time before you expose us. I guess you will take the Silence and sell that, too."

He runs his hand through his hair, clearly upset. "Now that's unfair. I've worked like a dog all these years. I think I've earned my success."

Mir is sitting very still. She is watching him. She looks at me with a shrinking expression, as though I have slapped a puppy.

"Inj, can't we find a middle ground? Here's the blue sky. I'm open. Tell me what you want to do."

I regret having brought Mir. We should have done this without her. But who could I have left her with? I am all she has. And I am at a loss.

"I have something of yours," I tell Rob at last. I put the bag on the counter. Inside, his soul twitches, chatters a little. Irritated at having been plucked from the happy oblivious mud under the bridge, I guess. "I've been keeping it for insurance purposes."

His eyelids clench into suspicious lines as he tilts his nose toward the bag. He doesn't seem to guess what's in there. Can't he smell it? I tried to clean up the bag, wiping algal smudges off the orange plastic, but it still looks disreputable and it reeks of his soul.

He stands up. I gather that I have insulted him, because he speaks with frigid courtesy.

"OK. I can see it's not going to work. I get it. We both need time to think this one through. Let me walk you to the station. Or maybe my car can take you somewhere?"

I take Mir's hand. I have to drag her away from Rob's system. I hope she is messing up his personal organiser.

"We'll walk."

He walks with us, and because I don't want to upset Mir, I let him. Out on the Strand he tries to make small talk. My heart is pounding. I don't know how to stand down. I don't know if I can stand down. I notice the wind on the river; I notice that the beech trees have been augmented. All the air is thick with transmissions. I hold my potted plant before me like a ridiculous shield. I am afraid.

"The trouble is, Inj, you're not stable. I know it. You know it. You could go down at any time, and then what happens to Mir?"

I stop walking. I can't believe he just said that in front of her.

"Just stop talking, Rob." I am impotent and he knows it. He is refusing to look at me, and at first I think he's ignoring me. Then I realise he's doing something with his cogs. He's ordering something up.

The beech trees overhead are boosting some creation of his, and emergents are crawling up from the ground. They quicksilver over my feet and up my legs. They drop like caterpillars from the trees and engulf me, thousands upon thousands of his trained vermin. They are in my eye socket.

It's happening again.

I know I'm hyperventilating. He has staged this whole thing: to scare her, to scare me, to force my hand. I'm the witch and he's thrown a bucket of water on me and I am melting.

It's the same old helplessness. I will end up in hospital and then he will take her.

I grip Mir's hand and push past Rob, beginning to run toward Charing Cross station. Seeking safety underground.

But the pavement folds and remixes my kinaesthetic perception: my insides are visible, my flesh begins to strain and pop. I know this sensation. Soon I will lose myself entirely.

I try to run but I'm going nowhere.

Mir is tugging on my hand, pulling me toward her.

"Don't run," she says. "Mum, don't run away."

She throws her arms around me. I can feel the singing of her foliage in my teeth and along the tracks of my tendons.

I can't see.

My intestines are spilling out through my vagina and my bones are gathering in my throat and poking through my eye sockets. The world is roiling away from me in a tide of dust, and there is a wordless power in the air that wills the end of me. Everything I have ever loved, every mercy, every kindness, is mown down by an ineffable storm of hate.

I am shit.

The worms are inside my head. They trawl through every pathetic effort I have ever made to pull myself together, every grant proposal and small article I have written, and they mock. Each tiny bit of progress I have made, they trash. Everything I have ever done or thought that was good, they take, until I can't remember whether it ever was my own.

They say they will come for my plants. They say they will come for Mir.

This is happening with breathtaking speed. I try to remember where I am, what is going on. I don't want her to see me like this. It will break her. He will break us both.

"I have to get away, Mir," I gasp. "I wish I could fight it, but I don't know how."

She says, "You don't have to fight it. Call the Silence. Close off. Play dead."

I don't know how to play dead. I only know how to be dead. That's where I'm going, right now.

Mir's mother never listens to her. She isn't like a tree. She doesn't know how to stand and take it. The plane trees that grow in a straight line along the Embankment, they are hard to kill. If you cut one down it would just sprout a bunch of new branches and keep going.

Mir's mother pulls away from Rob and drags Mir along the Embankment. Mir holds the plant they brought for protection. She calls on it for help. Just then her mother's legs go out from under her and she falls to her knees. Mir holds the plant as her mother is sick on the roots of a plane tree.

Mir can feel the killing thing in her own leaf follicles. She can taste it on the back of her tongue.

She calls the Silence. She calls it around herself and the potted plant from Dartford. The Silence falls over them like a shadow. Then she calls it into the plane trees. They try valiantly to help. They are already expert at transforming human pollution into clean air. Mir could teach them to do the same with ideas, if she only had more time.

Her dad has followed them. Mir senses him trying to contact his emergent, but he can't because of the Silence. He has only his own body. But he's still bigger than Mir. She can feel her mouth working and she's trying not to cry.

"I'm not upset," she tells him. "It's fine. She'll be okay."

He closes his eyes for a moment, like something is hurting him. Then he kneels down in front of Mir the way adults do when they want children to think they're being really fair. He takes Mir's hand in his hand. Their hands are alike.

"She isn't okay," he tells Mir. "You don't have to –"

"Stop killing her."

His hand withdraws. He doesn't know where to look. Mir is still calling the Silence. The plane trees ride her wave and hold the Silence. She smells their oxygen. Their leaves shimmer in the wind. People's heels are scuffing along the pavement and bike gears are clicking and a dog rattles its chain. She hears everything so clearly, and she hears him say some more rubbish but doesn't listen.

"I saw the emergent in your system," she tells him. "I'm not stupid."

He laughs.

"You're just like her. So sharp. I just want to know you, Mir. I want to save you so you won't end up like… like…"

Like her.

He is sweating. The Silence around them is cool. Mir's mother starts to pull herself together. She takes a tissue out of her bag and wipes her mouth.

"You should have this," Mir tells her father. "Then maybe you'll stop."

She holds out the plastic bag. He waves it away. He's laughing again in a fake way.

"Maybe you don't understand," Mir says. It's what her mother says to Mir when she's getting ready to tell Mir off in a big way. "I'm blocking your emergent, Dad. I know what it is. I know how to stop it."

"But… Mir, I can give you the best education. Your potential. You could go so far, just let me –"

"Take it," Mir says. She shoves the bag at him and upends it. His soul falls out. He just manages to catch it before it hits the pavement. There's this moment where he seems to recognise it, but then he shoves it in his jacket pocket and stands up and he's backing away from her.

"Please don't drive it away again," Mir tells him. Then she goes back to her mum, leaning on the plane tree. Mir is crying. She wanted it to be so different.

It takes hours for Mir and me to get home by tube, train and bus. As the terror subsides, I find myself thinking of the young green walls of London today, of Karranga's offer to help me grow the Silence. I am thinking of the plant I'm holding in my arms, how it saved me. I want to do something with the Silence. I know it's important. If the plants saved me, they can save others.

But even as the bus lets us out, a terrible weariness has come over me. I feel dark. Mir drags me through the industrial estate to the green waste beyond. I do not know how I will muster the energy to do everything that I have to do. It feels so much easier to run and hide. How can I find a way to carry on with this work when its outcome is something no one has ever seen?

It's too much pressure. The very air seems to weigh on me, making thunder in my mind. I nearly lost everything back there.

"Mum," says Mir, poking me. "Stop listening to the waves. Just stop."

I put my fingers in my ears but it doesn't help.

Mir's shadow is tall and gangly when we make our way to the

pewter coolness of the river, the weed-scrambled bank with its leaning tents and smoke-scarred air. Even as electric trucks glide along the A206 and over the bridge, our renegade plants lunge this way and that toward the sky. The Butcher is just finishing up a day's work of transplanting along the bank, and I watch him walking along the footpath with a spade over his shoulder.

At last the Silence reaches out and embraces me. My weariness dissolves, and that's when I remember it was never quite real.

Mir skips ahead of me, through the nettles and toward the restless treetops of our home.

As she runs, she waves the empty plastic bag in the air, like a flag.

The Time-Travellers' Ball

(A Story in Ten Words)

Rose Biggin

It took ages to organise.
Are you going? I did.

Dress Rehearsal

Adrian Tchaikovsky

In Doje we played *The Beetle* which, though everyone knows it as one of Molodori's more boisterous comedies, has a solemn little soliloquy in Act Four that I've always coveted. It goes to the old pantaloon role, of course, who spends the rest of the play being duped by his niece and her foreign-officer-of-a-lover as they parade their affair through his house without him being any the wiser. And then, just when the audience is practically howling in their contempt for him, he has the stage alone and gives them eighteen lines of utter gravitas, a guardian's lament of how he might have been a better uncle, and all the lost opportunities we recognise only when it's too late to act on them. And the audience – if you do this right – is spellbound. And the older amongst them see themselves in the man they've been ridiculing, and perhaps he gets a little extra applause at the curtain call.

I, of course, was the dashing foreign lover with his colourful past, and that's ostensibly the lead, but the uncle's by far the role they remember. "Next Time Doctor Kampfe dusts off this play," I promised myself, "I'll audition and give him such a risible old fart he won't be able to see anyone else doing the role." But Doje was the third time we'd done *The Beetle* since I joined the company and, unless something happened to our senior clown, I probably wasn't in with a sniff of a chance.

We were booked for seven nights in the Majestic Blood Theatre, the name of which might suggest *Grand Guignol* but instead derives from the place's use, in the middle-distant past, as a site of gladiatorial spectacle. The people of Doje are very aware of their barbaric history, and rather too fond of it. We filled the house on every night, but twice as many turned out for the public hangings in the square.

Seven nights of rapturous applause, and then Doctor Kampfe went to the Majestic's owner and haggled for another two because we'd been turning people away at the door all week. Sufficient lucre changed hands that the stage magician booked after us was persuaded to vanish for a couple of days to give us another two packed houses. After the last night we all came away from the standing ovation quite drunk on show business. There really is no feeling like that intense camaraderie with people you know you'll be bickering with come morning.

And then there was a fanfare, I kid you not. Some flunky with more scrambled egg on his uniform than I ever ate off a plate turned up and bugled the devil out of our little dressing room, shocking everyone into silence, and in came a big man in velvet eveningwear who I recognised from the local coinage.

Actors are good at bowing and we put our practice to good use, for here was Cornelius the Fifth, a.k.a. 'the Conqueror', King of Doje and its subject territories and Scourge of Nicrephos. I have no idea what Nicrephos did to deserve a scourging, but I'm willing to bet old Cornelius didn't spare the rod.

He was a rather angry man by nature, I'd heard, but right then he was charm itself because he was saying nice things about the performance. His had been that big booming laugh from the gilded box to stage left, and I let him off a bit of the scourging, because a good laugh in the audience is worth an encore all on its own. Especially when you're the king and everyone laughs with you. Anyway, Cornelius Five had most definitely had a good night and had come down to our level to tell us so. We were properly honoured. Felice simpered and flirted a little; Alfonso, senior clown, repeated some of his funnier lines on request, and I modestly said that I didn't really know anything about sword fighting, it was all for show, Your Majesty. I've found that's the safest line wherever there are strict laws as far as bearing arms is concerned.

And then His Majesty announced grandly that we would all,

of course, come to his Spring Palace for a command performance for the court.

We were looking at our lord and manager Doctor Kampfe, who was frozen midway through sipping his wine. I could see the very narrow slice of time in which he was going to say no. Now, there are Kings you can say no to, and Cornelius the Conqueror was not one of them. On his most recent campaign, he was notable for his treatment of captives whose religion differed from his own in some very trivial way. Impaled, don't you know. On spikes. So he wasn't going to react well to a group of travelling players – foreigners to boot – turning him down.

And so Doctor Kampfe gave his most ingratiating smile and said how *very* happy we would be to oblige the King, and Cornelius turned up his own enormous grin and told us how *very* rich such obliging would make us, and we all toasted everyone's health and the King's long reign.

The King went about his regal business assured that we would pack up our flats and properties and set our wagon on its way to the Spring Palace with all speed. And then Doctor Kampfe's Famed October Players jumped on our wagon and got the hell out of Doje.

It was Doctor Kampfe's iron decision, that. And we bitched and moaned and threatened to jump ship, but he would not be swayed. Almost everyone in every world will tell you there's no way to make a decent living as an actor, and this isn't actually true. If there's one way to put aside a decent nest egg, it's royal command performances. But our complaints broke against the Doctor's resolve like waves against the cliffs, and then we'd crossed the town limits and were gone into the night like thieves. I guessed that it was Cornelius' volatile reputation which informed the good doctor's decision. For myself I'd have risked a little volatility for the chance of that most legendary of things: a genuine pouch of gold. As it was, we left so quickly we didn't even get the takings from the last and most lucrative night, and the owner of the Majestic kept our deposit. All in all, a victory for neither art nor commerce.

You might have thought that the threat of pursuit would cross our mind. Cornelius the Fifth was likely to sally forth, surely, when his favourite actors didn't appear at the gates of the Spring Palace. A theatrical wagon doesn't exactly chip along and a king has a lot of resources when it comes to finding people. However, the lash of royal displeasure was the one thing we *weren't* fretting about. Where we were going, nobody would even have heard of Cornelius the Fifth of Doje. I tell a lie, they had a dirty little fairy tale about a king matching his description who was cuckolded by everyone from the boot boy to his own grand vizier – putting the cornuto into Cornelius – but he wasn't a historical figure, just a figure of fun. When we packed up our greasepaint and took the road out of Doje, it wasn't a road that led to any of its geographical neighbours. We are the very acme of travelling players, and we visit many places, and each of those places is a myth or parable or dirty limerick in one of the others. It all works out so long as we don't put on the wrong play in the wrong place. It can bring people over all funny, when they see the fifth act of their own life story being played out before they've actually got there themselves.

When we caught sight of our next stop the grumbling redoubled, because it was a dump. This was our first view of Sevengraves, which looked as jolly as it sounds. Sevengraves was a provincial town of a country that had until recently been at war. Someone had used machines or magic to punch that town full of holes and flatten its factories, and the war's end hadn't gone far towards getting things back on track. I couldn't actually tell you if they won or lost, even. It wasn't a topic of conversation any of the locals wanted to discuss.

Nobody would be getting rich out of Sevengraves. We'd be lucky to charge five of their pence for the good seats, and we'd probably take barter for the cheaps.

So we crept into town under cover of darkness. We had six

days to get ourselves in order before we played a run at the Municipal Hall, a venue whose roof was sufficiently unsound that if you had a seat in the stalls you were advised to bring an umbrella.

"Nine nights," Doctor Kampfe decided, examining the dingy, mouldering place as though it was the royal command performance we'd been denied. "We'll give them the works."

We actors tried a united front. "Three," I tried, as leading man. "We'll have no audience. Look at the place. Even three will leave us with a bare pantry."

"They can't afford us," agreed Timoti de Venezi, whom Kampfe was training up as assistant manager.

"I've never seen a city so under the black cloud," Felice backed us up. "You think they'll pay what they've got to watch Alfonso do fart jokes?"

"I think no place so needed the enrichment of life that comes with good theatre," Doctor Kampfe answered us all. "But no, I agree a comedy would grate. We'll play *Estelle and Alexander*."

"Saints preserve us," said Sidney Lord Essex. "They'll slit their own throats by the end of Act Four."

"It will be a grand success. I say it will." And Doctor Kampfe carried the day, as usual "Felice and Richard, you're Estelle and Alexander. Alfonso, you know Estevan still…" And he doled out the roles then and there, listening to representations from ambitious cast members but seldom being swayed by them, save that Sidney got a promotion to Stammers the Butler. There were still some objections about the choice of play, but not from me. Purely selfishly, I was looking forward to giving Alexander another go. Like the best romantic tragedies, *E&A* is riotous comedy for three acts, a spectacular declaration of love for most of Act Four and then a colossally depressing roll of deaths until the curtain call. In particular, there's a scene in the middle where Alexander takes a potion to give him courage and turns up dressed like a fivepenny pimp picking fights with his betters, and everyone laughs, and then everyone sighs when he and Estelle finally do get their act together, and then he dies and, if I've done my job right, you can cut the grieving silence with a knife. Some people say the death of Stammers in Act Five is even more heart-stringy, but they haven't seen *my* Alexander.

We got into rehearsals, which involved hiring a local named Magritte for the role of Laina because we only had one actress for the mature roles and the play called for two. It was heartbreaking, actually. When we put the word out; there was a queue of women from twenty to ninety stretching all the way down the street. Everyone in Sevengraves was hungry. Timoti di Venezi went down and picked Magritte from the line without auditioning anyone, but he's good at that sort of thing. The city where we picked him up, everything was numbered and measured to an inch of its life.

Maybe Magritte would travel with us when we left; maybe not. Looking at Sevengraves, I'd have done anything to get out of the place.

The play came together slowly, including a blazing row between Alfonso and Sidney over the senior clown's limelight hogging, and two days of icy silence between Felice and me about who had stepped on whose cues in Act Four. Act Five was still ropey, but Alexander was dead by then so I didn't need to worry about that. I could just sit back and make snide comments.

I was doing exactly that, pondering my next witticism, when someone tapped me on the shoulder and said, "Excuse me," in that nasal Sevengraves accent we were all getting used to.

I jumped up and plastered a winning smile on, because when a local turns up mid-rehearsal they're the local law or the local gang, and anyway they want money. This chap looked too well-dressed for either, though. He was a tall fellow with a neatly-pressed shirt with a little lace at the collar and cuffs – not a fashion seen amongst the strata of Sevengravers we'd been associating with. He had a broad-brimmed, round-crowned hat in his hands, and he wore a red-lined cape with a high collar, enough so that any actor worth their salt would instantly have a certain stock character leaping into mind. His face was mild-looking, though, with thinning grey hair and round-lensed spectacles over watery eyes. He might have the get-up for the most pantomime of villains, but certainly not the presence.

As no menaces for money appeared to be forthcoming, I ushered him a little ways from the stage and asked him what he was after.

"I'm very sorry to trouble you," he said, in a voice that positively reeked of comfortably old money, the sort that didn't mind spreading itself around. "I saw that you were putting on *Estelle and Alexander*."

"We'll be up in three days," I confirmed, and then I rattled off the prices and pushed a handful of fliers into his hand, that Timoti had cranked out on our little printing press. "Tell your friends."

"Ah well, it's the matter of a friend that I wished to talk to you about," he said, voice properly hushed. Mr Collar was someone who showed the proper respect when a rehearsal was underway. "I have a ward who is inordinately fond of the theatre, and this piece in particular. However, her condition restricts her to her bed, and I was wondering…" He wrung his hat a little, twisting the felt. "I don't suppose you do house calls?"

"This condition, is it catching?" I asked, because Sevengraves looked like a plague-pit.

"Lord, no! No, it's an illness she's had from birth. It denies her access to what little entertainment is to be had in our poor town." His shoulders hunched. "This is very impertinent of me to ask, I know. I've offended your professional –"

"No, no." I was thinking quickly. We were in rehearsals right now; we had a couple of days before the dress… I looked over at the stage, where Felice was getting into a serious strop with Timoti after forgetting her lines, while Sidney, as the deceased Stammers, shifted about to find the most comfortable position to be dead in. We were not ready to put on any kind of performance right then.

"Is there some way I can contact you?" I asked, and Mr Collar took a card from his hat, deftly as a conjurer. At my raised eyebrow he gave a weak smile. "Some of us wanted to be performers, before other duties called on us." When he left, I saw that he had the sort of limp you get after someone tries to kill you.

Mr Collar plainly had money, but he'd never mentioned parting with any of it. A private show for a bedridden ward smacked of performing purely for the exposure, which is notorious for being hard to eat and not keeping the rain off. Nonetheless, I was confident of extracting some sort of reward, if only I could make this happen, and it was plain I wasn't getting any other kind of bonus out of Sevengraves. For even the distant chance of a few more coins, I decided to play the generous giver.

The problem was that I couldn't exactly walk off with the company. Doctor Kampfe was rehearsing everyone very hard, and the harder we rehearsed the more it became plain that we needed it. I needed an ally to help me enrich myself, which meant I'd have to share whatever meagre enriching Sevengraves had on offer. In the end I confided in Timoti, because he had a mind like a calculating engine and, if there was a way, he'd find it. And Doctor Kampfe listened to him, which was a singular honour.

"Can't be done," he said at first, but I knew him and waited. Then he said, "Not with the full company. Sidney's terrible as Stammers. Kampfe will lock him in a room until he knows his lines. And Edith keeps doing Lady Deerling from *Marshwic's Ball* instead of the Contessa. The Good Doctor's going to blow an artery if she doesn't keep straight what play she's in." And he thought a bit and made some tea and scribbled some notes on the back of a flyer, and then he told me, "But if we had you and Felice… and John's been understudying Alfonso and Sidney as well as playing Villon, and he can just about do all three if we jockey the script. And Magritte's really quite a find and she can do Laina and the Contessa if she changes hats quickly enough.

You four, and I could read in the other roles as needed."

"Which leaves us with the *when*," I pointed out, but I was only play-acting. I could see he'd already thought of that.

"Dress rehearsal in two evenings' time," Timoti stated. "I could suggest to the Doctor that he spends that day working with Sidney and Edith, and that the rest of you really need some time to yourselves or you'll be no good on the night. And we could sneak off to this kid's bedside and do a very rough rehearsed reading, because that's all it can be. But she'll get something."

"I could kiss you," I told him.

"You can give me half what you get."

"I might not get anything. He made this sound like a charity do."

Timoti gave me a sour look. "You're telling me I did all that thinking for nothing?"

"Think of it as doing a good deed to appease the gods of the theatre," I told him. "Maybe it'll guarantee us good houses."

Timoti di Venezi didn't believe in gods. Still, he didn't pull out. Like me, he was holding out for the chance to pass the hat round, even if it was just to Mr Collar.

We talked to Felice and Magritte and John Worthing, and they were all game. Mostly it was the chance of getting away from the rest of the company, who were wound up tighter and tighter as we got close to the dress. I'd never have thought a day out in Sevengraves would actually hold any attraction, but it beat a day in with Sidney Lord Essex swearing and putting his boot through the flats because he couldn't remember his death speech. I may also have over-egged the idea of how open-handed Mr Collar was going to be. We were all still smarting at losing that royal command performance.

So I sent word to Mr Collar and he sent a little card in reply with an address printed on it. I showed this to our local talent, Magritte.

"That's the Saint Agatha Orphanage." Her eyes accused me

of false representation. "No way any of us are getting rich out of those kids."

"They've got a rich benefactor," I insisted.

"There ain't any rich benefactors in Sevengraves." Her opinion of her home town was even lower than ours.

"Don't bail on me," I begged her, with the implied rider, *Don't rat on me to the others*. She gave me a sour look, but she didn't need the leading man of the company pissed at her, so she kept quiet. That way, I at least got Felice, Timoti and John to the place before they realised the whole venture was fool's gold.

"Oh you are kidding me." Felice threw up her hands in grand theatrical tradition. "This place has more holes in it than the damn theatre!"

I put on the face I used when playing sanctimonious bores. "I told you this is for a poor child who can't leave her bed. This is good karma."

"They don't have karma in Sevengraves," Felice spat. "That was that other place. They had money there, too."

"So what, we're going to turn around and go back, are we? I mean, they'll feed us, at least. A free hot dinner's nothing to be sniffed at right now, eh?" Horrifying to admit it, but I had a point. Food was scarce in Sevengraves and we'd been on short commons since we arrived, especially as our Doje coinage had come across the worlds-border as tin and nickel. So we, Doctor Kampfe's Famed October Players, would do our charity gig at the orphanage just in case they had some gruel going spare.

Mr Collar met us at the door and ushered us in. The place gave a bad name to dingy and escaped being run-down only because it had never been up. Crowded, too: orphans were the only war surplus Sevengraves had going spare. Timoti went first, alongside Mr Collar's awkward limp, giving our excuses ahead of time – the reduced cast, the need for books, the general cack-handedness of the tat we were about to foist off on his bedridden ward under the name of art. Mr Collar rallied magnificently.

"Gentlemen and ladies of the stage," he addressed us. "It

matters not the missed cues or entrances, but I beg you, place your hearts and souls into this. Make this not a rehearsal but a true performance of your piece. It is likely the only chance my ward will ever have to see it played."

As you can imagine, that extra pressure made us all feel delighted with ourselves for the rubbish we were about to perpetrate.

And then we were in the poor moppet's room, and true enough she was a wan little creature, propped up on pillows and wearing a nightdress gone sepia with age and washing, but obviously fine once. Timoti arranged some screens to give our fourth wall some boundaries and sorted the props out, and we had a quick huddle to agree entrances and exits. Then we turned around and they were all there. They had filed in so meekly none of us had noticed.

Either side of Miss Ward's bed the orphans were crammed in shoulder to shoulder. They sat on the counterpane, too, and in front, lined up all the way to the screens. We were confronted with a genuine sea of faces, all dirty and hungry and pale and huge-eyed, ages from ten to seventeen. I've never known children sit so quietly. I think it was because they had absolutely no hope whatsoever. I don't think they actually knew what they were about to see.

"Erm…?" I signalled Mr Collar, who had been displaced into the doorway.

"My ward was insistent that the performance must be for all, not just for her," he said, sounding choked up with pride at the sentiment. From my point of view, it's very easy to be generous with someone else's time and effort, but I couldn't exactly say anything in front of that massed and hollow attention.

And besides, part of me was thinking, *this is probably the biggest house we'll see in Sevengraves.*

With that sentiment, I turned to my fellow thespians. "Let's make this count," I told them.

We made it count.

I don't know how we did it, putting on a ten role play with five of us, and half of us having to crib from the book. It should have been as terrible a piece of coarse acting as any amateur rep company ever mishandled, but instead…

I was glorious. I have never been better than that matinee at the orphanage. I swear I *was* Alexander. Actually, that's not true; Alexander could never have Alexandered as well as I. They screamed with laughter when I was funny and they sighed when I was a lover. And when I died – when I *died,* my God they were weeping – those children without parents from a town without a future, and I made them weep.

And the others were all right, I suppose. Felice was word perfect, and when she took the poison at the end I saw half the audience get halfway up to beg her to stop. Magritte played the comic duo with John to perfection – better than ever she could with scene-stealing Alfonso. And Timoti clicked through his roles with clinical perfection that, if it did not move hearts in itself, allowed the rest of us to move them more through his support.

And when we took our bow, there was no applause. Now mostly that's bad, but sometimes you play a tragedy *just right*, and the audience is shocked to stillness by the sheer intensity of what they've seen, and it means more than all the standing ovations in the world. And that's what we got from them. They'd have given us anything we asked for, in that moment, so it was a shame they were penniless orphans who didn't have anything to give.

But we didn't care, because we were full of that elation peculiar to actors post-performance. We bad farewell to the children and were just about to exit with empty pockets and full hearts when Mr Collar met us at the door.

Well, he was thankful, of course, and extremely complimentary, and we would have taken that as our due except that he was holding out a decent-sized pouch.

"It's not very much," he explained to us. "Obviously Saint Agatha's can't reimburse you, but I have a little put away myself. I hope it's in order."

It was a pouch of gold. It was something we had only come across before in stage directions. The coins looked old and pure and a world away from the worn coppers the Sevengravers measured out their lives with.

And you might not believe it, but we did actually try to turn him down. We were so high on the performance that even Timoti told him that he should find more deserving beneficiaries of his largesse, but Mr Collar was insistent. "This was a real performance," he told us, "and deserves real remuneration. Please, take the purse with my blessings."

So in the end we took his money and everyone lived happily ever after.

Well, not quite.

We returned to the Municipal Hall and went on with a dress rehearsal in which absolutely everything went wrong. At one point Sidney and I very nearly fought to the death with prop swords over a missed cue. The next night, we went up.

We filled about a third of the dry seats, which meant about a sixth of the house. The Sevengravers watched us strut and fumble our way through the play as though they'd only just been introduced to the concept of drama and didn't much like it. There was some desultory clapping at the end. The total take hadn't been quite enough to buy everyone a pint. At around that point, those of us who had received Mr Collar's little dividend talked very seriously about sharing the wealth around, just to cheer everyone up. But somehow we never quite did. It was out little secret.

The second night was more than half full. I spotted some return faces from the first. Our spirits began to pick up and so did our performance. From the third to the ninth we were sold out and there were people standing in the aisles by the end. They were weary and poor, and some paid in coppers and others in firewood and root vegetables, but by God they came to see us play. I don't think anything the full company put on quite matched that magical afternoon in the orphanage, but we came together even so. Sidney mastered his role and played that marvellously understated death scene to a tee, and Edith remembered which play she was in, and Alfonso and Magritte made them laugh right up to the point where we all made them cry. They cheered us after each house, and if it wasn't that rapt silence we'd had before, it was good enough.

I met Alexander once, you know – in that world where he was real and not just a character in a play. You'd never have picked him as someone to inspire a great romance of the ages. And I, having studied the part before I met him, didn't have the heart to tell him how everything would work out.

All too soon we came to the end of our final night, and there were even some bouquets for the ladies, and some jugs of homebrew for everyone, and if half our takings were in coppers then at least the other half were generally edible so we weren't going to starve. Doctor Kampfe went round the company and shook everyone's hand, and made sure we all acknowledged how right he'd been about the nine nights.

That was when Mr Collar turned up. None of saw him enter: he was just there in the dressing room, waiting politely with his hat in his hands.

I went over to him, still bubbling with the joy of a good performance, and offered him a drink. He declined politely. "Actually, I was rather hoping for a word with Doctor Kampfe."

Well that was awkward, because of course the Good Doctor didn't know what had been going on behind his back, but there was nothing I could do about it now. I decided I would sell the whole thing as a bit of extra rehearsal and hoped nobody would mention the money.

So I let Mr Collar between happy actors intent on inebriation until we got to Doctor Kampfe.

I saw something was wrong the moment they laid eyes on each other. The Good Doctor knew Mr Collar instantly, and Mr Collar's air of genial whimsy was gone as though it had never been. When he smiled, you could have shaved with it.

"I thought that was rather a good show," he remarked.

"Thank you. We do what we can with the material given us," Doctor Kampfe replied with precise cordiality.

"So you always said," Mr Collar observed. "I'm glad to see you've been honing your skills, Doctor, but I would remind you that your presence is requested."

Doctor Kampfe leant back and took a swallow from the jug we were passing around. "Your master can request as much as he wants. I'm still on tour."

"Not any more." That shaving-sharp smile glinted. "Come on, Doctor, you know the terms of your contract better than anyone."

"I do." Doctor Kampfe was utterly unconcerned. "Come back when I finish a run of something. Until then, bark all you want, but don't pretend you'll bite."

By now everyone was listening, ready to manhandle Mr Collar out the stage door if he got nasty.

"Your run is finished," said Mr Collar, with masterful double meaning.

"The small print is quite clear on the subject," Doctor Kampfe disagreed. "'A run shall constitute ten performances of the same play before the Players move on…' I have the contract about me if you want to check…"

Mr Collar was also good at deadpan. "And congratulations on a fine tenth performance."

Doctor Kampfe went very still. "Nine," he said. "Sometimes less but never more than nine."

In the wake of his words I was left feeling as though I had done something very unwise indeed. And I had been manipulated, surely, but an actor, of all people, has no business complaining he has been tricked.

"A matinee for the orphans of Saint Agatha's," Mr Collar stated. "Truly a masterpiece. Performed by your company and paid for, handsomely. The day before you opened here."

The Doctor's eyes sought mine and then Timoti's. He must have known the truth by the way we avoided his gaze. He fumbled from his jacket a cracklingly old document and unfolded it with shaking hands. He really did have the contract on him. It was that important.

"Don't look so downcast. You're still my master's favourite, and think of the actors you'll have the pick of," Mr Collar told him. "They almost all come to us in the end, after all. It's such a venal profession."

Doctor Kampfe looked up from the contract. I knew he must have been looking for some clause that rendered our little charity gig null and void. I think it was the payment that did it, though. When we took Mr Collar's gold, the performance was entered in the books as official.

"It has been a while since I saw the old place." Doctor Kampfe looked older than I'd ever seen him.

"Three hundred years of nine-night runs," agreed Mr Collar. "Everything is as you left it."

"Of course it is." He didn't rage, our Doctor Kampfe. He didn't curse me for my greed or folly. He was the manager, after all, and had to retain his dignity before mere actors.

"And perhaps my master will allow you another sabbatical, some time. Albeit one with more rigorously worded terms. You'd think, with all the lawyers we have to hand, we'd have spotted that one." Mr Collar gestured grandly and one of the walls of the dressing room opened up as though hidden machinery had moved it. Behind it was…

I don't want to say just what I saw behind it. If you want to imagine the usual mummery of flames and tormented souls and red-skinned goat-men with pitchforks, then I won't say you're wrong, but it doesn't do it justice. And deep down in all of that, on some distant lower circle, I saw a stage.

Doctor Kampfe turned to us and spread his hands. "My friends, my companions," he said, "I leave Timoti to stand in my place. He knows where everything is, and is good with money.

There's little more to the craft of a theatrical manager, truth be told. And, as and when each of you should find your way to join me, you may be assured of a sympathetic audition. You've often heard it said that there is a special place down below reserved for actors, and now you know this to be true, but it's a place of privilege. Even the Lord of the Pit enjoys a good show."

And then he bowed and stepped back past the notional boundary of that fourth wall, and abruptly all that we had seen there was gone, and we were within a conventionally-bounded dressing room once more and staring at each other.

Needless to say the orphanage business got a full airing and we had to spread the gold around or risk the company coming apart at the seams. I consider myself justly chastened.

Later that night most of the company were either asleep or swapping anecdotes about when other actors not present had royally screwed up. Nobody was talking about our lost leader, though everyone was thinking of him. Timoti di Venezi was already poring over the Doctor's maps and working out which town we'd play next, while the old man who adapted our scripts was scratching the first pages of a new tragedy. I didn't want to look at the *dramatis persona*. I knew who'd be at the head of it.

Instead I found Felice, who had been fending off John Worthing's sodden advances, and we went out into the stalls to look at the moon through the holes in the roof. We had the last jug of the Sevengraves homebrew, and were comfortable enough with our general dislike of each other that nothing untoward was likely to happen. What we had not expected was to find Mr Collar, red-lined cloak and all, sitting and staring at the stage as though all the world were contained there.

We were sufficiently drunk that we accosted him at once, utterly forgetting who and what he must be. Felice went so far as to prod him in the chest and snap, "I suppose that was all fakery then, the orphanage, your bedridden ward? All just a trick to get to Doctor Kampfe?"

I waited for the explosion, but Mr Collar just shook his head sadly. "Not at all. Do you think I can show no real kindness or charity? What else do we do on vacation abroad, but those things forbidden to us at home?" He rolled his shoulders and stretched in a way most inhuman, as though the shape was constricting him. "Count yourself lucky that you are an actress, my dear. Some of us spend our entire lives playing the demon king."

The Tenth Man

Bryony Pearce

"You've got the paperwork?" The nurse held out his hand. Or was he a nurse? My eyes went to the cuffs on his belt, the walkie-talkie.

I stuttered a reply, offering the folder I had almost forgotten to bring in from the car. "A letter from the university, permission from his wife, notes from his doctor."

The nurse, guard, care assistant – what was he? – nodded. "It all seems to be in order." But he didn't move.

I glanced at my watch. "I don't have –"

"Of course." He shuffled, suddenly less intimidating. "What do you know about Professor Macguire, Mr Thomas?

"He's the leader in his field at Oxford – particle physics, he believes in multiple universes –"

The nurse held up a chapped finger.

"About his illness, I mean."

It was my turn to fidget. I cleared my throat. "Dissociative Identity Disorder, that's what I was told."

"And you know what that is?"

I glanced at my own reflection in the glass below the exit sign. "It's like schizophrenia, isn't it?

The nurse shook his head. "Schizophrenia has a number of symptoms, including hallucinations, delusions and muddled thoughts. It's usually diagnosed between the ages of fifteen and thirty-five. Professor Macguire was sixty when he was brought in; he suffers no hallucinations, his thoughts are clear." The nurse returned my folder. "Professor Macaguire has the most astonishing case of D.I.D that we have ever seen."

"Which means what?" I leaned forward.

The nurse touched my arm. “Professor Macguire has *ten distinct personalities* inhabiting his body.”

“Ten …” I cleared my throat again. “How do you know there are ten?”

“As I said,” the nurse rubbed his chin and I heard the rasp of five o clock shadow, even though it was barely ten am. “They are *distinct* personalities. All are male and seem to be the same age, but they have very different histories, mannerisms, beliefs and even knowledge. Professor Macguire, as you know, was a world expert in his field. Number two, for example, can barely count to ten – and needs to use his fingers for that.”

“*Is.*” I snapped.

“I’m sorry?”

“You said he *was* an expert in his field.” I tucked the folder back into my rucksack. “Even with his… problems, Professor Macguire remains the foremost expert in multiple universe theory and dimensional research in the world. That’s why I’m here.” I straightened. “I’m doing my PhD on his work, hoping to take it forward towards completion.”

The nurse took a step away from me, less friendly. “Look, this is standard information for a new visitor. A warning if you like. Professor Macguire himself – he’s a nice guy. Two’s a bit on the slow side - childish, but you’ll like him if you meet him. Three, Four and Five, are almost … primitive. Six thinks he’s from some kind of world of the future. Eight and Nine seem like normal businessmen; you can tell the difference between them because Nine thinks he has kids and Eight is a foul-mouthed bastard, mind my French. But Seven and Ten…” He hesitated, touched his cuffs. “It’s not always easy to tell, which is why we don’t usually allow visitors, but there are signs. If the Professor begins to limp, or seems to be having trouble using his left hand, it’s Seven. Get as far away from him as possible – put the bed or desk between you – and hit the panic button.”

“Why, what does he –?”

“There’s a reason he was hospitalised, Mr Thomas.”

"The… incident?"

"That was Seven. At least we think so."

"And Ten?"

"If Ten surfaces, stay calm, but hit the panic button. He's not violent, or hasn't been yet, but –"

"How will I know?"

"It's hard to distinguish Ten from Professor Macguire himself, but there are signs. Ten will start talking about the end of the world."

"If he's not violent, why is it so important to get out?"

"Ten's a sociopath. He'll manipulate you. He talked another patient into killing herself, which is why we keep the Professor in isolation. Even after that he was able to persuade one of my colleagues into attempting to free him. People who speak to Ten don't come out the same, Mr Thomas. He does something to them. The rate of violence and suicide among his visitors is significantly above the national average. We can't prove anything but…"

"You think he can talk me into, what – setting fire to the student union?" I snorted.

The nurse sighed. "This is *your* warning, Mr Thomas. The hospital won't be liable if something happens to you during your visit with Professor Macguire, or afterwards."

"Of course."

"Then will you sign this, thereby freeing the hospital from liability?" The nurse pushed a clipboard at me.

Impatiently I scrawled my name with the pencil stub provided.

"Now, if you'll go through the metal detector." He gestured. "It's like an airport – can I confirm that you have no sharp objects, nail scissors, penknives, nail files or anything similar you might have forgotten to leave in your vehicle?"

"Nothing like that." I shook my head. "All I have is my tape recorder, notebook, pen –"

"You'll need to hand that in." The nurse held out his hand.

"The tape recorder?" I frowned.

"The pen." He took it from me. "If you have to write we've got crayons."

"Are you serious?" I frowned.

The nurse mimed stabbing me with the biro by way of explanation and I flinched. "Or stamp on it and you've got yourself some plastic shards." He chose a blue crayon from a box beside his screen and handed it over.

I turned the Crayola over and stared at the blunted end. "Bloody hell."

"Are you sure you want to go through with the visit?"

I nodded. Without Professor Macguire I had nothing for my PhD. The only science related career I'd be able to hope for was teaching it. I shuddered. "Lead on."

The Professor's room was one of several on the floor, but the others seemed unoccupied. I frowned as we walked past yet another empty unit.

"We had to clear the rest of the corridor." The nurse said, correctly translating my raised eyebrow. "Ten kept speaking to them through his door. There was mass hysteria and we can't keep him permanently sedated."

"Or gagged." I quipped into the awkward silence.

"Right." The nurse stopped outside the only closed door and handed me a button on what seemed to be a small box. "Your panic button. Remember – limping, having difficulty with his left hand, or talking about the end of the world. I won't be far."

I swallowed and took the box. Then I watched the nurse loosen his cuffs and unlock the door.

The Professor sat at his desk with his back to me; he was staring out of his small window and I could see papers under his elbow; numbers, equations. My heart beat faster: he was still working.

His hair was longer than in the photographs: a dark salt-and-pepper grey, it curled over the back of his collar to brush against his broad shoulders, thicker even than mine.

He made no move as the door opened and the nurse guided me in.

"Professor?" The nurse curled one hand around his walkie-talkie. "Professor Macguire?" The nurse looked at the papers crumped beneath his patient's arm.

The man sighed. "Yes, William, it's me." He turned slowly. He was bigger than I'd expected. He must have spent time in the gym, using weights, driving his thoughts on treadmills. Now he was starting to sag, to waste away.

"You have a visitor. I'll have to look after your pencil until he's gone."

The Professor looked me up and down with a slight frown.

"He's from the university." The nurse picked up the pencil that was lying on the Professor's papers and tucked it into his pocket. He pointed me towards the guest chair beside the desk. I started forwards.

"He has a panic button?" The Professor's dark, almost girlish lashes dropped as he looked at my hand.

"Of course." The nurse nodded. "No need to worry, you won't be able to hurt Mr Thomas, he's been warned."

"And forewarned is forearmed." The Professor smiled then, his blue eyes warm, and I smiled back. All those warnings and the Professor was fine; lucid, worried about hurting me even. Everything was about liability nowadays. The floor was probably just empty because of cut backs and all those warnings were to make sure I couldn't sue if I stubbed my toe or something during the visit. I didn't watch the nurse walk out and lock the door behind him. I was already setting up my tape recorder.

"You want to speak to me about my work, Mr Thomas?" The Professor had caught my unsubtle glances at his notes.

"Call me Dean." I sat down, carefully. "I'd like to do an interview, at least to start with. I've read your papers, but I want to know in your own words, what you were doing and what…"

"What went wrong?"

"Yes. I hope that I can replicate… I won't say improve… but if I can look at things in a different way, from a different angle." I cleared my throat.

"You're from a different discipline?"

"More maths oriented." I looked again at the pages beneath his arm.

"You want to see these?" He pushed them towards me. "Take them."

"Take them?" I breathed raggedly, my fingers hovering over the paper, as if he might change his mind and snatch them back.

"What good do they do me? If Two doesn't scribble on the bloody things, Three'll eat them, or Four'll wipe his –" He stopped, spread his hands. "You understand my condition?"

I was horrified. "You destroy your own work?"

"Not *me*." The Professor shook his head. "Two through Five." He sighed. "I don't know how long I've got, so you'd better ask your questions."

"You mean…"

"I mean I'm driving right now, boy, but one of the passengers will likely take over in a while."

I swallowed. "So, I know your work involved multiple universe theory and you were trying to create a – a wormhole I suppose is the best way to describe it, into an alternative universe. You wanted to communicate across worlds, with the ultimate aim of swapping knowledge, scientific advances, perhaps even resources."

"In broad layman's terms." The Professor nodded. "Imagine if we could create a doorway into a world where they still have plentiful fossil fuels and strike a trade deal just as we would with the US or China. Imagine if we could open a doorway into a world that could give us the secret of cold fusion, a simple way to clean up our oceans, repair our atmosphere, or travel across the galaxy."

"Mathematically speaking, these couldn't possibly be worlds close to our own."

"Then you do understand multiple universe theory." The Professor leaned forward on his elbows, suddenly animated. "Go on, tell me what you know."

"Every single time a decision is made, an alternative universe is created, so that there are infinite universes; some very, very similar to our own, others that diverged thousands of millennia ago and took totally different paths." I felt as if I was in a supervision and worried that I sounded as if I was hoping for a good grade from him.

Instead of mocking me, the Professor shook his head quite seriously. "Not *that* long ago."

The tape recorder whirred quietly between us. "Why not?"

"Decision implies consciousness. If, as I posit, alternative universes are created by decision, then the overwhelming majority of universes spurred from ours will have been created after mankind developed thought from instinct. The number prior to this, generated by random decisions when faced with a choice of little consequence – whether to go to the left or right in order to pass a boulder blocking the way, for example – would be negligible compared to the myriad generated since."

"Of course. Instinct means that for most situations there is only one possible course of action. It wouldn't be a conscious decision whether or not to run from a sabre tooth tiger." I grinned.

"Right. I believe the development of symbolic culture, language and specialised lithic technology signified the start of universe mitosis. Around fifty millennia ago."

Excited, I scribbled a note. Then I looked up "Still, the universes most different from our own and therefore potentially most useful to us, would be the ones created millennia ago. But it would be easiest to open a door to the universe least divergent from ours."

It was the Professor's turn to smile. "But then, how would we know we had done so?"

"I'm sorry?"

"If the universe were the same as ours in every conceivable way, except one - that Mrs Brown from number ten had curry for dinner instead of casserole perhaps – how would you know that you had managed to open a door to another universe?"

"Readings – air, background radiation…" I faltered.

"All are unlikely to change in a universe so close to our own."

"And that was your first problem." I nodded, sagely.

The Professor leaned back in his chair and laughed. "*That* wasn't my first problem! Think. How much energy would you need to open an actual door into another universe? What would you use to build the door? What materials should I be looking at to tear a hole through our own reality and into another? Should I be looking at magnetism, sucking atoms from space, dark matter? My *first* problem was that the whole thing is utterly impossible."

I gaped. "What?"

"Go home, son." The Professor knitted his long fingers behind his head and looked down his nose at me. His blue eyes twinkled. "This, whatever it is you're doing, your PhD, it's tilting at windmills. There is no way you can open a physical gateway into another universe, another dimension, or even into another spot in our own world. The best you can hope is to go to B&Q, buy yourself a new front door and tell yourself it opens each morning onto a new day… Fucktard!"

"What?" My eyes widened.

"You heard me, you whore-son, go home. Go home before your arse-wittage creates a cluster-fuck of a problem that even your mother can't buy you out of." The Professor's eyes continued to twinkle merrily and I gaped.

"You – you –" I fingered the panic button, my thoughts racing. "Eight?"

The Professor shoved his chair back from his desk and crossed his legs. "Rude fucking kids. My name is Ray."

"R-Ray?"

"Ray Macguire, dickhead."

There were subtle changes in the Professor's demeanour, now

that I knew to look for them. He sat now with his arms dangling by his sides, utterly relaxed, like an old boy on a barstool, missing only his pint. His twinkling eyes had a hard edge, not true good humour. He'd laugh at you, but only if you fell from your own stool and injured your coccyx.

Was the Professor gone then? For how long? I exhaled shakily. I had a time limit – a single morning with Professor Macguire. Was a ten-minute interview and a statement that his work was all hokum, all I was going to get?

"Ray?" I dragged a shaking hand through my dark blonde hair. "Do you know what the Professor and I were talking about? Were you… listening?"

He snorted. "Opening a door into another universe so you can swap recipes or some bollocks. You don't know the first thing about shit."

"I need the Professor." I pleaded. "Can't you… put him back on the line or something."

Ray threw back his head and laughed. Then he spoke into his closed fist. "Sandra? Yes, dear, would you kindly transfer Professor Macguire to line one? I have a right twat here who wants to speak to him." His laugh petered out, as if it had run down a drain. He regarded me with his head cocked to one side. "You're a bloody little nerd aren't you? What the hell're you going to contribute to the world?"

I blinked. "I'm sorry?"

"You heard. Never done a day's work in your life, have you? Never even done a paper round, or washed glasses in a bar. Wouldn't know how to run a business if yer life depended on it. No good with people, no good with money."

"And you are?" I raised my eyebrows.

Ray snorted. "Just look at any business index. My company was top one hundred four years in a row."

I swallowed, shakily. "And what does your company do?"

"Do?" Ray sneered. "We don't *do,* we *make.*"

My head swam, I was totally out of my depth, struggling to

find any kind of response that made sense and wouldn't anger him. "What do you *make*?"

"We *make* portants, carriers, dozer components, e.c.cs." He sighed and turned away. "Not that you'd…"

I frowned, the pencil turned in my fingers and I looked down. "Those things … I don't –"

The professor sighed. "Portants – personal teleporters – no?" He shook his head. "Trapped here, in this body, in this crappy world without even an e.c.c. for entertainment…"

His voice faded. I sat up.

"Trapped here? In *this* crappy world, what do you mean?"

"Trapped." The professor hunched in his chair and looked up at me wide eyed. He combed his fringe over his face with his fingers. "Ray-Ray go home?"

"Home?" I echoed. Despite the Professor's age, I suddenly felt like the older one in the room.

He frowned. "Go bye-bye - go home." He stood, stamped his feet and then spotted my blue crayon. He grabbed it with an expression of pure joy, skipped to the wall and began marking lines on the white paint.

It felt as if the floor was moving under me. I gripped the table edge. "Two?" I fumbled for my phone and took a picture of the growing piece of art on the wall. Trees, they had to be and, I tilted my head to one side, a cave perhaps.

"Is that… home?"

The Professor dropped the crayon and started to stroke the wall, patting the cave entrance with one hand, thumping his forehead with the other.

"Professor?" I called gently, then louder. If he could swap personalities that fast, perhaps I could get him back. What would do it? My gaze fell on the papers he had been working on. I picked them up. His writing was neat, small curlicues on the ends of the fives and threes, almost calligraphic. "I see your equations here – you know you made a small mistake in the integral on the third line?" I picked up the fallen crayon, and made a change which looked like a child's scrawl among the neat lines of algebra.

The Professor fell silent.

"It has an effect on the differentiation further down the page, and you know what maths is like – one tiny mistake early on and by the end it's a vast amount of difference..." I was babbling, trying to catch the attention of a man who might or might not be listening, buried beneath at least two other personalities.

I kept my head down, pretended to ignore the Professor, made notes on his pages as I scanned them. Apart from the small mistake early on his mind, as laid out to me here, was brilliant. What were these equations meant to prove? Was this an answer to the gateway problem?

Out of the corner of my eye, I saw him approach, felt him lean over me. I shivered. What if this was Seven? I had nowhere to run. I imagined his hands around my neck: large hands.

My memory fed me the reports of his arrest and subsequent insanity plea. A laboratory burned to the foundations. One dead, two injured. Not all burn victims. I shuddered again, but kept scanning the papers, drawn into the numbers almost despite myself.

A hand on my shoulder. I froze. Then a finger pointing. "You made a correction here – you're sure that's right?" His voice was once again that of the man I had met when I entered the room.

I sagged slightly, relieved. Then I turned. "I'm sure. What do these do? You said the gateway wouldn't work."

The Professor smiled. "It can't, not in the way you think?"

"Not, the way I think? Then it *can* work." My eye fell on the notes I had been taking, almost unconsciously. Three words were written in capitals, encircled. PHYSICAL GATEWAY IMPOSSIBLE. "Physical gateway impossible." I read. Then my own eyes widened. "A *physical* gateway, but what about a *non-physical* one?"

The Professor sighed, walked around me and sat down again, crossing his legs at the ankle. "What do you think you know?"

"I'm not sure. Do you mind if I think aloud?"

The Professor gestured, a sign to go-ahead.

"My friend, Beth, is a researcher in the particle physics lab, that's one of your specialties, isn't it? She's been running experiments on atoms. We already know that measuring an atom seems to affect its course. She hopes to prove that our mere *expectations* of an atom's direction can change its eventual position."

The Professor's brows raised. "I'd like to know how she intends to prove that."

"You'd have to speak to Beth." I folded my hands. "If she's right, though, that means that our own observation of our universe, our own expectations of it, have a hand in creating it."

"Mind over matter," the Professor commented mildly, but his eyes were glittering.

"So if *decisions* create universe mitosis and our own *expectations* shape the universe we end up in…" I floundered. The Professor waited. "If we essentially create our own universes, it should be possible to access other universes… by creating a gateway…" I stopped and the blood ran from my cheeks.

"In our own minds." The Professor finished.

My hands started to shake. I rose from my stool and backed away until I hit the wall. I stared at the Professor, then at the artwork behind him, the life-size cave crayoned onto the paintwork.

"You – you're telling me that you did manage to create a wormhole? A-a gateway inside your own head. You don't have D.I.D, you have… a portal to another universe – in your *head*?"

The Professor steepled his fingers. "Not *an*-other universe."

"Nine. Is that right? Nine other selves: nine universes. You have ten distinct personalities because you have nine versions of yourself from other universes trapped inside your mind."

The Professor clenched his fists. "I didn't realise what I was doing would be a trap for them. I should have seen it, but I didn't. They got into my mind, into our world, but they can't get out."

"Why not?"

"I made a mistake. I thought what I was doing would allow *me* to perceive other universes, to travel across realities, but instead I created an open space which instead draws others *in.* I shut the experiment down as soon as I realised. Now I'm trying to work out –"

"How to get them home?" I looked at the sheets of maths. "How did you open this wormhole in the first place?"

The Professor rose and walked to his door, he leaned on the jamb. "Everything we know about the world is based on what our brain tells us, do you understand that?"

"Of course." He was lecturing now, I his willing student.

"Our brain perceives the world based on the stimulation it receives through neurons?"

"Right." I nodded.

"You think your conscious self is interacting with the world directly, but this is an illusion created by the brain. Your brain receives an *enormous* amount of information and it filters that information before it reaches your consciousness."

I nodded.

"So then, how can you know that anything you see is real?"

I paused before answering. "I... I don't know."

"You know people used to believe that we only utilise around ten percent of our brain?"

"I'd heard that."

"Proved to be nonsense, of course, but I now wonder if there was more truth in the notion than we knew, if a good portion of our mind is active in ways we never suspected. My theory is that in reality our brains are exposed to, or perceive, a vast number of alternative universes at a level we cannot possibly comprehend, but are constantly filtering out the information that doesn't apply to the one relevant to us. So, as you said, expectation informs matter; not by changing it, but by filtering out the other versions of reality."

I sat up. "That's brilliant."

He folded his arms. "So then, how did I create the gateway?"

"Somehow you have to cancel out your expectations, fool the brain into showing you other realities?"

"Something like that. I worked with Professor… Frith, in the neuropsychology department."

The small hesitation before he spoke the name caught my attention. "Professor Frith." I rolled the name around my tongue, trying to remember why I knew of him. Had one of my friends had him as a supervisor? Then the answer came to me like striking lightning: Professor Charles Frith: Charlie Frith, strangled and then burned. By Seven.

The Professor looked at me coldly, and I suppressed my instinctive shudder. This was important. I needed to know. I had a future to think of. "Sorry, go on."

"Professor Frith and I created a machine which forced both my conscious and unconscious mind to totally focus on one single task. It made sure that the part of my mind that set expectations of the universe had no way to communicate with the other part, in effect, we switched it off." His face fell. "I thought this would enable me to perceive other universes; instead it left an empty space which was filled…"

"By other versions of yourself," I gasped. "But the information you can get from them…"

"That's why I… we… carried on." The Professor turned his attention to the window. "One of my selves comes from a world where they have teleportation. If he would only write down the formula... Others are from dying worlds; if they could just tell us what they did wrong... One of them is from a world so far ahead of ours it's almost alien, he must have so much to share with us…"

"But they won't share."

"Even if they would be willing to help the person who trapped them in a world not their own, no one would listen." The Professor seemed to be talking to himself now. "I'm insane, remember? Why would anyone…?" He looked at me.

"*I'm* listening." I sat up. "If you could get Ray to tell me how the teleporters work…"

"You can claim to have come up with the idea yourself." His voice had hardened. "Become a billionaire."

"Do you want the world to have these ideas or not?" I snapped, suddenly angry. "You say your aim was to find out wonderful things, but you don't want to share if there's a chance someone else will get credit." I stopped, stood. "Is that what happened to Professor Frith, was he going to get credit?"

The Professor laughed. "It wasn't about credit, you fool." He turned his attention back to the window.

"Then what?" My palms itched.

"He was like you, he wanted to *know things*. When he couldn't persuade the *other* Rays to give up their knowledge for the good of our world, he decided that it was a fault in *me*. He decided to try the machine for himself. Thought that the other versions of him that came through would be more altruistic." He snorted.

"Weren't they?"

The Professor's laughter was bitter. "What we didn't realise was that there are worlds out there, universes, where humanity is no longer… human. We… they evolved, destroyed their own worlds, and have been waiting for us, or others, to open this gateway and let them escape their own wastelands. The Frith that took over Charlie's body wasn't human, he was… horrifying." The Professor visibly shuddered. "And there are whole worlds, whole *universes* of beings like that who want to come through – to take over our bodies and live here. It took me a while to see it – weeks. Frith seemed so reasonable at first. He showed us how to create the gateway without using the machine. It's so simple a child could do it. He wanted us to share the technique with the whole world, to open up completely to *his* universe and let his people through to take ours."

I sank back into my seat. "But you saw through him in the end."

The Professor's eyes grew wet. "Somehow, Charlie managed

to take charge of his own body again, just for a short time. When he'd finished screaming and begging for death, he warned me that if I let the secret of the gateway out it would be the end of our world. *Everyone* would end up like him, imprisoned in a corner of their own mind. Our only hope was to kill the project before anyone else from Frith's world broke through into ours. And to look out for others who might have found the secret of the gateway. Stop them spreading the knowledge."

I swallowed. "That's why you killed Charles Frith and set fire to the lab."

The Professor bit his lip and his eyes slid away. "It's what he wanted."

"So you're the only one who can open the gateway now."

The Professor cocked his head. "You want me to tell you the secret."

"If you tell me how to open it, I should be able to work out how to close it, to set all those versions of you free. And someone else should know, don't you think? Should recognise the technique it if it gets out?" I leaped up.

The Professor seemed to think, then he limped over to me and whispered in my ear. My eyes widened.

"It's that simple?"

"That simple." He sat down, rubbed one hand with the other. Then he looked back up at me, "Hey, have you seen my kids, how are they doing?"

I gathered my things. "Nine? Ray?"

"Yeah. Listen, tell Elaine I'm coming home soon, okay."

"Sure." I backed towards the door, pressed the panic button and waited for the nurse to come and let me out.

The Professor watched as the PhD student – what was his name? Dean Thomas – almost ran back to his car. A smile played across his lips. The nurse stood behind him.

"Do you think he'll use the mantra, Professor?

"Of course, William. In the end you all do, don't you? It's

irresistible. I warn you, give you a fair chance, but you must *know*."

The nurse nodded. "And you think he'll be able to spread the technique."

"He seems stronger than the last and he has the potential to be influential, in time."

"Will you let the original out for a while?"

"Why not?" Number Ten closed his eyes.

When the eyes opened again, they were bleak and haunted. Professor Macguire dove from his chair and scuttled into a corner, pinning himself between the bed and the wall. His hands flew to his face. His screams were soul-wrenching, but there was no one on the empty floor to hear.

Only William, whose home universe was an empty shell, and he just smiled.

Rare as a Harpy's Tear

Neil Williamson

Dust of the Mesa

The first drop is sand. It skitters, slides soft from the corner of my eye, coming to rest on my crag cheek. Familiar as ghosting dust on the red mesa, although our home is long away and far down from here. And we almost made the air, my love. We almost did.

I have dragged you to shelter, hidden now from the Birds of the Air. I shield you with my own wide wings, though I'm certain we are safe. We will rest here. Soon enough you will wake. And then we shall leave, as heroes.

Sweat of Honest Valour

The second drop is salt. Crusted sweat, it cracks when I close my eyes to rest. When I open them, scintillating, a diamond in the corner of my vision. Paltry treasure for hours of toil. I have blunted my talons on the Djinn Lord's wall, scraping out mortar, heaving at the blocks. Bloody claw marks mar the Cloud Palace marble.

Almost there, my love. A little longer and this block will rock loose. Then we valiant thieves will have our escape. The relief of arid air! But first, let me rest in the cool palm shade.

Bile of the Forgotten

The third drop is spit. If you can call it that, this gob of froth flecking my hide. Feeble, but no less ire-filled, no less heart-felt.

That one being should own such fabulous riches and guard them so jealously, for so long, that they become less than a myth.

All we wanted for our kin was a pocketful of treasure to plant out in the world, seeds that might grow into rumours and bring men sniffing along the desert roads again. Oh, to feast on more than snakeflesh and scarabs. Is that too much to ask?

Many the Dead

The fourth drop is blood. A jewel of ruby rage, shed with my defiant shriek, a carrion cry that I cannot still. Even knowing that, as it rends the air, shivers the tranquil pools and still halls, I risk calling the *ifrits*, the *djinn*, the Birds of the Air upon us.

We have battled them, and can do so again. Are we not furies? Didn't we once terrorise travellers, painting the desert paths with their entrails? Let them come, these tyrant's vassals.

Many are the corpses in paradise today. One for each of our own, wasted away.

Seed of Salvation

The fifth drop is a carnelian. It tumbles down my face, jostled free of its setting while I laboured at the last of these blocks. *Look, a door*, I say. *Now we can fly.*

I would give up this fire-gem, tear-shaped and polished by a master craftsman. I would return all of the jewels in our plunder sack, spill them, skittering, onto those glittering mountains of undreamt-of wealth locked away in the Djinn Lord's treasure rooms. And, with them, relinquish the last hopes of our kind.

I would do this, my love, if you would only look.

Seed of Life

The sixth drop is a seed.

Oh, Meghis Tree! We tarried; swords bloodied and scorched, limbs weary from the fight and for the thought of flying, barely able to heft this brimful sack between us.

Meghis, the first tree. Heart of the oasis. Those succulent, life-giving leaves, miraculously capable of flourishing anywhere, even the mesa.

These jewels, you said, *may return prey to our lands. But this one seed, will save us all from thirst.*

I tilt your head towards the hole, and would return even that seed to see you revived by the zephyrs of home.

Seed of Love

The seventh drop is semen. It jets forth with an unbidden jag of memory, sweet and sticky on my leather as when we are at play. Deep in the cool caves, our bodies acoil, wrapped in darkness and echoes of sighs, of cries, of wingtips whispering against the rock. Dust and come lie tangy on our drowsy tongues.

Or else, gliding over the mesa, riding the highest thermals, wings beating together; hearts and flesh joined in an ecstasy of soaring.

My love, I would give up even this if you might just once more whisper my name.

Birds of the Air

The eighth drop condenses from my resigned exhalation. Squanderful, uncaring. In this palace water is plentiful. In the caves we lick the walls.

We were too proud, too glorious. The *ifrits* fell to our claws, the *djinn* snuffed by our blades, but we had no defence against the Birds of the Air. Owls and eagles are easy, they fight as we fight, but it was the sparrows and finches, too small, too fast, too numerous, that undid us.

Under our frond shelter, by this rough, useless door, I sigh again. The breath of half a man.

Wicked Waste of Water

The ninth drop is bitter loss. It shivers on my eyelid. A semblance of animation. As much a mockery as the way the sweet garden breezes ruffle your feathers, stir your hair. Your chest does not swell for breath. Your heart no longer squeezes your lifeblood from your wounds. Your beautiful eyes, black as baleful coals, my love, pecked and wrecked and stolen by the Birds, will never look on me again.

Our people are rock, and rock does not weep. Yet, as these drops accumulate in my eye, I accept the inevitability of my sorrow.

The Last Drop

No harpy's tear will fall where all is hoarded, nothing valued. The Djinn Lord takes everything. He'll have nothing more.

I bring you to the wall. Your wings, ever graceful, catch the air as you dive your last. The roaring sands welcome you home. The sack follows. What use luring seekers to the mesa without you to share the sport of their slaughter? Our people will persist a while yet regardless.

I take but one thing from the tyrant: the Meghis seed, for its beauty. I will plant it in shade. And water it with my grief.

Utopia +10

J. A. Christy

The first time it happened, I was on the canal at Ancoats. Me and DJ Bin Tony had been into the city to try to find work but there was nothing. Nothing at all. So we'd gone fishing. We had to do something with our day. Dianne's always moaning that I get under her feet and the kids are all hypnotised by PS17a Utopia game where their world is still green.

So we got our rods and headed for the water. I say water, and I do remember water, but this is more like a rusty soup with plastic chunks. Even so, there are still fish. DJ Bin Tony's a bit of a philosopher and his take on it is this:

"That Darwin bloke had it worked out. The fish adapt, don't they. We tip the shit in; I've seen it, mate, when I worked the refuse, straight into the water. Reckoned it'd dissolve or something. Put stuff in with it to help it along. Anyway. Them fish. The thicker the liquid, the harder they have to work, yeah? Big fuckers now."

They were massive. We'd leaned over the canal bank, lying on our bellies as we did when we were ten, and peered into the soup. They were there, all right. Moving around. We could see them, huge shadows moving through the thick molecules, stirring it up. We could sense them.

"It's primal, mate. Primal. We're made to hunt. Hunters, we are."

I think DJ Bin Tony was trying to convince himself. It's hard to think in those terms now. How we used to be. I knew he was right, and when I saw the fish I did feel it, but it was cancelled out by the hopelessness of mass produced, plastic wrapped portions that pass as food these days.

So I got it into my head that I wanted some real food. I'd wake in the night, hot and sweaty and somewhere in the past when we could kill and eat our food on the same day. Where we knew what it was we were eating. Where we cooked it, instead of the instantaneous heat of the hole in the wall in modern kitchens. I could remember fish and chips from Leo's on Oldham Street, fried in front of you and steaming in the night air. The salt and vinegar smell. The grease.

The urge to hunt grew and grew. Tony felt it too. I could tell. We went out every night, staring into the canal, neither of us speaking, but sharing something from deep history. Planning our campaign. Us against them. Once or twice we saw them, pulsing through the rust in groups. Tony licked his lips. I just nodded and narrowed my eyes. I could almost taste them.

I think we always knew that one day we would find ourselves sitting on that bank, our lines drawn tight by the thick flow. Watching, waiting. Hours passed and people walked by, on their way to the tree museum at Castlefield. The only trees left in the wild now, outside the manufactured forests in the wastelands. You could sometimes hear the birds singing from here, and people stopped and cocked their heads, hoping.

We smiled and nodded at them, but our minds were match fit. Focused. Staring at the bobbing pieces of cork that Tony had found in his mam's cupboard. He'd held them in both hands with reverence and whispered over them.

"Me dad's. He was a fisherman. She kept them after he… Well. She kept them."

Tony's dad was the first person I knew to suffocate. That would be ten years ago, at the beginning of the Earth warming. It was awful to watch, the slow gulping of breath over weeks and months, then, eventually, collapse. The summit, as it was called now, was unpredictable. People were dropping dead all over the place back then. "Not rocket science really. The lack of trees and the air pollution could only lead to one thing. Naturally, Tony had a theory.

"Survival of the fittest." He'd stated this at his Dad's funeral, just as the plume of smoke emerged from the crematorium chimney, adding to the air pollution. Our own personal contribution to the grey doom skies. "Weed out the wheat from the chaff, it will."

He was right. The first sign of a cough or asthma and you were pumped with medication. It still happened, that blue-faced death, but not on the streets any more. There were people. Rescuers. People were trained to spot the signs and pull you into a building if you keeled. Me and Tony had applied for a jobs as rescuers but, like everything, you had to have the right postal code. The right face. No genetic defects. Survival of the fittest was about right.

We stared and we stared that day, watching and waiting, our breath shallow. The murky grey day turned a little darker and Tony took a sip of his bottled water. I turned to reach for the bottle before he put his top back on and it happened. I didn't see it, but when I turned back, the cork was gone. Tony's was still there but mine had gone.

We jumped up, bouncing on our toes and heaving the rod.

"It's a big one! It's a fucking big one."

Even in the excitement, I remembered that time Tony's dad had taken us fishing, taken us down Daisy Nook and shown us how to cast. How it'd rained and we could stay out in it because it didn't burn then. How we'd looked up and seen a rainbow. Tony looked a lot like his dad in that moment when we caught the fish.

It took a few minutes to reel in, but all of a sudden the fish was there in front of us. Gasping for air. It was real. Tail flipping, scales somehow shining in the gloom, it stared at us. Tony's fingers curled round my arm.

"What we gonna do, Charlie, mate? How we gonna kill it?"

I hadn't considered that. No one really killed anything these days. Everything was grown or made. No need to kill. People died, obviously, but not in public, if possible. No. These days it was all about survival and hope. Like PS17a Utopia. I didn't know how to kill a fish. I'd never seen Tony's dad kill one. He'd always put them back.

Suddenly I felt ill. Strange. And really hungry. The fish was thrashing now, and I knew if I left it there long enough it would die anyway. Even so, something inside me, deep down, in the same place as my hunter dreams, told me to hit it hard. Put the creature out of its misery. So I grabbed a piece of concrete and dropped it. On to the fish. And it was still.

We both stared. Its eye was dull now and the mouth gaped. Tony started to cry. Big clear tears. We lifted the fish onto my jacket and wrapped it up. It took two of us to carry it back to my place near the old Dispensary, through the back streets so no one would see us and rob us of our quarry. I was emotional. Horror that I had killed mixed with a visceral hunger I had never felt before.

We carried the fish into the kitchen. Dianne was in the lounge with the kids, all of them safely plugged into the mainframe Utopia server. I shut the middle door and we unwrapped the fish. Tony was busy on his phone, finding pictures of fish and eventually he matched.

"Carp. That's what this is. Carp."

He held up the picture of the fish and we both looked from one fish to the other. It did look similar, but more muscular and much bigger. I washed it and stroked it. Tony took some pictures and then we came to the inevitable moment we had both been avoiding. Tony sighed.

"Who's gonna cut it up then?"

I looked at the fish, trying to decide how to do it. Tony googled and, of course, there was a tutorial. There's a tutorial for everything, even things that don't exist any more. We watched in horror as a fisherman, in the wild, beside a river and surrounded by trees, sliced open the stomach of a bream and chopped off its head. Then he filleted it and threw the fillets on an open fire. His envirnment couldn't have been more different to my stark, sterilised kitchen. We weren't allowed fires any more, even if there had been any wood to burn. Ironic really, as everyone knows that the ability to make fire is what sets us apart from animals. Makes you wonder when they're going to ban thumbs.

There we were with this huge creature, leaning in so that we could smell the death, and we didn't know what to do. I knew the instinct was there inside me somewhere. I knew that if I didn't do something it would be too late. I wanted the fish. I wanted to eat it. I wanted to snatch the headphones away from my children, pull them away from Utopia and give them real food. Give them the fish.

Would they ever feel this? They're trapped in the memory of an artificial world they can't get back to. I suddenly realise that they'll never have memories like mine. My granddad's house, the tiny goldfish in the clear water sphere. The apple tree outside the window swaying in the breeze. Sunshine. And songs about sunshine. That fish on the table was a giant red version of my granddads goldfish.

I grabbed the knife. Tony stepped back and paled.

"You're not going to cut its head off, are you?"

I lowered the knife.

"Course I am, you stupid sod. I'll have to cut it up if we're going to eat it. Go on. Get out if you're too scared. I'll shout you when it's done."

He waited a few seconds, shuffling from foot to foot. He had a look in his eye that my mums dog used to have when she was carving the Sunday roast. I put the knife down and put my hands on his shoulders.

"I'm not going to eat it without you, Tone. We're in this together, yeah?"

For some unknown reason we clasped hands and did the gang handshake that we hadn't done since we were at school. Then he left, looking over his shoulder at the glassy-eyed fish lying on my kitchen table.

It was just me and the fish. I realised I needed more time to consider this. To make a plan. I walked around the table, eyeing the carcass and nodding. Then I looked around the kitchen. How was I going to cook it? More flickers from the past: my class teacher, Mr Ellis, rolling bits of wood between his palms against a hollowed log and some grass. Sparks. Flint clicking together. No chance of any of that. No wood, no trees, no flint. I wrapped the fish up and pushed it under the table. I knew that Dianne kept a box upstairs with stuff from our past. From when we met.

I remembered that day, when we'd sat behind a bush in Alexandra Park. There was music playing and people sitting around on the grass. Immediately, the smell of freshly cut grass brought tears to my eyes and I almost went back to the kitchen and sat and cried for the feel of soil between my fingers. For tall sunflowers and yellow daffodils. Day to day you forget the details of life, don't you? But now I remembered. Oh yeah, now I did.

Dianne's box was tucked under our bed. It looked shabby in the pristine room, stained brown and checkered with newsprint. I ran my fingers over the texture and I never felt so alive. But a little bit scared, too. I knew that the box contained my life, freeze-framed before things changed. Before we were too busy having kids to notice the melting icebergs and the flood. Before we made the connection.

Before the sea became waves of plastic and the canal was the only place left to dump our waste. Before the last blade of grass and the last tree.

I opened it all the same. I needed to go back there, to ease this ache in me for the past. But most of all, to find that lighter we used that day in the park. The one I lit Diane's ciggie with before we held hands and smoked it between us. I rummaged in the box, tossing aside pictures of us and the kids, me and my mam, our dog Buster and the old house we used to live in before it was torn down to make way for the Units.

It was there. A cylindrical plastic lighter with a Union Jack on the side. I shook it and it was still half full of fuel. I'd be able to make a spark at least. I looked around for something to burn, but there was nothing. No wood, obviously. Everything was made of plastic which wouldn't burn. Believe me, a lot of people have tried, but all they get is spirals of black smoke and a ten day minimum prison sentence.

I looked back at the box. Dianne would kill me, but I wanted to eat that fish. I got that mad urge, like I used to get when overpackaged Amazon parcels arrived, where I wanted to tear it up there and then. Tear it up and set light to all the combustable materials and cook my fish.

Reality kicked in. I hurried downstairs with the case and pushed the fish and the knife inside. Dianne and the kids were completely engrossed in Utopia, but I called out to them anyway.

"Just goin' out. Be back later." I listened as the soundwaves rippled through the clarified oxygen and hit the plastic. It sounded like a previous, optimistic version of me, when there was somewhere to be. Something to do. No reply, so I flung the front door open and strode down the street, Tony in tow. I was heading for the forest. Or at least to where the forest used to be. Something in my soul dragged me along through the plastic and concrete jungle, along the rusty canal bank and over the steel and plastic bridge.

We were taking a chance. A risk. We're allowed to keep artefacts in private, but not in public, as if there's an invisible tax on reminiscing. Dianne's brown suitcase would have been a class one penalty, with its manky pateen corners and mouldy covering. The photos inside would have been severely frowned upon. We were all brown and smiling and surrounded by trees. Rumours were that no one wants us to remember that. That it'd do strange things to us. I can't see it myself.

I'd played in the forest as a child and my muscle memory guided me back there. I knew instinctively where it was, which direction, and when I saw the boulder that marked the outskirts I punched the air. It was paved for miles, with the odd boulder sticking out. A kind of unspoken memorial to how the world used to be.

I picked a large boulder to sit behind. Tony sat opposite, legs crossed.

"My Dad used to say that these were meteorites. Come from space. Dead stars."

He pointed upwards, and we both looked into the murky air. I nodded.

"Yeah. Stars. It's been a while."

I reached into the box and produced the fish. Tony gasped.

"Bloody hell. I though you'd chopped it up. Bloody hell, Charlie."

He got up and sat round the other side of the meteorite. I could still feel it, the primal urge and I smiled as I thought that I was sitting right next to a star. I unwrapped the fish and took out the knife. Grabbing a handful of photographs, I ripped them up and made them into kindling. Dianne and me ripped to shreds. Me and Mam, separated and decapitated. The greenery backgrounds merged together and I almost imagined that I was burning real wood. Well, I was, wasn't I? Paper was made of wood.

I even ripped up the suitcase. A label inside told me that it was made in 1938. It belonged in the artefact museum, really. I pulled it apart all the same. By the time everything was torn into tiny pieces there was a fair pile of my former life. I clicked the lighter a couple of times and it lit. An orange dancing flame, so beautiful that I stared at it for longer than I should and it went out.

I panicked and clicked again, but there were only sparks this time. I could hear Tony shuffling around.

"Have you done it yet? Have you?"

I took a deep breath. The knife was in my hand and I held the fish firm. It was starting to smell a bit and a dark green liquid was leaking from its eyes. I pushed the knife home just below the gills, as I'd seen them do on the YouTube demonstration. The flesh moved under my hands as I hit something hard and I winced and pulled out the knife.

It was no good. The bile in my mouth made me feel like a

fucking wuss, and the warrior instinct took over. I hacked at the dead flesh and sawed through the fish. Its head wouldn't detach from the body so I sawed more frantically. My sweat dripped onto the scales, running off in rivulets. Fragments of meat splattered the paving stones and there was a thud, thud, thud as the end of the knive hit hard stone in rhythm.

Finally, I threw the knife aside and grabbed its body in one hand and its head in the other. I pulled and pulled, but it wouldn't come away. Scales scraped off and fell to the ground and the flesh mangled around the cut as I tore at it. Suddenly, I realised that Tony was watching me. He was standing a few feet away, horrified. He moved forward and touched my shoulder.

"Mate. Stop. Look at the fucking state of you."

I dropped the huge fish and it flopped onto the floor. Somewhere in the back of my consciousness, something scanned it and told me that it was still fit to eat. But my senses were fixed on something else. Something that glinted from inside the fish. Something mechanical. I wiped my hands on my jumper and wiped the slippy handle of the knife. Cutting away the flesh above the gills, the metal hit metal. I carved around the object. Tony gasped.

"Jesus Christ. What is that? What is it?"

It appeared to be a steel rib. I dug deeper and it was attached to a steel spine. It wasn't right. This wasn't a fish.

"What the fuck is it, Charlie? It's some kind of monster."

I butchered the fish. I scraped every single scrap of meat off its metal skeleton and put it neatly on one side. On top of the meteorite. I picked it up by the tail and shook it. It reminded me of one of those key rings you used to get in Christmas crackers. Flexible and slinky. It was perfectly engineered. It glinted in the light that pose as sunshine through the murky clouds. It was perfection.

I heard a click and Tony stared at the lighter in amazement.

"It worked! I saw a…"

"Spark. You saw a spark. Probably the last one. Jesus, Tone, I was gonna use that to cook it."

He stared at the pile of debris.

"You're not seriously going to eat it are you? We don't even know if it's real."

So we sat there in the middle of the concrete forest, our backs against the boulder. The sparkling hope of all things past dropped out of the air and stunk all around us of rotting flesh. To make it worse, the Manchester sunshine we hardly ever saw these days broke through and made the fish stink even more.

Tony picked up one of the eyes and held it up to the light. He squashed it just like we used to do back when we were kids and there were spiders to pull the legs off. It didn't pulp between his white-from-the-force fingers. Instead, it caught a ray and cast a huge rainbow through the damp air of Ancoats. The first one either of us had seen since that day we went fishing with Tony's dad.

A stray sunbeam bent in a fluke turn of the atmosphere and directed the light at my former life, which promptly went up in smoke. I could have sworn I saw Tony's dad through the smoke, fishing rod over his shoulder, walk off into the distance shaking his head. As if time had stood still ten years ago and only just found the balls to move on. I looked at the mutant fish and the smouldering photos and suddenly realised that now I had no past, there was only the future.

"Dianne's gonna fucking kill me."

Tony's shoulders slumped and we wrapped the fish bits and the metal back up and walked home. I left the bundle outside and pushed the door open, not really relishing the thought of telling Dianne what had happened. But there was no need.

They all stood there laughing and cheering. It was party central and there I was, stinking to high heaven. No one cared. Dianne hugged me and kissed me.

"You did it, Charlie. You only went and did it."

She pulled me over to the console on the wall and pointed.

"You passed the test. We've been elevated. Don't you

understand? You passed the decade test."

Tony was as confused as me, but he took a bottle of beer from her. She handed round more alcohol to the neighbours who had joined the celebrations. The kids had old fashioned sweets and Dianne opened a box to reveal a cake.

"Ta-da!"

I stared at her.

"Your box…"

"Never mind that. Come on! Enjoy the moment. You know what this means, don't you?" I shook my head. I didn't know. I had no idea. "We're on the next level! Utopia. We can move on."

I looked at the ground.

"Okay. Utopia. So you're at ten years ago now. Yeah. And we've completed a decade."

My son, Michael butted in.

"Synched, dad. Synched."

"Whatever. So if you're moving on to the next level, where do you think you're heading? To now, Dianne, and the only way that can look like Utopia is if the real future is worse."

Her eyes narrowed, but she kept smiling.

"Don't spoil it, Charlie. Come on, have a drink. And they've sent us this too."

She opened the food portal and pulled out a great big steaming pile of fish and chips. I looked at Tone, who turned a funny shade.

"You can't..."

But it was too late. They were eating them.

Me and Tone went outside and the fish was gone. So we sat on the concrete and thought about the next ten years and wondered what challenges Utopia would bring for us tomorrow so that our families wouldn't be faced with today.

Ten Love Songs to Change the World

Peter F. Hamilton

I met Jesus once. Well come on, we all do it. He was one of us after all, a fey. Our hero, venerated by us the way baseline humans worship him for something else entirely. It was his stand which makes our history, our world, possible.

I was fourteen years old, and dreamed myself all the way back to his time. A relatively peaceful segment of his life, mind you, when he was starting to quietly gather his disciples from across the Roman Empire and beyond, and before the ghouls started showing an interest. It was on the shore of a lake. I don't remember where. It's not important.

He saw me and recognised what I was. Not hard. Fey can see each other when we're manifesting, and I must have been quite a sight. I was wearing a white summer dress from Top Shop and some frayed Nike trainers. My hair was fairer than you got in the Middle East at that time, and cut in a wavy bob that was never really in fashion even in my time, never mind back then. All very different to First Century styles.

To look at he wasn't anything remarkable. Average height, average build, small beard. His eyes though, they were sad. But I could see how much anger he could bring forth. Maybe that's what made him the one, our saviour.

"You're from a long way ahead," he said. Or rather didn't say, we don't use words, of course, not in manifested state. As in all dreams, you can talk to whoever you want and understand each other. "I can always tell."

"The start of the twenty first century," I admitted.

"That's risky. You'll get the Guardians come and talk to you. There will be finger wagging."

"I know. But I had to see you. To thank you."

"You're welcome."

"You won. Or you will win, but then you know that."

"Yes, enough of you tell me."

'I live thanks to you. I'm grateful. I wanted you to know. That's all."

"Well thank you for making the trip… "

"Malinda."

"Malinda from two thousand years ahead. I appreciate it."

I looked round at his band of followers. He'd gathered over forty fey already, and not just timedreamers like me, there were sidedreamers, fardreamers, soothers, and more. But all of them were fighters, I knew that from their attitude. "Thank you all," I said. And I saw someone else approaching. Some boy in late eighteenth century clothes, who was walking over to us with his feet not quite touching the ground.

I wondered what it must be like for Jesus, to have a constant stream of visitors from every century there will be, arriving in every spare moment, all praising him for the fight he would have and win. What must it be like knowing you were going to win? And die?

The disciples basically ignored me. They must see a dozen awestruck timedreamer kids a day. All of us breaking the guidelines.

"I should go," I said. "It's a long wave back."

Which truly made me very nervous. The longer you stay in the past, the further back you go, the more chance there is that you change something, especially if you talk to someone backwhen. The universe, the timeline, it adjusts to every dream we have, every impact we make. Every word we speak to a fellow fey alters something, not by loading them with foreknowledge which is just damn stupid. But even if you only speak for a moment, you delay them – that changes things in a physical way, and that has consequences. The example Guardians always give is that a pause makes a pace different, every step they make thereafter is fractionally altered. Dislodge a pebble that wasn't dislodged before (step on a Butterfly! – the timedreamers' very own ultimate horror story) and it has consequences. That pebble can start a temporal avalanche if you're not very careful. Was it the stone that got caught in a sandal, which made another traveller on the road stop, and if it doesn't get caught in his sole and he arrives a minute early, he might see someone he didn't before, a friendship springs up, lives are altered and so – history is *different.* Too different and you might not get born.

So you ride the consequence wave home. And you get to see what you've done rushing around you like you're watching the whole world in IMAX, watching the changes ripple out to become temporal tsunamis that wipe away everything you know, the timeline that produced you.

I did change things. I watched my consequences from a couple of the disciples admiring me, talking about me later that evening. Their movements were different, they trod on ground left clear before. Dirt was dislodged, tiny specks only, but some soil was compressed. A couple of grass seeds never germinated. But others came and took their place – were chewed on by animals. It was a ripple – circular, small. It washed out. The timeline didn't change. I woke up safe on my bed on a sunny afternoon August 2000.

I'm never going back that far again.

Jesus is history to me for evermore.

He made his stand back there when we fey were becoming hunted to extinction. Not that there have ever been many of us. But nature being the bitch she is creates predators for everything, locking life in an eternal rock paper scissors battle. Humans are deadly to most animals, we can swat a scorpion, but a scorpion sting can kill humans just as asteroids kill dinosaurs (don't laugh, asteroids are part of nature too, a very big nature).

We timedreamers were stalked and our minds devoured by ghouls as we contained the richest thoughts of all the fey. Just like us, ghouls were physically indistinguishable from baseline humans; but once they latched on, they savoured the memories and sensations of others, sucking them out to leave husks behind. And us, with our ability to visit anywhen, well we were the ultimate hit; the high they all craved. They sought us out first before feasting on the other fey. We were on the verge of dying out until Jesus decided to make his stand and fight back. He was a fardreamer, so he gathered other fey to him, which was a remarkable achievement in its own right. We always prefer to live quiet lives, keeping our heads down. Even today the prejudice against us is nasty. Back then, with Rome dominating Europe, any *difference* to the baselines was a death sentence. But he convinced the fey we were doomed anyway, and rallied our ancestors.

That many of us together acted like nectar for the ghouls. They came from all over the globe. Unfortunately for them, it turned out the disciples were a wasp trap. There are no more ghouls now. Not in this universe. Oh sure, they're still out there in the endless parallels of the multiverse. But us, here, now, since the Time Of Christ, we're clean.

Jesus knew the outcome, because stupid awestruck teenagers like me came back to tell him, but still he fought on. He died to save us. Others have different versions of the conflict. They're all good.

I'm wondering if one day when I'm older and supposedly wiser I'll put in a stint as a Guardian. Lecturing and nagging kids to be careful how they dream themselves back in time, warning them of the consequence wave. Emphasising how history has to be preserved, because we've tried altering it, and frankly this is the best version there is -Hitler, Genghis Khan and all the other bastards included.

Except I'm not sure I believe that. I still think we should be bolder.

After that visit, when those missing blades of grass really did scare the crap out of me, I did what all of us with half a brain do, and stuck to the recent past.

I'm rich, of course. Our family always has been; using the talent to do very nicely thank you – the trick is not to overdo it and call attention to yourself. Mum is a reasonable fardreamer, and Dad can soothe, so my talent came as quite a surprise.

I have a nice life. Loving parents. Nice house by the sea. Housekeeper and gardener. It's easy. I want for nothing. I travel as I please. Mum and Dad encourage that, always telling me there's so much to see and enjoy in this world, this time. "Get out there, girl, and live it."

But I'm human. I want more. So I dream.

Everyone has dreams that they think are so real. That's because they are. Baseline humans view what's happening all over the multiverse. But they don't manifest there, they don't take part. They're observers only, and never really understand what they see anyway.

So after that stupid rite of passage I was a lot more cautious about when I went back to. It's thrilling to see history for real. Not that I'm one for politics (exception: Nelson Mandela walking out of prison is a must) or war or disasters, there's way too much suffering going on in my realtime, I don't need to add to it. Instead I did what most of us do, and go for the uniques. Concerts, sports matches, and of course everyone goes to watch the Vostock 1 and Apollo 11 launches, festivals, Woodstock (naturally!) Live Aid, I even went to the first Glastonbury – wow was that different: no yurts for the mega-rich back then.

I guess that's when I fell in love with Sixties music. I know, I know. That's a cliché. But I loved it. Music was raw and new back then, it meant something in that era, it wasn't a business. Bands and singers believed in their art, they were musicians not celebrities. All of it was exciting, and it spoke to the hearts of a whole generation. Inspired them. People had a buzz.

So back I went, again and again. The Who, the Stones, Joan Baez, Pink Floyd, Dylan, Jefferson Airplane, Cream, Janis Joplin,

Hendrix, The Beatles, Grateful Dead, Credence Clearwater Revival, I even sat through some Ravi Shankar – not really my thing but the audience vibe, man o man!

Then I found *him.*

"You're dreaming your life away," Mum says. "Look, I know it's like when you discover sex –"

"Mum!" she is the classic parental embarrassment at times.

"All right. But there's so much this world has to offer, too. Take a couple of trips further back, see the poverty and squalor everyone lived in just two hundred years ago. That way you might appreciate what you have a little more."

"I don't want to risk the consequence wave," I tell her.

Her eyes narrow. "Ah, you went to visit Jesus."

"Did not."

"Really?"

I sometimes think fardreaming is code for mind-reading. "Maybe quickly. Once. It didn't have consequences."

"But riding a wave that far must have scared you, so I get how you're just dipping shallow right now. But what we have is a gift, especially you; don't waste it."

"It's not a gift, it's natural. And really, apart from the money, it's not terribly practical, is it? It's for enjoyment. So I'm enjoying."

So she sighs in that waiting-till-it-runs-its-course patience she has. "Life is a gift, darling. Timedreaming enriches it like no other. Don't waste your gift, but don't let it dominate."

"We could do so much, though. We could have stopped 9/11. We still can." I still think about the attack most days. I saw it all on the TV. The first thing I wanted to do was go back, warn the CIA or FBI or someone. Mum sat with me watching events unfold, telling me I couldn't. That the Guardians already knew about 9/11, and were ready to stop any attempt to prevent it.

Life was simpler back in the sixties, another reason to spend all my time there.

"We could have," mum says sadly. "But the Guardians said no. The

fanatics would have come back with nukes in Paris and Washington."

"Then we could have stopped that, too."

"We're not the police."

"We could be. We should be."

"Sweetheart, please. You're young, and that's a gift as precious as any. I just want you to be happy. Now, have you been seeing any decent boys?"

"Mum!"

"All right. Girls?"

"Arrrgh. Stop it."

I manifested in the Tulip Bulb Auction Hall in Spalding, 29th May 1967. Cream and the Jimmy Hendrix Experience were headlining, with Pink Floyd supporting. Gabriel Ivins played a couple of songs first, an unannounced warm up for the support, when Spalding's young and restless were still clustered round the bar. He was nineteen, an electrical engineering student at Cambridge; up on stage all by himself, him and his acoustic guitar. All dark curly hair, weak sixties sideburns, gangly frame, big thick-knit pullover, and flares wider than some of my skirts. Dylan was clearly a big influence on Gabriel, he was almost a tribute act. Except he wrote those two songs himself. And his voice was mellow and kind of appealing.

I saw quite a few girls in the bar crowd turn round and listen, and watch. He finished, bowed nervously while no one applauded, and scuttled off stage. Just before he left, he caught my eye and quirked a grin.

I drifted after him. Caught up in the green room. The green room being where they stored bulb crates in an annex at the back of the hall. He was putting his guitar away in its case while the Floyd were getting ready to go on. I should have been interested in them, Syd Barrett was still part of the line up at that point.

Instead I went over to Gabriel. "Hi."

"Hi yourself," he said, and looked round the annex to check that he was right, and only he could see me. It was just him, looking like he was muttering to himself in the corner like a true wacko artist. "Cool threads, man."

"Thanks." I was wearing a ridiculous purple and green tie-dye shirt with a long vintage turquoise-blue skirt, gold daisies woven into my hair. I hadn't cut my hair since I was fourteen, so now aged seventeen it was halfway down my back – I had a real hippy-chick look going. "I liked your songs."

"Thanks. Where are you from?"

"Two thousand and three."

I could see the surprise in his eyes. "Yeah? You look… today, man."

"I like today."

"I thought you were a maybe a sidedreamer. I'm always kind of surprised to hear the twenty-first century exists."

"Barry McGuire, Eve Of Destruction," I grinned.

"Something like that." He produced a half-burnt reefer, and lit it.

"He was too pessimistic," I said. "Things aren't perfect but they're not too bad. So are you writing any more songs?"

"Some. They're not good enough to sing in public yet."

"The ones you sang tonight, *Rainbow Smile* and *Flower Sun*; are they recorded?"

"No. Not yet. Hey, you can tell me if they ever are, future girl."

"I can't. Sorry. Too many consequences."

"Heavy."

"Like neutronium."

"Wow, are you sure you're not sidedreaming from the land of the fairies?"

"Nah. Is that what you do?"

"A little. My talent's not too funky. I never get far enough to see anywhere groovy. My old man, he says there are wonders out there in the alternates."

"So I hear."

Gabriel took a deep drag. "I'd offer you some, but…"

"I know."

"Gotta split. Gotta hitch back to Cambridge."

"Have you got another gig lined up? Maybe I could come and hear if your other songs make it to the stage."

"Uh. I dunno. The scene man, it's not as cool as I thought. Unless you're the Beatles."

"Yeah, two-thousand-three remembers the Beatles."

"Take care, future girl."

"And you."

Google is not my friend. Yahoo is not my friend. The internet has nothing on Gabriel Ivins. No bootleg sites have recordings of Rainbow Smiles and Flower Sun. I can't believe it. They were good. How did he sink away without being signed by a record company?

I so much want to hear them again. They'd be a comfort right now. I'm sitting here in this cold February, with the TV showing the build-up of troops on the Iraq border. There's going to be war. Bush and Blair are really going to do it, they're going to let thousands of people die.

There must be another way, there must! I'm thinking in a few months I could go back to now. I could tell other fey how many died, that it wasn't worth it. They'd be outraged. They'd do something. Wouldn't they?

It's taken me a few dreams backwhen, stalking I suppose. But I found the student newspaper with the announcement, and manifested in the Cambridge Corn Exchange 23rd July 1967.

Gabriel took to the stage just after eight o'clock. Still in his thick woolly jumper (does he have any other clothes?). He sang four songs, and this time people drifted away from the bar, starting to groove along. They're sweet songs, his new two, about love and fate and hope. He got a big round of cheering and applause when he finished. It was great. This little gig must be the start of his success, I'm sure of it, and I'm one of the witnesses. Go history! But then he looked straight at me from the stage, smiled shyly, and started his fifth song of the evening. And OMG!

The Future Fairy by Gabriel Ivins was issued in 1968, a limited pressing vinyl single on the Calibre label (an independent Cambridge record label – declared bankrupt in 1970). It is a love song by young poet musician Gabriel Ivins, dedicated to 'my sad and lovely vision'. Ivins was a solo singer songwriter guitarist until this recording, when he was joined by Calibre session musicians, adding electric guitar and drums.

Ivins died in November 1971 from a drug overdose. A good copy of The Future Fairy will cost £87.00. V Rare.

Google is my friend after all. It doesn't matter how many times I shake my head in disbelief, the words on the screen stay the same. The consequence wave I rode back after the concert was exhilarating. Nobody dies. Nobody is worse off. It's changed the timeline.

I. Changed. Things.

The Guardians haven't noticed.

And Gabriel died.

But before he did, he wrote a song about me. Me!

It was cold on February 15th 2003. I'd never gone back such a short time before. But the crowds I saw on TV just a few months ago thronged all around me. Marching through London's streets, chanting and calling. So many people, so much good humour. And desperate hope. I've seen that kind of belief once before, back in the Sixties. Back when music and good people were going to change the world.

There are plenty of fey among the marchers. I flit between as many as I can find. And all the time I tell them. "There are no Weapons of Mass Destruction, there never were. I know. I'm a timedreamer from the future. They're lying, Bush and Blair. Tell everyone. It's all a lie. They don't exist."

After it was over, after the crowds went home and the night claimed the empty streets, I braced myself and rode the consequence wave back to late summer.

There was nothing, no real disturbance. February 15 was a

day of chaos and determination. Everyone I told believed anyway. One fey girl with long hair and a desperate smile telling them they were right changed nothing. Nothing. Around my pathetic little consequence wave, tens of thousands of people died in pain and fire.

The Future Fairy single hit the timeline harder, for fuck's sake.

Mum knocks on my door. My knuckles screw the tears from my eyes and I say: "Come in."

She does, but she's not alone. There's this old woman with her, wearing a neat grey suit and sensible black shoes, like she's on her way home from her city desk job. Except I know she never worked at any desk.

"Sweetheart, this is Ms Remek," mum says, slightly nervous.

"You're a Guardian," I say. There's only four or five in any generation. We don't need more, there aren't many timedreamers. We're kind of like fey royalty I guess.

"I am, dear, yes."

And she has this sympathetic voice, too, all understanding, an I-was-young-once voice. But stern, too.

"Nobody listened," I tell her miserably. "Nothing changed."

"I know. But the point is you tried to change it."

"There are no Weapons of Mass Destruction. There never were."

"All the fardreamers knew that last year. You weren't telling anyone anything new."

"But it's a lie, and now it's over and all those people are dead."

"It's not over," Ms Remek says. "The war doesn't officially end until December two-thousand-and-eleven."

"Eleven!" I squeak.

"Fraid so. We screw up the peace even worse."

"Then stop it!" I yell.

"It's not that simple," she says kindly. "It never is. You heard about Paris and Washington, didn't you?"

"Nukes. If 9/11 is stopped."

"That's right."

"So… stop that as well."

"And if we do, which we could, it would be another target, another atrocity. Bin Laden is a persistent man."

"So tell the CIA where he is."

"A compound in Bilal, that's in Pakistan."

"What? You know?"

"Yes. He's going to be killed by a navy Seals team in two thousand and eleven."

"What is it with two-thousand-eleven? And why not assassinate him now?"

"You tell me."

My shoulders sag. "Consequences."

"Yes. If we keep chasing down the bad guys, what does that make us?"

"What do you mean?"

"We become official. True world Guardians of Peace. The baseline governments will turn us into an agency or service – at best. We are unique, my dear, us timedreamers. At most there are a hundred of us in any generation. But our talent makes us possibly the most powerful people ever. We can strike down an enemy before they even become an enemy. And what will happen if baseline humans ever discover we exist? Have you thought of that?"

"They'll be frightened, I guess."

"No. It will be worse than the age of ghouls. They will be utterly terrified. Because if we do stop terrorists and wars, we poor few will become the rulers of the world. We decide everything, including who lives and who dies."

"So that's what you're really Guarding against?"

"It's half of it, yes. We carry on the work Jesus started, and protect the fey. First they'll come for us, then the others will be hunted, and we won't be there to protect them."

"But we'll always be able to warn ourselves if anyone comes for us."

"And so we become rulers out of self-defence. There are parallel worlds where it has happened. Where it is happening."

"What's the point of timedreaming if we can't help people?"

"We are helping people. Guardians talk to each other across eras, and

keep the timeline stable."

"So what you're saying is Guardians do have a purpose. I don't. Are you trying to recruit me?"

"Nobody is ever forced to become a Guardian; that would be wholly counterproductive. And not every fey has your compassion and goodwill. We Guard against that, too. I watch history and warn my predecessors against rogues and inadvertent consequences; as I am warned by those in the centuries to come."

"What if I don't listen? What if I keep trying to expose the lies?"

"You don't succeed. And if you were to, and make things worse, then there's always one person who will come backwhen to your moment of failure and convince you beyond any doubt that you're making a mistake."

"Who?"

Ms Remek smiles in compassion. "You, of course."

Gabriel's digs are truly *eueeew*. I mean, I don't need to go back two centuries to witness people living in poverty and squalor. Sixties students would envy medieval hovels for their luxury.

He doesn't seem to mind. January sixty-eight was cold. His gas fire had five wavy flames, which all seemed to burn yellow, producing no heat. The inside of the windows were frosted over. I was lucky I couldn't feel the temperature, at the time my body was snug at home, curled up on my bed in the early autumn, with the central heating on.

Gabriel wore his thick sweater – of course – with three T-shirts on underneath. He sat on the threadbare bed-settee, strumming his guitar, writing possible lyrics in his big notebook.

"What do you think?" he asked.

"I like it. Sort of like *Perfect Day*, but harder. Sharper."

"Oh, man, you mean it's not original?"

"Oh it is. Lou Reed writes *Perfect Day* in the early seventies, I think."

He brightened. "I write like Lou Reed?"

"Better."

"Nahh."

"You do, seriously." I'd manifested in five of his gigs now. He was gaining quite a reputation locally.

"So how come I haven't got a record deal?"

"They take time, Gabriel."

"Do I get one?" he pleaded.

"I can't say. You know that."

"I was thinking of giving up my course. Just concentrate on my music."

I didn't know what to say. He only had three years left to live. If I knew I was going to die, I wouldn't spent what time I had left sitting in lectures. "Follow your dream."

"Yeah?"

"Gabriel, I'd say that to anyone."

"You're infuriating, you know that."

"You ever thought of going electric?"

"Naww, it's a sell out. I play my own music. I express what I have to say myself."

"I love your integrity."

"This geezer, Matt, he was interested at the gig last week. Said he's got his own record company, Calibre. But he wanted me to go electric, too. Said acoustic is dead."

"Your choice. Do you want people to hear what you have to say or not?"

"Is that a hint, future fairy?"

"Don't call me that."

Then there was a commotion outside. His friends had arrived, and he let them in. Fellow students, bringing cheap wine and homemade beer. Gabriel had more friends now, people who liked hanging out with a musician. It was party time. Two of the girls made sure they were sitting next to him, hanging off every word. I smiled. Waved goodbye.

Mum's happy for me.

His name's James. He's nineteen and says he's a musician – when he's not working behind the bar at the local pub. He lays down electro-pop tracks on his PC, and lets anyone download them for free from his website. Twelve people have logged on in the last three months.

His dream is a record contract. At night, when we cling together, he confesses once he's discovered he's going to be mega, and super-rich, with homes here and in the Caribbean. He thanks me for listening, for believing in him.

I tell him to write a protest song about the war.

His answer? "Aw come on, that's so sixties."

He's tall and skinny. He has thick dark hair which is long and curly. In the dark, with his body lying on top of mine, I can't see his face. I can't see it's not really Gabriel.

Amid the final joy I call a name. I'm not sure whose.

"Have you met me, man?" Gabriel asks.

It was late summer sixty-eight, and we walked around Cambridge a week before all the students came back. He carried a bag full of Future Fairy singles, which he was trying to flog to the city's independent record shops.

"Er... what do you think I'm doing?" I ask.

"Not now," he laughs. "In the future. Have you come to see me?"

"No."

"Did you try? I'll be what? Fifty five, yeah? Did my bodyguards stop you?"

"You have a very high opinion of yourself."

"Is it justified?"

I haven't seen him so happy for a while. Musicians can be moody prats at times. Adds to the mystique, I suppose.

"Stop trying to wheedle stuff like that out of me. You know I'll never say."

"Okay, all right." He stopped in the middle of the market square, and almost made to grab me. His arms came up before he remembered – he was the wild student talking to himself in public. "How about this, man. What month is it with you now?"

"September."

"I'm going to remember November the first, 2003, okay? On that day I do solemnly swear I will be right here on this spot. No bodyguards, no managers. Just me. Please please please, be here. Just to talk." He faltered. "Just to touch you. To know you're real. I need that."

"Gabriel…"

"Promise me!" he yelled.

Now half the market was looking at the crazy boy.

"I promise." I turned away so he couldn't see my tears.

So now Google says Just To Touch You the second single by Gabriel Ivins charted at number 47 in the nineteen-sixty-nine January top fifty chart.

And on the radio the news is a High School shooting in the American Midwest. Seven dead. I wait and I wait, and future me doesn't manifest to tell me not to go and warn the school.

But I'm scared. Scared of my power. I don't want to rule the world. I want the world to be a better place. But I want those kids not to have died.

I don't know what to do.

Winter sixty-nine, and the Gabriel Ivins band is on tour, promoting their first album. I haven't been to see him for a while – his time. That last consequence wave was a large one. I almost expected a visit from Ms Remek. But she didn't come, so I manifested in a pub in Newcastle.

The band is mainly session musicians put together by Calibre records. Older than Gabriel. Competent but without his verve.

I drift through the audience watching the show. And Gabriel is bad. You can tell the roadies have turned down his guitar feed. His hand is strumming in a jittery way that's out of tune with the rest of the band. And his lovely smooth voice is all harsh – like he's inventing death metal twenty years too early.

That gave me a chill, but I'm pretty sure I've never mentioned future music trends to him.

The audience drinks. They don't pay him much attention.

Backstage in the green room after the gig, and he's got three groupies groping him on the couch. Nobody drinks beer, it's all whisky.

Gabriel was knocking them back, but then he finally sees me. He lets out this stupid wolf howl of greeting. "Man, I missed you. It is you, isn't it?"

One of the groupies who's got the whole Goth thing right before there were any, frowned in my direction. But she was smoking a thick reefer so she didn't really think anything was wrong or weird.

"It's me."

"Cool. I thought you'd left me."

"No."

"Do you like the album?"

"I do." The album had some neat songs; on the recording Gabriel's voice had been appealing and evocative. *Downcountry* was a protest about 'Nam. It was charting, number seventeen last week – its highest. He was doing something, making his voice heard, inspiring others. I was so proud of him when I discovered that.

Trouble was, up on stage he'd just been awful.

"Thanks, man. Hey, did we meet up in futureland like we said?"

The groupies giggled at that.

"Yes," I lied.

"Cool. What's life like up there?"

"We gave up. We stopped protesting. The whole world's going to hell."

"Bummer, huh?"

Then one of the roadies came in, and gave Gabriel a nod. He lumbered to his feet and staggered across the room. The roadie slipped him a small leather wallet. Gabriel went into the toilets.

My Gabriel is doing hard drugs.

Gabriel Ivins died March 17th 1970 from a drugs overdose. Although his band's first album was moderately successful, Ivins had to cancel the promotional tour half way through due to 'exhaustion'. He spent the following months alone writing new songs. Recording for his new album, *Paradise Unglimpsed,* was scheduled to begin in April 1970. His record company, Calibre, was declared bankrupt a month later.

I'm in the lounge, crying, when Ms Remek comes in. She gives me a thoughtful look, and asks: "Have you been seeing Gabriel Ivins?"

"No. Yes. He dies anyway."

"There have been consequences."

I nod miserably. "I know. The wave wasn't very big."

"That's because you're only surfing it for twenty years. There are significant consequences later on."

"Oh." I try to make out like I'm interested. "I see future me hasn't manifested. So how bad is it?"

"Not enough to warrant a full intervention against you. Soothers were called in to calm certain situations."

"Oh good, so the future stays perfect then."

Ms Remek frowns, determining how much sarcasm and sass I'm giving her. Because just this month Anna Lindh was stabbed to death by some religious nutter, Iran is refusing to cooperate with the nuclear inspectorate, Osama bin Laden says Al-Quaeda is developing biological weapons, the British National Party got a councillor elected in a Thurrock by-election, a suicide bomber killed eight people in Israel, airstrikes in Zabul province killed seventeen people. And Johnny Cash died. I could have stopped those bombings and killings. I wonder what consequences that would have? People getting to live their lives and have a chance at happiness.

"The future doesn't get any worse," she says tetchily.

"What's the point?" I ask.

"The point?"

"Of our ability? If all we do is use it to keep everything the same. Why do we have it?"

"You just answered your own question. This is as good as it gets."

I shake my head. I refuse to believe that. "There must be somewhere out there in the parallels, a world where we get it right. We could use it as a template."

"Maybe there is. But if it is out there, it's beyond any sidedreamer I've ever talked to."

"So now what?"

"So be careful, please."

I nod. I know she's being reasonable, and semi-sympathetic, but it still makes no sense to me.

I want to make a difference. I want to stop the ugliness that contaminates this world.

When Ms Remek leaves I make myself a promise. In the future, I'll come back to now and tell me something that can be stopped. If I can't influence other people, then I can use facts; if someone's going to get shot or bombed then I can warn them or the police myself. I will make a difference.

But I don't manifest in front of me. I break my promise. Why? Why why why?

Gabriel's new digs weren't any better than his student ones. He'd got a flat in a grand old house overlooking the Cam, with two more rooms than last time, an extra bedroom and a tiny kitchen. The squalor remained the same.

When I manifested, he was lying on the worn settee, a week's stubble on his cheeks, and looking so thin I could believe he hadn't eaten for the whole of that same week. A guitar lay on top of him. There was a syringe and all the rest of his drugs crap on the carpet beside him.

He was dozing fitfully. I almost left, then. Except it was mid-afternoon on March the seventeenth, nineteen seventy. Gabriel Ivins would be dead before the end of the day.

I drifted round the room. He had been writing, bless him. There were pieces of paper scattered about, some scrunched up on the floor. All of them holding his lyrics, lines crossed out – re-written again and again. Ten sheets had been laid out neatly on the table: his songs for *Paradise Unglimpsed*, the album he never got to make.

As always, Gabriel's lyrics were profound and eloquent. He spoke of worlds where people don't kill, where peace breaks out not war, where hunger and hatred is a memory. A world far far away from ours.

The world I want to live in.

"You came back," he croaked.

I went over to the settee and gazed down on him. His eyes were brutally bloodshot. I saw now how the fluffy stubble disguised sunken cheeks. "Yes, I came back."

"I thought you'd given up on me."

"No, Gabriel." I forced a grin. "I've spent too much time to abandon you now."

"That's stupid, man. I am just one giant fuck-up."

"No you're not. I read your lyrics. They're beautiful, Gabriel. Congratulations."

"Matt wants me to lay down another album. I can't do it. Touring, man, it's too heavy. I'm not built for it."

"You went sideways, didn't you, a decent world a long way sideways into the parallels?"

He dropped his head in his hands. "I don't know. Maybe. I was out of it. I don't know if it was real or a real dream."

"There's no such thing."

"Yeah." He nodded weakly.

I stared at his syringe. "Have you been trying to go back there, Gabriel?"

"Yes."

"You can't."

My beautiful sweet Gabriel started to cry. "I hate myself."

"Sing for me," I told him. "Play the songs you wrote. I want to hear Paradise Unglimpsed."

"What's that?"

"Ooops. That's the title of your next album."

"Not bad, man. Hey, you're not supposed to tell me that."

"I know. I'll put up with the heat just this once. Hearing you sing them will make it worthwhile."

"Okay. Yeah, groovy." He picked up his guitar.

Gabriel Ivins sang his unmade album to me in that bleak grey, cold Cambridge afternoon. He sang his songs the way they were meant to be sung, with hope and pleading.

"That's what music is for," I told him reverently when he finished. "To give people courage, to inspire them."

He grinned nervously. "Are you crying future fairy?"

"Yes, Gabriel, I'm crying. I'm crying because we can never go to that parallel world you dreamed. The only way we will ever live it, is to turn our world into it."

His gaze dropped down to the syringe.

"Listen to me, Gabriel." I knelt in front of him, imploring. "You have to tell people a life like that is possible. You can do it. You can inspire them. Sing it loud, Gabriel. Sing it to the whole world. This is the only age when music counts. After this, the companies and producers take over. The money wins. It's never about the music again."

"I just want to go back there," he said brokenly.

"You never do," I told him. Suddenly I was standing, my expression stern. "You're going to die, Gabriel. Today."

"What the fuck, man?"

"You die. Here in this god-awful rat's nest. You overdose on the shit you're injecting yourself with. Nobody will ever hear *Paradise Unglimpsed.* This world will carry on along its vile corrupt course. It needs to be changed, Gabriel. You can do that. Sing for me Gabriel, show people what a decent life full of love can be. Sing that they don't have to live like this. Be my angel, Gabriel. Save the world."

And I leave him like that, gaping at me in astonishment and fear. I surf the consequence wave into the new realtime. I'm not afraid, it is exhilarating. I watch him make his choice, the right choice, stamping on the syringe, breaking it.

Gabriel lives. He goes on to record Paradise Unglimpsed, which charts high. Then goes on to record his next album. People flock to his gigs. They hear his songs and sing them loud.

Changes flood out from the wave. Multiplying. The changes carry his message of love and hope with them, spilling right across the world. The difference builds and builds.

Until the Reading Rock Festival in '77. Thousands of happy people sailing across a sea of mud swirl around me. The consequence means it's now Gabriel Ivins who headlines on Sunday night, not the Sensational Alex Harvey Band.

My mother is in the crowd, her arms raised above her head, swaying from side to side as she chants Gabriel's anthem: Beyond A Dream. Absorbing the love he evokes. Questions about the way we live are kindled in her deepest thoughts. But she doesn't meet dad there. The consequence has put him somewhere else.

And I'm witnessing the world I want born. It is the most exquisite moment I know. Ten simple honest songs, my gift as I am unborn –

Ten Days

Nina Allan

Ten days, ten hours, ten minutes. A man is murdered and a woman is charged. The hangman winds his watch and then goes home. I don't suppose you remember that old Cher lyric, you're too young. *If I could turn back time, if I could find a way.* My best friend from law school, Frieda Solomon, used to play that track at the end of every party she ever threw, when we were solidly pissed and everyone was dancing, even those of us who never danced, when discussion had dissolved into barracking and all the ugly home truths began to come out.

The song is about someone who's said something stupid and wishes she hadn't. Hardly a crime, when you think of the appalling things people do to one another every day and can't take back. What are mere words, you might ask, in the face of deeds? I'm not so sure, myself. What if the person Cher is singing to happens to be some hot-shot international trader with revenge on his mind? Or a fighter pilot? Or a president with his finger on the button? Who knows what someone like that might do, if you caught them at the wrong moment?

One thoughtless comment and it's World War Three. Who knows?

If I could turn back time, my dear, I wouldn't change a thing.

It takes about two minutes for a time machine to get going, in my experience. Nothing happens for what seems like forever, then just as you're telling yourself you were an idiot to believe, even for ten seconds, that such a thing would be possible, the edges of things – your fingers, your sight lines, your thoughts – begin to blur, to stumble off kilter, and then you're gone. Or not gone as such, but *there*. Your surroundings appear oddly familiar, because of course they are. The time you have left seems insubstantial suddenly, a peculiar daydream fantasy. Vivid while you were having it but, like most dreams, irretrievable on waking.

There was a man who lived next door to us when we were children whose house was stuffed to the rafters with old radios. The type he liked best were the wooden console models from before the war, but he kept Bakelite sets too, and those tinny little transistors from the nineteen fifties. His main obsession was a hefty wooden box full of burnt-out circuits and coils he claimed had once belonged to a wireless set used by the French resistance in World War Two. He was forever trying to restore the thing but I think there were pieces missing and so far as I know he never got it working again.

I used to spend hours round at his house, going through the boxes of junk and watching what he was doing. Our mother couldn't stand Gary Tonkes. She would have stopped me having anything to do with him if she could. Looking back on it now, I suppose she thought there was something peculiar about his interest in me, but there was never anything like that, nothing you could point a finger at, anyway. When I was thirteen, Gary Tonkes was sectioned under the Mental Health Act. His house was infested with rats, and he kept insisting that one of his radios had started picking up signals from Mars. I remember taking pictures of the house afterwards with the Kodak Instamatic Uncle Henry had given me for my tenth birthday, pretending I was working for MI5. I still feel bad about that. I think now that Gary Tonkes's radio might have been picking up not signals from Mars, but the voices of people who had lived in the house before him, or who would live there in the future, after he'd gone.

Time doesn't give a damn about the laws of physics. It does what it wants.

I think of Helen's basement living room in Camden, the ancient Aubusson carpet faded to a dusty monochrome, the books, the burnt-orange scent of chrysanthemums. I sometimes wish I could go back there, just to see it again, but I know I can't. I've had my turn. And stealing more time could be dangerous, not just for me and for Helen but for you as well.

When I was eighteen, I contracted leukaemia. I was very ill for about ten months and then I recovered. Against the odds, the doctors said, and only after the kind of clichéd regime of brutal chemo you read about in the colour supplements. And yes, there were times I wished they'd give up on me and let me die. I suspect – in fact I know – it was my brother Martin who persuaded me to stick around. His white face at my bedside, I can still see it now. His terror, that I wasn't going to pull through, I suppose. I don't think I've mattered like that to anyone, before or since, and that includes Ray. I hung on and hung on, until suddenly there I was, washed up on the shore of life once more and the tide of those months receding like some lurid sick joke.

But there were side effects. I'd been offered a place at Cambridge, to read mathematics. Following my illness I found something was missing: the instinctive affinity for numbers I had taken for granted as an inseparable part of me was, if not vanished, then noticeably blunted. It was like thinking through gauze. My professor seemed confident that I was simply exhausted, that any diminution in my ability would soon be restored. Perhaps she was right. I'll never know now, will I? The university offered me the option to defer my entry for a further year, but I refused.

I turned down my place, partly from the terror of failure and partly to match the drama that was playing out inside my head with something concrete that could be measured in the world outside. I was having a breakdown, in other words, and in the aftermath of that I switched to Law. I know it doesn't sound like much, when you put it like that, but the decision hurt a lot at the time. It felt like the worst kind of defeat. I won't say I ever got over the loss, but I learned to live with it, the same as you do with any bereavement. And in time I even came to enjoy my legal studies. There is a beauty in the law, in which the abstraction of numbers is countered by the wily and intricate compromises of philosophy. Call it compensation, if you like. An out-of-court settlement that, if not generous, has at least proved adequate.

I'm good at my job, I think, and it has provided me with a decent living in return. And whenever I find myself growing maudlin for what might have been, I remind myself that the law has also provided me with what Martin sometimes jokingly refers to as Dora's file on the doomed: an interest that began as a tree branch of curiosity and grew into a passion.

If I am known to the public at all, it is for my articles and radio broadcasts on the subject of capital punishment, and the fatal miscarriages of justice that have been associated with this barbaric practice. For many years, the essays I wrote for various history and politics journals formed the limit of my ambition for my researches. It was Martin – of course! – who first suggested I should write a book, and the more I thought about the idea the more I liked it.

My first thought was to write a monograph on capital punishment in general: a philosophical treatise, to be accompanied by a thorough debunking. A literary bollocking, if you like. I soon came to realise how dull such a volume would be, unless you had an interest in the subject to begin with, which would make the whole thing pointless, a sermon to the converted. I came to the conclusion that a more personal approach would work better, an in-depth study of specific cases, of one specific case even. What better way to demonstrate the brutality of state-sanctioned murder than to tell the story of one of its victims? To show that murder is always murder, even when enshrined in law, with the same practical margin for error and moral depravity that murder entails?

My decision to write about Helen Bostall was made quickly and easily. As a story, her case had everything you might look for in a decent thriller. The condemned criminal was also a woman, which made the case a cause celebre, even at the time. People are fascinated by women who kill in much the same way as they are fascinated by genetic freaks, and with the same mixture of self-righteous indignation and covert repulsion.

For my own part, I became interested in Helen because I admired her writing, and also because from the moment I first encountered what passed for the facts of her case, I found myself convinced she was not guilty. Not that I would have ceased to admire her, necessarily, if she had been a murderer – Edwin Dillon was an arrogant prick, if you ask me – but her innocence made her the perfect candidate for my thesis. I would do her justice, I decided, if not in deed then in word, at the very least.

I've read interviews with biographers in which they wax on about having a special kinship with their subjects, a personal relationship across time that could never have existed in reality. I would once have dismissed such speculation as sentimental codswallop.

Not any more, though.

Helen Bostall was born in 1895, in Addiscombe, Croydon. Her father, Winston Bostall, was a doctor and lay preacher. Her mother, Edith, had worked as a teacher, though she gave up her career entirely after she married. The two were well-matched, forward-thinking people who gave their only daughter Helen every opportunity to develop her intellectual awareness of the world and her place within it.

I might have been content, Helen wrote in her 1923 pamphlet essay "On War, on Murder", *content to take up my place among the teachers, preachers, poets and painters I had learned to admire as a very young woman, to speak my protest, but timidly, from inside the very system I was protesting. It was the spectacle of war that made me a radical, that fired in me the conviction that the system I was protesting had to be broken.*

The war, and more specifically the death on the Somme of her cousin, Peter Arnold Bostall, the son of her father's brother Charles. Peter and Helen, both only children and of a similar age, had been close throughout their childhoods. At the outbreak of war in 1914, Peter had just graduated from Oxford and was considering whether to take up a junior fellowship offered to him by his college, or to embark on a research trip to Madagascar with his other uncle, his mother's brother, the entomologist Rupert Paxton.

It is not known whether Peter and Helen had plans to marry, although judging by the letters the two exchanged while Peter was at Oxford it is certainly a possibility. There is no doubt that Helen was devastated by her cousin's death, locking herself away in her room for several weeks afterwards and ultimately falling ill with pneumonia. She emerged from her illness a different person, determined to play her part in creating a more just society, a society in which a death such as her cousin's would not be possible. When the war ended she took up lodgings in Hampstead, close to the house where John Keats once lived, and began taking in private pupils. During the hours she was not teaching, she was studying and writing. She also joined a suffragist group. Her parents, though initially upset by her abrupt departure from the family home and concerned for her health, were tentatively supportive of her aims.

Until she met Edwin Dillon. Then everything changed.

Edwin Dillon was thirty years old, a journalist on the Manchester Guardian who had written a number of inflammatory articles on the employment conditions of factory workers in the north of England. He had lost three fingers of his left hand in an unspecified industrial accident, although there was some talk that he had inflicted the injury himself, to avoid conscription.

He came south to London in 1919, quickly establishing links with the community of Russian anarchists and dissident Marxists living there in exile from the Bolshevik revolution. It was likely to have been Dillon's views on free love that set Helen's parents so thoroughly against Dillon, although it could simply have been that they didn't much like him.

Hector Dubois, the proprietor of the Liberty Bookshop in Camden and a former associate of Dillon's, testified in support of Helen Bostall at her trial. He described Edwin Dillon as 'a man you needed to be careful around, a man who held a grudge'. There were also rumours that Dillon's original motive for coming to London had to do with a woman he had made pregnant in Manchester and later abandoned. Attempts to trace this woman ended in failure and so the rumours could not be verified.

Whatever the reason, Winston and Edith Bostall were determined that their daughter should have nothing more to do with Edwin Dillon. When Helen announced that she was intending to move into Dillon's rooms in Camden, her parents threatened to cut all ties with her. Perhaps they hoped to call her bluff. If so, it was a gamble that backfired. In the February of 1927, Helen gave up her Hampstead lodgings and moved into the basement flat at 112 Milliver Road.

I soon found myself accruing vast amounts of information, not just on Helen Bostall but on her whole family. I can imagine many editors dismissing most of it as irrelevant – who cared about Winston Bostall's run-in with a colleague in 1907 (over the involuntary committal of an unmarried mother to a mental asylum, if you're interested) when the incident had zero connection to the case in hand? But the more I dug into the private lives of the Bostalls and their circle, the more I became convinced that they were important. Crime does not arise in a vacuum. A murder is simply the flash point in a gradual accretion of narrative. The various strands that make up that narrative – Winston Bostall's mortal hatred of violence, Edith Bostall's inability to conceive another child, Peter Bostall's ambiguous relationship with his uncle, Rupert Paxton – may all be contributing factors in its final outcome.

And besides that, I was interested. The Bostalls were an unremarkable family, on the face of it, and yet their lives provided a snapshot of an entire era. In the conflicts and setbacks they encountered, it was possible to discern the birth of the modern age and the decline of empire, the fireworks and anxieties that occurred when the two collided. Was it any wonder that a woman like Helen Bostall – educated, resourceful and unwilling to settle for the life that society had preordained for her – ended up finding herself directly in the firing line?

The shadow side of my researches was the strange vacuity surrounding the person of Edwin Dillon. Information about the Bostalls proved plentiful, and easy to come by. This was partly because of the crime, of course – call someone a murderer, and suddenly every detail of their life becomes interesting, becomes *evidence* – but that was not the only reason. The Bostalls – Helen herself, but also Winston, Edith, Peter, Rupert, and especially Rupert's wife Marina, who was Russian and embraced the literary arts as the birthright they were – were all copious, inveterate letter-writers and journal-keepers. Their histories remained bright, remained present. Searching for information about Edwin Dillon came to seem like staring into a black hole. I became convinced that if Dillon hadn't been murdered, he would have disappeared from history altogether. I turned up odd pieces of his journalism here and there, but finding images of the man himself was another matter. Aside from the blurry photograph that so often featured in the newspapers at the time of Helen's trial, Edwin Dillon might as well have been invisible.

In the end I decided it would be better to set all the background material aside for the moment and concentrate on the timeline of the case itself. It was like working on a proof, in a way – carry one distinct line of enquiry through to its logical conclusion and the rest will follow.

The actual order of events was easy enough to assemble from

the trial records. A little before eight o'clock on the evening of the 20th of January 1928, a Mrs Irene Wilbur, a widow who lived in the ground floor apartment of 112 Milliver Road, was disturbed by what she called a 'furious altercation' in the flat below. Concerned by what she heard – "It sounded like they were bashing each other's brains out," was what she said on the witness stand – she left her flat and hurried to the Red Lion public house, approximately a minute's walk away, helping to enlist the aid of the publican in locating a police constable. When asked why she did not call at Dillon's apartment herself, she insisted she was afraid to. "The noise they were making," she said. "It was as if the devil had got into them."

The publican of the Red Lion, Gerald Honeyshot, confirmed that Irene Wilbur came into the pub soon after eight o'clock. He left with her more or less immediately and they walked together to Camden Town underground station, where they were able to secure the services of PC Robert Greystowe, who passed by the station regularly on his beat.

The three then returned to 112 Milliver Road, where on entry into the hallway they found the house silent, and the door leading to Dillon's apartment standing ajar.

"I knew straight away there'd been a murder done," Irene Wilbur claimed in her statement. "You could feel it in the air. Something about the silence. It wasn't right."

At this point, Greystowe gave instructions for Wilbur and Honeyshot to remain upstairs in the hallway while he entered the basement apartment alone. He called out to 'Mr and Mrs Dillon' as he entered, but there was no reply. A short time later he re-emerged, and informed Wilbur and Honeyshot that they would need to report to the police station on Highgate Road immediately, in order to give their witness statements. He did not offer them any further information at this point, but by the end of the evening both Wilbur and Honeyshot knew that Edwin Dillon had been murdered. According to PC Greystowe, he had discovered Dillon within moments of entering the flat. He was in the kitchen. His clothes were soaked with blood, and more blood was spreading in a large puddle across the kitchen tiles.

Edwin Dillon was pronounced dead where he lay. He had been stabbed five times. Two of the wounds were serious enough to have killed him.

There was no sign, anywhere, of Helen Bostall. An officer was left on duty outside the house, and when Helen eventually returned home at around eleven o'clock she was taken immediately into police custody. On being asked where she had spent the evening, she said she had been at the house of a friend, Daphne Evans, who lived in Highgate. Daphne quickly confirmed Helen's alibi, but when officers asked if they might search her flat, according to PC Greystowe she became agitated.

"I suppose you have to come in," she said in the end. She had been about to go to bed. When asked why she was reluctant to let police officers enter her apartment, she said it was because she was in her dressing gown.

The apartment was tidy, with no signs of disturbance, let alone the murder weapon. Two porcelain teacups – according to Daphne Evans they were the same teacups she and Helen had been drinking tea from earlier that evening – stood drying in the drainer beside the sink. It was only after half an hour's searching that officers discovered the small valise on top of the wardrobe in Evans's bedroom. The valise contained clothes that were later positively identified as belonging to Helen Bostall, together with a forward-dated ticket for the boat train from Victoria and a number of notebooks and letters, either addressed to Helen Bostall or filled with her handwriting.

It was clear that Helen Bostall had been planning her getaway, that she had been keeping her plans hidden from Dillon, that she had not intended for him to accompany her on her journey. When asked why this was, she stated that she had decided to break with Dillon permanently and was determined not to get into an argument with him. "Edwin's temper had become unreliable. I didn't want there to be a scene."

When the prosecuting counsel pressed her on whether she was, in fact, afraid of Dillon, she hesitated and then said no. "Edwin was domineering, but I was used to that," she said. "He would never have done me physical harm."

When questioned about the row she'd had with Dillon on the evening of his death, Helen Bostall seemed completely bemused. "I barely saw Edwin all day," she said. "I was working in the library for most of the morning, then in the afternoon I saw three of my private pupils at Milliver Road. I have no idea where Edwin was at that time. He came back to the flat at around six o'clock. He seemed tired and irritable, but no more so than usual. I told him I was going to Daphne's, that I would be back around eleven. Those were the last words I spoke to him. I left the flat soon afterwards." She hesitated. "We really didn't have much to say to each other any more."

The police seemed determined right from the start that Helen was the killer. She had a motive – Dillon's coercive behaviour – and she had her escape already planned. A further breakthrough came the following day, when the murder weapon – a serrated steel kitchen knife with a scratched wooden handle – was discovered jammed into a crack in the wall separating the back garden of 112 Milliver Road from the garden of 114. The blade was caked in dried blood, later proved to be of the same blood type as Edwin Dillon's. Three clear fingerprints were found on the handle – all Helen's.

Helen freely admitted that the knife was hers, that it had come from her kitchen. She strongly denied that she had used it to murder Dillon. When asked who she thought had killed her lover, she said she didn't know. "Edwin was always falling in and out of love with people. He thrived on dissent. He didn't have friends so much as sparring partners, political cronies, most of them – people he knew from before we met. I gave up having anything to do with them a long time ago."

When asked why that was, Helen Bostall stated that she no longer cared for their company. "They were all men, obsessed with themselves and their own self-importance. They barely knew I existed. I'm sure some of them hated Edwin – he could be obnoxious. Whether any of them hated him enough to want to kill him I have no idea."

For two or three days, attention veered away from Helen as the police went in search of Dillon's political associates, many of whom, as Helen had suggested, turned out to have grievances against him. Then on February 5th, just as things were starting to get interesting, officers received an anonymous tip-off concerning a Louise Tichener of Highgate Village. This person – or persons – insisted that Miss Tichener had been conducting an affair with Edwin Dillon, and that Helen Bostall had known about it. When found and questioned, Tichener, who belonged to one of the suffragist groups also attended by Bostall, readily confessed to the affair, with the additional information that Dillon had been planning to leave Bostall, and marry her.

"We were going to leave London," Tichener said. "We were happy."

Helen confirmed that she knew Tichener by sight from the women's group, but denied she knew anything about an affair between her and Dillon. She reaffirmed that her own relationship with Dillon was as good as over, and the idea that she might have murdered him out of jealousy was ridiculous. "What Edwin did with his time or his affections was none of my business," she said. "If it is true that this young woman put her trust in Edwin, I would have been afraid for her."

But the tide had turned. Louise Tichener's evidence, together with Irene Wilbur's statement, the clothes and travel tickets hidden at Daphne Evans's flat – the evidence seemed damning. Paradoxically, Helen's fortitude under questioning – her refusal to break down on the witness stand – may actually have helped in securing a conviction.

Helen Bostal was found guilty of murder and sentenced to

death. She was hanged at Holloway prison on the morning of August 14th, 1928. Three weeks after her execution the hangman, Arthur Rawlin, resigned from the prison service and took up a position as a warehouseman for a minor shipping company part-owned by friends of his brother, a decision that meant a considerable drop in his standard of living. More than one enterprising journalist clamoured for Rawlin's story, but he refused to comment, saying merely that he was done with the hanging game and that was that.

I found that interesting. Rawlin wasn't the first hangman to lose his stomach for the profession, either. John Ellis, who executed Edith Thompson in 1923, ended up committing suicide. Although some said it was his alcoholism that did for him, most people agreed that Ellis never got over the appalling brutality of Edith's execution. There have been others, too – look them up if you don't believe me. It was thinking about Arthur Rawlin that prompted me to call on Lewis Usher. Lewis was an old client of mine – I'd helped him fight off the property acquisitions company that wanted to tear down the historic Methodist chapel that backed on to his home in Greenwich and turn it into a Tesco Metro – and it was during our war with Sequest Holdings that I happened to find out he was an expert on British murder trials as well as an enthusiastic collector of murder memorabilia. I always enjoy going to see Lewis – he tells the most amusing anecdotes, and his house on Crooms Hill contains more weird and wonderful collectibles than you'd hope to see in most provincial museums. When I visited him on that particular afternoon in late November, I was hoping he might have something enlightening to tell me about the Bostall execution and I was not disappointed.

"Do you think Arthur Rawlin gave up his job because he came to believe that Helen Bostall was innocent?" I asked him.

"It's a strong possibility," Lewis said. "There was more to it than that, though. People gossiped that Arthur Rawlin was in love with Bostall, that he believed he was, anyway. The prison governor reported that he used to visit Helen Bostall in her cell, during the run-up to her execution. There was a strange little article about it in the Evening Standard afterwards. You'd probably put his behaviour down to Stockholm Syndrome now, but it really was quite odd." He spooned more sugar into his tea. "You do know I have his watch?"

I felt my heartbeat quicken. "Arthur Rawlin's watch? The one he used to time his executions?"

"I think you'll find it was Albert Pierrepoint who used to do that. Rawlin might have copied him, I suppose. There was certainly a cult of personality around Pierrepoint at the time. It's Rawlin's watch though, definitely, whatever he used it for. I have the full provenance."

"Could I see it?" I found myself becoming excited in a way that seemed completely out of proportion with what Lewis had told me. It was just a watch, after all. But it was as if I knew, even then, that I was about to make a significant discovery, not just about Arthur Rawlin but about Helen Bostall.

"Of course. Won't be a tick." He eased himself out of his chair and shuffled off towards the side room where he kept most of his collection. I couldn't help noticing he relied on his cane more than he had on my last visit. Still, he seemed in good spirits. I gazed around the living room – the ancient red plush sofas, the fake stuffed dodo in its glass case, the walls and mantel shelf crowded with photographs of his wife, the stage actress Zoe Clifford, dead from a freak bout of pneumonia some ten years before. The place had become something of a haven for me during the Sequest case, which had happened to coincide with the first stage of my breakup with Ray. How glad I had been to come here, to escape from my own thoughts and misgivings into this cosy little corner of theatre land, where the fire was always lit and the stories were always larger and more preposterous than my own.

A place suspended in time, a lacuna in the fraying fabric of the everyday world.

"Here it is," Lewis said. I jumped, startled. I'd been so absorbed in my thoughts I hadn't noticed him come back into the room. He was carrying a small bag, made from yellow silk with a drawstring opening. "I can show you the papers too if you'd like to see them, but this is the watch."

He passed me the bag. I reached cautiously inside. Things inside bags make me nervous. You don't know what you're getting into until it's too late. In this case, Rawlin's watch, which was a full-case silver pocket watch about two inches in diameter. The front of the case was engraved with a lighted candle. On the back was a skull, the eye sockets and nasal cavities etched out in darker relief. The classic *vanitas*, life and death, light and darkness, the universal allegory for time's passing.

Perfect for a hangman, I thought.

"He may have commissioned the engraving personally," Lewis said, as if reading my thoughts. "Although the design isn't unusual for the time. The Victorians were heavily into mourning jewellery, as you probably know."

"Yes. Though it's more my brother's area, to be honest." I flipped open the front of the case. The watch's white enamelled face was simple and plain, as if in deliberate contrast to the gothic extravagance of the case. There was a date stamped on the dial, 1879, and a name, I supposed of the maker – Owen Andrews. The name meant nothing to me but I made a mental note to ask Martin about it later.

"It's a tourbillon watch," Lewis added. "Very expensive, even at the time. An ordinary working man like Rawlin would have had to save several months' salary to purchase this."

"What's a tourbillon?"

"A means for stabilising the watch's mechanism, so that it doesn't lose time. Here." He opened the back of the watch, revealing its workings, which resembled a complicated mechanical diagram, all gears and levers. "Have a look at this."

He angled his hand, showing me the inside back of the watch's case, and the photograph that had been secreted there.

The image showed a young woman, with short dark hair and light eyes, a narrow, straight nose and a high lace collar: Helen Bostall.

"There is a possibility that the photograph was placed inside the watch later – after Rawlin's death, I mean," said Lewis. "It's unlikely though. You won't read much about this in the newspapers, but if you delve a little deeper you'll find there are several contemporary accounts, from colleagues and family and so on. All of them agree that Rawlin was living in a fantasy world."

"About him and Helen being in love, you mean?"

"Yes, that, but it went even further." He chuckled. "I read one letter from Rawlin to his younger brother where he was going on about travelling back in time to prevent the execution he himself had carried out."

"That's ridiculous. Poor man."

"Plenty would say he got what he deserved. Not everyone would feel sorry for a hangman."

I did, though. We can't all choose our jobs, and was Rawlin so different from the soldiers sent out to kill other soldiers on the battlefields of World War 1? I tried to imagine how he must have felt, becoming properly aware for the first time of what his job meant, what it was he did. The imagining was not pleasant.

"Too bad we can't bring him back to talk to the Americans," I said. I smiled to myself, thinking how Martin would disapprove of my poor taste in jokes. He would love to see this watch, though, I thought, which gave me an idea. "Please say no if you want to," I said to Lewis, "but could I possibly borrow this? Just for a day or two? I'd like to show it to my brother."

"The watch?" He fell silent, and I was fully expecting him to demur, to begin explaining how he didn't like to let items from his collection leave the house, especially not an item such as this, which was valuable even aside from who had once owned it. "I'd like you to have it," was what he actually said. I felt so surprised and so shocked that for a moment I couldn't answer him.

"Lewis, don't be silly. I couldn't possibly. I'm sorry I asked," I said, when I could.

"I mean it," he insisted. "I've been wanting to leave you something – in my will, I mean. To say thank you for being such a good friend to me. But it's difficult to know what someone might like. If I know you like this, then you've made my task easier. You'll be doing me a favour."

"You're not ill?"

"Dying, you mean? No, no more so than usual. But I am eighty-six."

"Lewis," I said. "Thank you."

"It's my great pleasure. So long as you don't use it to go running off after repentant hangmen."

We both laughed at that. Both of us, at the same time. But I've sometimes had the feeling – call it hindsight, if you want – that neither of us actually thought it was funny.

Helen's defence rested on the fact that the evidence against her was circumstantial. No one – not even Irene Wilbur – claimed to have seen her in the vicinity of Milliver Road at the time of Dillon's death, and no matter how many times the prosecution cross-examined Daphne Evans over Helen's alibi, she never deviated from her original statement: Helen had arrived at her apartment just before seven, they ate some sandwiches Daphne had prepared and talked about Edwin. Helen still felt guilty for what she was planning – to walk out on him without a word of warning – but Daphne remained adamant she was doing the right thing.

"I never liked Edwin," she said. "He wasn't trustworthy. I was glad when Helen decided she was leaving him. I knew she wasn't happy."

When asked whether she considered Dillon to be a violent man, Daphne hesitated before replying and then said yes, adding: "I would have said he could be capable of violence. I was afraid for Helen, just sometimes, but she always told me I was being foolish so I had to believe her."

The prosecution's most important witness was Irene Wilbur. Her insistence that there had been a 'furious altercation' at 112 Milliver Road just before eight o'clock was more instrumental in securing a guilty verdict than Helen Bostall's fingerprints on the murder weapon. You didn't have to be a lawyer to understand that anyone could have used that knife, that the killer would have been likely to grab the first weapon to come to hand, especially if the murder had been opportunistic rather than planned. That Helen Bostall kept a carving knife in her kitchen drawer was hardly damning evidence.

On the other hand, Irene Wilbur was adamant that she had heard two people yelling at each other, that one of them had been a woman. And she had Gerald Honeyshot of the Red Lion to back her up regarding the time.

Why would Irene Wilbur lie? When asked by the prosecution if she had any reason to dislike or resent Helen Bostall, if there was any previous bad feeling between them, Wilbur was equally adamant that there hadn't been. "I barely knew her," she stated. "I'd not been living at Milliver Road for more than a fortnight. I'd seen her a few times to say hello to but that was all. She seemed friendly enough. A bit aloof perhaps but not what you'd call unpleasant."

In fact, Irene Wilbur had been resident at 112 Milliver Road for just ten days. The defence did not appear to find anything suspicious in that, and why would they? People move house all the time. Wilbur's assertion – that she had moved to Camden from Putney in order to be closer to grandchildren and because she had numerous friends in the area – seemed entirely reasonable.

I don't know what kept me picking away at Irene Wilbur, but I did. I didn't like the way she had been so relentless in the way she'd given her evidence, so determined, almost, that Helen was guilty. Wilbur had persisted, even while knowing that Helen might face a death sentence if convicted. Why such animosity towards a woman she claimed not to have known? I didn't get it. Those who thought to criticise Wilbur at the time did so on the grounds that she was a natural attention-seeker, altogether too enamoured of seeing herself in the newspapers. An interesting hypothesis, but I wasn't so certain.

Was it possible, I wondered, that Irene Wilbur had been a stooge? Most newspaper accounts of the trial made mention of Wilbur's 'smart' attire, and several made particular mention of a jade and diamond broach she wore. Everyone seemed to agree she was 'a handsome woman'.

After pursuing the matter a little further, I discovered that Irene Wilbur had moved away from Milliver Road less than a week after Helen's execution, that she had returned to her old stamping ground of Putney, and to considerably smarter lodgings than she had occupied previously.

If Irene Wilbur had been paid to provide false evidence, it suggested not only that Dillon's murder had been carefully planned, but that Helen had been intended to take the blame all along.

If this was so – and once I stumbled upon the idea I found it difficult to give up the conviction that it was – then Irene Wilbur would have to be connected with Edwin Dillon in some way, or rather with his enemies, who would scarcely have risked employing a stranger to do their dirty work.

On top of my research into the lives of Helen Bostall and Edwin Dillon, I now found myself grubbing around for any information I could find about Irene Wilbur. I soon discovered she had been married at the age of twenty-one to a Major Douglas Wilbur, who had been killed at the Battle of Amiens in World War One. They had one child, a daughter named Laura, born in the February of 1919, a full six months after her father's death.

Those dates seemed odd to me. Of course it was entirely possible that Major Wilbur had been afforded leave prior to the Amiens campaign, that Laura could have been conceived then, but it didn't fit somehow, not to my mind anyway. Douglas Wilbur had been an experienced, valuable and loyal officer. It was inconceivable that he would have left his post immediately before such a crucial offensive.

There was also the fact that Irene Wilbur was thirty-eight years old at the time of Laura's birth, that during the whole of her twenty-year marriage there had been no other children.

What had changed?

If Douglas Wilbur was not in fact Laura's father, who was?

I looked back once again over the trial records, focussing on any mention of Irene Wilbur's home life, no matter how minor. Which is how I came to notice something that had not registered before, namely that Laura Wilbur had not been resident at Milliver Road, that at the time of the murder she was staying instead with a person Irene Wilbur described as a 'near relative', a Mrs Jocelyn Bell, close to the Wilburs' old address in Putney. When questioned about why her daughter was not in fact living with her, Irene Wilbur said it was a matter of Laura's schooling.

Once again, it was possible. But by now I was coming to believe it was more likely a matter of Irene not wanting her daughter anywhere near a house where she knew there was going to be a murder. Wilbur would not be staying long at Milliver Road, in any case. Far better to keep Laura at a distance.

I was filled with a sense of knowing, the feeling that always comes over me when I understand I have discovered an insight into a case that has hitherto kept itself obstinately hidden. I knew that I was close to something, that the pieces of the truth were more than likely already assembled, that it was simply a matter of arranging them in the correct order.

The first step, I decided, was to try and find out a little more about Jocelyn Bell. And in the meantime I still had to talk to Martin about the hangman's watch.

People say we're alike, Martin and I, but I'm not so sure. We look alike, and I suppose what our mutual friends might be picking up on is our shared tendency towards poking around in subjects no one else gives a damn about. We both like finding things out. Of the two of us, though, I believe Martin is the better human being. Martin cares about people, which is why he is so good at his job. When I tell him this, he always insists that I must care about people too, or I wouldn't put such time and effort into fighting their corners.

Perhaps he's right. But I still think what I enjoy most about my work is the thrill of argument, the abstract battle of opposing forces. If 'doing good' happens to be a side-effect of that I'm not going to knock it, but it isn't the driving force behind what I do.

I don't think so, anyway. You'd better ask Martin.

I hope he meets someone else. He's borne up remarkably well since Miranda died, but that's Martin all over, never one to make a fuss.

I was always the one who made a fuss. Getting cancer then going crazy then marrying Ray. Martin was there for me through all of it, no matter how much I managed to screw up.

He can cook a mean curry, too.

"Have you ever heard of a watchmaker called Owen Andrews?" I asked him once we'd finished eating. I poured us both another glass of wine. It was odd, the way his face changed. A lot of people might not even have noticed, but I'm used to watching other people's body language and I know Martin back to front. The moment I said the name Owen Andrews, it was as if someone had suddenly switched a light on inside him, then just as rapidly flicked it off again. Something he didn't want to talk about? Or felt uncertain of? Could have been either. I'd been telling him about my research, my various theories about Irene Wilbur. I'd deliberately held off mentioning Arthur Rawlin because once you get Martin on to the subject of watches it's difficult to get him off it again.

I knew he'd be interested, but the extremity of his reaction surprised me, all the same.

"I've heard of him, yes," Martin said finally. "But what does he have to do with Irene Wilbur?"

This is going to sound strange, but I decided more or less in that moment that I wasn't going to tell Martin I had Rawlin's watch in my possession. Not yet, anyway.

It wasn't that I didn't trust him. I would trust Martin with my life, and perhaps that was the problem.

It was as if – and I know how bizarre this sounds, especially coming from an unreconstructed rationalist like me – I sensed already that something was going to happen, something involving the watch. I think I was afraid that if Martin got wind of what I meant to do, he would say it was dangerous and try to stop me.

I'm not good at taking advice – once I have a mind to do something, you might as well try *advising* a stampeding mare with a swarm of bees on her tail. No one knows this better than Martin and normally he'd stay out of it but in this case?

Let's just say I wanted to keep my intentions under wraps.

"Nothing," I said. "At least nothing directly." I told him about Arthur Rawlin and Arthur Rawlin's posthumous obsession with Helen Bostall, and then added that my old client Lewis Usher knew someone who knew someone who'd purchased Arthur Rawlin's watch in a private auction.

"It's by a London maker, apparently, this Owen Andrews," I said. "Lewis seems to think that Rawlin attached mystical properties to the watch, that he believed it could reverse time, or something. He's going to try and dig out the documents for me – Lewis, I mean. I wondered if you knew anything about this Andrews guy, that's all."

"Only that he trained in Southwark, and that his watches are vanishingly rare," Martin said. He sighed. "There are entire internet forums devoted to Owen Andrews. He's one of those people other people are always talking about, probably because we know so little about him. People are still having arguments over exactly when he was born. There's speculation that he had access to Breguet's late notebooks. I don't believe it myself. I don't see how he could have done. The notebooks weren't in the public domain for at least a century after Breguet's death."

"Who's Breguet?"

"Abram Louis Breguet, a Swiss watchmaker. He's best known for making a watch for Marie Antoinette and almost losing his head for his trouble. But for horologists, Breguet is most famous for inventing the tourbillon."

Martin went off into a long-winded explanation of what a tourbillon was and how it worked, how before Breguet, no pocket watch could keep accurate time over a long period because of gravity, which acted as a drag weight on the mechanism, speeding it up or slowing it down by as much as sixty seconds in every hour. Breguet placed the whole mechanism inside a revolving metal cage he called a tourbillon, or whirlwind. The tourbillon kept the mechanism in stasis, twirling it around its own axis like a sidecar on a fairground ride.

The tourbillon watch was like a planet, spinning in space. In every sense that mattered, it was weightless.

"Think of a tornado," Martin said. "A wind itself has no substance, but it has incredible power. It renders everything weightless before it, even massive objects like houses and cars."

I zoned out a bit towards the end, not because what Martin was telling me wasn't interesting, but because I couldn't see how any of it related to Arthur Rawlin and a possible time machine. Then Martin said something else, something jaw-dropping. I was dragged back into the conversation with a physical jolt.

"What was that about the notebooks?"

"Breguet's notebooks," Martin repeated. "His doctors always insisted he was senile by then, but according to his son, Breguet was lucid and rational right up until he died. His late writings suggest he had been trying to create a kind of super-tourbillon, a mechanism he believed would eventually enable human beings to travel through time. He called it the time-stasis. I can't believe anyone would take it literally, quite honestly, but some of the people on the forums believe Owen Andrews made it his mission to put Breguet's theory into practice."

"To make a watch that could turn back time?"

Martin shrugged. "If you like."

"That's incredible."

"If it were true, maybe. But I've seen some of Andrews's pieces and they're just watches. Andrews was gifted but he wasn't a magician. All that time travel stuff – it's just the horological equivalent of urban myth."

I thought there was something heroic about it, nonetheless – the lone mechanic, pitting himself against logic like a gladiator fighting a tiger. I reminded myself that all the most radical advances in science seem like lunacy before they are proven.

"It's a beautiful word," I said to Martin. "Horological."

"Are you still convinced Helen Bostall was innocent?" he asked.

"More than ever. And I believe Arthur Rawlin thought so, too – that's why he felt so guilty over her death."

"You're determined to prove it, aren't you? Through your book?"

I laughed. "I suppose I am."

I didn't just want to prove it, though – I can admit that now. I wanted to change it. But I wasn't about to blow my cover to Martin.

Three days later I performed an experiment. Just one little trip back, five minutes or so. *Brain of Britain* was on the radio, which made it easy to tell if anything had actually happened. I had a second go at some of the questions, which would have upped my score if I'd been keeping tally, which I wasn't. It would have been cheating, anyway.

Jocelyn Bell turned out to be Jocelyn Leslie, an artist. She won a scholarship to study at the Slade, and when her father – a successful Yorkshire businessman of a conservative cast of mind – refused to let her go, she continued to paint in secret, making her own way to London two years later. She enjoyed moderate popularity for a time. Although there were those who dismissed her efforts as 'primitive' or 'naive', Lavinia Sable, who wrote art criticism for several London papers under the pseudonym Marcus Fell, insisted that in spite of having almost no formal training, Bell's work showed a keener understanding of European modernism than many of her better-known contemporaries.

I liked the sound of Lavinia, who apparently attended private views and press gatherings for years as Marcus, with no one being any the wiser. Lavinia was easily interesting enough to fill a book in her own right, but Lavinia was not my mission and after spending a day or two reading up on her I laid the material reluctantly aside and went back to the matter in hand, namely Jocelyn Bell.

On arrival in London, Jocelyn found work first as an assistant housekeeper at a private boarding school for girls, then as a secretary and assistant to the curator of one of the more progressive galleries on Cork Street. It was here, I'm certain, that she first encountered Leonard Bell, who was friendly with several of the artists represented there.

Leonard Bell was actually Leonid Belayev, a Russian émigré and a member of the radical socialist group based in Camden called the Four Brothers. The group was founded in the 1890s and, unlike many similar loose associations that fractured and splintered at the outbreak of war, the Four Brothers remained intact as a group well into the 1920s.

At some point during 1924, Edwin Dillon began attending their meetings.

Here at last was the breakthrough I'd been searching for. Jocelyn Leslie married Leonard Bell in 1902. They had one son, Malcolm, in 1903, although letters sent by Jocelyn to a friend in Manchester reveal that differences were already making themselves felt between the couple and by 1905 their marriage was over in all but name. Leonard Bell kept in close touch with his family, though – I think he was probably still living under the same roof for some years after he and Jocelyn separated, a fact that would almost certainly have led to gossip amongst the neighbours. Not that Jocelyn or Leonard gave much of a damn for bourgeois convention. They remained friends, and when Leonard eventually began a long-term affair with another woman, the woman quickly became Jocelyn's friend, also.

That woman – and you can imagine my satisfaction when I was able to prove this for sure – was Irene Wilbur. There were in fact several dozen letters from Leonard to his lover, preserved amongst Jocelyn Bell's papers at the Women Artists Forum in Hammersmith.

As a bonus, the letters also revealed to me the identity of Malcolm Bell's soon-to-be fiancée: Louise Tichener.

Frustratingly, I was never able to find out much about Irene Wilbur herself, and I can only assume her willingness to go along with the murder plot had more to do with her wanting to protect Leonard Bell than with any active animosity towards Helen Bostall. The true identity of Dillon's murderer also remained hidden from me, although I'm more or less positive it wasn't Bell himself. Leonard was a hardened activist – he would have known better than to put himself directly at risk.

After weeks of rooting around in various archives of obscure research papers, I came to the conclusion that the most likely suspect was a much younger man, Michael Woolcot, who seems to have known Dillon when he was living in Manchester. The two had some sort of falling-out – either in Manchester or soon after Woolcot's own arrival in the capital. So far as I know they were never reconciled, although mysteriously there was one final meeting between them, in a Camden public house, just ten days before Dillon's murder. The meeting was remarked upon by a moderate socialist named West, a journalist who wrote a satirical column for an independent newspaper called The Masthead, lampooning many of the personalities associated with the more extreme wing of the movement.

They say that if you sup with the devil you should use a long spoon,

West wrote in his January 20th column, just one week before the murder. *Judging by the outbreak of cosy camaraderie at The Horse's Head last Thursday evening, it would seem there are those who set little store by such sage advice, even those we might consider our elders and betters.* West goes on to reveal the identities of both Dillon and Woolcot, referring to the latter as 'an upwardly mobile cur of the Belayev persuasion' and to the meeting itself as 'a council of war'.

Which can only beg the question, West writes, *of who exactly is at war here, and with whom?*

Whether the police were ever made aware of West's column, or possessed enough insider knowledge to make head or tail of it, I have no idea. Leonard Bell was questioned briefly, along with two dozen or so other regular and irregular members of the Four Brothers group, though the comrades' universal disdain for the official forces of law and order would have meant the chances of anyone letting anything slip were practically nil.

Helen Bostall's ticket for the boat train was forward-dated to February 3rd, a date that turned out to be less than a week after Dillon's murder. It seems likely that someone – someone friendly with Leonard Bell or one of his cronies – knew about Helen's travel plans. For Bell's plan to succeed, it was crucial that Dillon be killed well in advance of Helen's departure for the continent. I believe it was Dillon's meeting with Woolcot, staged by Bell as an opportunity for reconciliation, that set the stage for the murder. No doubt Woolcot had been instructed to arrange a second, more informal meeting, to take place at Dillon's flat.

Putting all the evidence together, it finally became clear to me that it was those ten days that formed the crucial time period, the ten days between Dillon first meeting Woolcot at The Horse's Head, and his eventual death.

If Helen Bostall could have been persuaded to bring her journey forward – to leave London soon after New Year, say – then Bell would either have had to shelve his plans, or risk being exposed as complicit in Dillon's killing.

Regardless of Dillon's fate, Helen Bostall herself would have been saved.

If only someone could have told her, I thought, and almost immediately afterwards I thought of Arthur Rawlin. Had he tried to use the watch? I wondered. If so, he had obviously failed.

As to why Bell wanted Dillon dead in the first place, the reasons remained obscure to me. All I could think was that it must have been down to some intricate power struggle within the Four Brothers. Truth be told, I didn't care much. Not then.

I knew from the start that the best place to approach Helen would be at one of her suffragist meetings. The very nature of such gatherings meant there would always be new faces in evidence, strangers who might turn up for a couple of meetings and then disappear again. It ought to be relatively easy to mingle with the women without drawing undue attention to myself. The main thing was not to go overboard in trying to fit in. I chose clothes that were unobtrusive rather than authentic: the three-quarter-length coat I normally wore to court hearings in winter, a dark, paisley-patterned skirt I hardly ever wore but couldn't bear to throw out because I liked the material so much, a pair of black lace-up shoes. Plain clothes, in every sense of the word.

By now you're either wondering what on Earth I'm talking about, or if I can possibly be serious. Which is fine.

I kept putting off the actual – journey? I told myself I needed to do more research, which was at least partly true. To keep myself safe, I had to know that particular bit of Camden well enough to be able to walk around it blindfold, if need be. But mostly I was just scared. Scared in case the watch didn't work and scared in case it did.

Five minutes and a hundred years were not the same thing.

What if the watch refused to bring me back, or marooned me in a time that was not my own?

I wanted to know though, I wanted to *see*. The closer it came to the date I'd set myself, the more impatient I felt. Impatient with my fear. Impatient with my delaying tactics. When Ray phoned me the night before to ask me if I was going to some private view or other his agent was organising, I almost bit his head off.

"Are you okay, Dottie?" he said. He hadn't called me Dottie for years, not since we separated.

"I'll be there, don't worry," I said, not answering his question and not knowing if I'd be there, either. "I've got a lot on at work, that's all. Say hi to Clio for me."

Clio is Ray's daughter, the child he has with Maya. I should make more of an effort with Maya, I suppose, but it's difficult. We're such different people, and although chumming up with her ex-husband's new wife seemed to work for Jocelyn Bell, I'm not sure it's for me.

Clio, though. She's eight years old and a miracle. I could never tell this to anyone, not even Martin, but occasionally it breaks my heart that she isn't mine.

There is a lever inside the watch, a silver pin that slides from side to side inside a moulded slit – imagine the back of an old wind-up alarm clock, the little lever you use to engage the alarm function, or to turn it off. There is no clear indication of what the purpose of this lever might be, and when you first engage it, nothing seems to happen. Say 'nothing happens full stop', if you like. I won't mind.

I once had a conversation with Martin, years ago when we were kids, about whether ghosts existed. When I asked Martin if he believed, he said it didn't matter. "If ghosts exist, they'll go on existing whether we believe in them or not."

It's the same with this. And if I tell you that what time travel reminds me of most of all is the time before my illness, I wonder will you believe that either? The time when I was so in love with numbers – when I could listen to numbers conversing the same way you might listen to music, when I felt the thrum of numbers in my blood, intricate as a crystal lattice, sound and rhythmic and basic as the beat of a drum.

I turned the lever, and the rush of numbers filled my head, blazing in my veins like alcohol, like burning petrol. The music of the primes, du Sautoy called it, and I could hear it again. I closed my eyes and counted backwards. I could feel the boundaries of reality expanding, unfurling. Bobbing deftly out of reach of my hands, like a toy balloon.

I ducked under the boundary wire and followed. Time filled me up, chilly and intoxicating.

Yes, but what's it *like*? I can hear you asking.

Like a triple slug of Russian vodka that's been kept in the icebox, that's what it's like.

I started going on practice runs. Just silly things: walking past my front door in the middle of last week, going to a concert at the Barbican I'd wanted to attend when it was actually on but happened to miss. I thought that getting the timing right would prove difficult, but in fact the mechanism was extremely accurate, once you got the hang of it. I found it mostly came down to imagining: knowing where you wanted to be and forming an image of the place and time inside your mind. This sounds irrational I know, but that's how it was.

I spent a lot of time in Camden, just walking around. You'd be surprised how little it's changed. Even when houses, whole streets have been torn down and built over, the old shadows remain.

The city has a shape. You can sense it, if you feel for it, even if you're sleepwalking and perhaps especially then, London's presence wrapped closely around you like a blanket.

The suffragist meetings took place in rooms about the Quaker meeting house, on Bentley Street. During the day it was mostly quiet, but in the evenings things livened up considerably, mainly because of The Charlady, a public house and pie shop on the corner of the street opposite. I went in daylight the first time, just to be safe. Muggings were common then in this part of London and I saw no point in exposing myself to unnecessary risk.

You think of the past as cleaner, but it really isn't. Horse shit, engine oil, smoke, blood, piss, beer, the rotting detritus from the market, piled at the kerb. Not London as it might be in a theme park, but a London you'd recognise instantly, just from the stench. Cars are creeping in already: hackney cabs and omnibuses, gentlemen's conveyances. And the bikes – the thrilling tring of bicycle bells, boy couriers speeding along. *Oi Miss, get on the pavement, why dontchyer? Bleedin' 'eck.* A flower and matchbox seller, a puckered scar across one cheek and her left hand missing. I reach into my pocket to find the right coins, then remember I don't have the right coins, not at all. Exactly the kind of stupid blunder I'm supposed to be on guard against. The peddler gazes at me with tired eyes and I look away in shame. The next time I come I bring her a paper packet of corned beef sandwiches but she is no longer there. Not in the same place, anyway. I remind myself of what I'm here for, and move swiftly along.

Another time, I stand in a shop doorway opposite and watch the women arrive for their meeting. I'm amazed to find that I recognise some of them, from the letters I've read, from the blurred photographs in the Women's Studies archive in the British Library. One of them, a young poet named Kathleen Thwaite, is accompanied to the door of the meeting house by her husband, Austin Gears. I know that Kathleen is to die in 1937, on a protest march against Franco's fascists in Madrid. It makes my heart ache to see her, and the urge to do something, to warn her in some way, is all but overwhelming. I turn quickly away, hoping to catch a glimpse of Helen Bostall instead. On this occasion at least she appears to be absent.

Has my being here, even to stand motionless in the street, altered things somehow, and for the worse? I push the thought away. It is coincidence, that's all. She will be here next week, and if not then, the week after. It need not matter.

The next time, I file inside the hall with the other women. No one talks to me or takes particular notice but many smile. I feel accepted as one of them. More than that, I can *imagine* myself as one of them. Almost as if I have experienced this life, this version of my life anyway, this Dora Newland who attended suffragist rallies in Hyde Park, who conducted furious arguments with her uncle about being allowed to travel down through Italy with another woman friend. Casting Henry – dear Henry, who indulged our every whim when we were children – in the role of domineering guardian makes me smile.

We sit on hard wooden chairs in the draughty space – three small attic rooms that have been converted into one larger one – and listen to a Mrs Marjorie Hennessey tell us about her experience of studying politics at the Sorbonne. She is an impressive woman, commanding and authoritative, and I cannot help wondering what happened to her, how come she failed.

So many women. It is depressing to consider how many of us have been discouraged, disparaged, forced to reconsider, turned aside from our dreams.

I want to rush up to Marjorie Hennessey and tell her not to give up, not to drop by the wayside, not to fall silent.

"She's wonderful, isn't she?" It is the interval and we are queuing up for tea. The woman who speaks to me seems shy and rather young, and I have the feeling this is her first time here also. Her cheeks are flushed pink.

"Admirable," I say, and for a second I experience a sensation close to vertigo. I am here, and I am speaking to someone. I hug my bag as if seeking support from it. Inside the bag are the keys to my flat, my purse, my Kindle ereader, my mobile phone, all those other insignificant trifles that don't exist yet. *I come from the future*, I think, in what Martin always calls the MGM voice. I want to laugh out loud. I glance over at the chalk board, where Marjorie Hennessey has been drawing diagrams illustrating the economic implications of women withdrawing their labour from the home.

I wonder how my new friend in the tea queue would react if I were to tell her that almost a century later we're still fighting the same battles. Again, I want to laugh. Not that it's funny.

"We need more like her," I say instead, because that also is still true. Now, more than ever, we need more anger, more knowledge. "Shall we sit down?"

We take our tea and sit at one of the wooden trestles at the side of the hall. The woman tells me her name is Barbara Winton and she's a socialist.

"They say there's going to be another war," she says. "We have to join with our sisters in Europe – we must prevent war, at all costs."

She is learning German, and corresponding with the daughter of a friend of her father's, who lives in Frankfurt. "Her name is Gisela. She's a sculptor. Don't you think that's marvellous? She's asked me to go out and visit her and Daddy says I can. It feels – I'm not sure how to explain – as if a whole new life is beginning."

"I hope you're right," I say. I tell her that I'm studying law, that I am hoping to practise at the bar. I see confusion on her face – my age, probably – which is swiftly succeeded by a kind of wonder, mixed with mischievous delight. Women have been allowed access to the legal profession for less than a decade, after all.

"Well done, you," she says. "I think that's marvellous."

Her excitement is contagious. It is only as we are about to resume our seats for the second half of the programme that I finally catch sight of Helen Bostall. She is near the back of the room, talking to a woman with an upright posture and hawkish nose whom I recognise at once as Daphne Evans.

I gaze at them, dumbstruck. I feel like a spy. As I move

towards my seat I see Helen turn, just for a moment, and look directly at me.

Instead of the blank, flat gaze of a woman casually scanning the crowd, what I see in her eyes – indisputably – is recognition: *you're here.* I feel cold right through. My hands begin to shake. I'm going to drop my cup, I think, then realise it's all right, I no longer have it. Barbara Winton has taken it from me and returned it to the tea bench at the back.

That was when I lost my nerve. Instead of sitting down again I pushed through the crowd to the door and then rushed down the stairs, almost tripping over the paisley skirt in the process. Once outside I felt better. There was the usual rowdy hubbub coming from The Charlady, the same stink of greasy Irish stew and overloaded dustbins. I made my way to an access lane between two rows of terraces and took out the watch. I engaged the lever without looking at it – not looking had become a kind of superstition with me – and stood there in the dark, counting primes and feeling that odd, trembling dream state take hold until I became aware of the sound of traffic – motor traffic, I mean, buses and police sirens – on Camden High Street.

I was back. I breathed in through my mouth, tasting exhaust fumes and the tarry scent of someone's spent cigarette. I stood still for some moments, letting the world come back into focus around me and feeling the relief I felt each time: that I had conducted an extremely risky experiment – heating flash powder in a petri dish, say – and managed to get away without blowing my hands off.

I never experimented with going forward, not even by one day. I had a terror of it, a paralysing phobia. It was a deal I made, I suppose – with God, the devil, myself, Owen Andrews? *Bring me safely home, and I'll keep our bargain.* Well, I guess it worked.

The next time I went back, I was prepared. So, it seems, was Helen. She was waiting for me this time, at the bottom of the stairs outside the meeting house. She told me later that she'd waited there at the start of every meeting since she'd first seen me, knowing I would be returning but not knowing when.

"Dora," she said quietly. "You're here at last." She caught my hands in both of hers. Her fingers were cold. It was December, and she was smiling in a way that suggested she was greeting an old friend, someone she knew well but hadn't seen in a while. Pleasure, and sadness, as if she knew our time together would not be long.

"I don't understand," I said, and sighed. Who was I to talk? "How did you – how do you know me?"

"Knowing everything you know – do you need to ask?" she said. "The order in which things happen doesn't matter, surely? Just that they happen. I'm so pleased to see you."

She leaned forward to embrace me, and I found myself almost believing – there was such joy in seeing her, such emotion – that this was indeed a reunion and not, as I knew it to be, our first meeting.

"Come," she said. "We can go back to the flat. Edwin's away – in Manchester. That's what he says, anyway."

"You don't think he really is?"

She shrugged. "Edwin tells me what it pleases him to tell me. Sometimes it's the truth and sometimes it isn't. I had to give up caring which a long time ago."

We came to Milliver Road. I'd been to the house of course – what I mean is I'd stood outside it many times. I knew 112 as a spruce, bay-fronted terrace with replacement windows. The house in Helen's time seemed smaller, meaner, the exterior paintwork chipped and blistering. A flight of steps led steeply down to a basement forecourt.

"We've had problems with damp," Helen said. "The woman who lives upstairs says there are rats, too, but I've never seen them."

"Mrs Wilbur?"

She gave me a puzzled look. "Mrs Wilbur? Mrs Herschel lives on the ground floor. There's no Mrs Wilbur."

"It doesn't matter," I said. So my researches had proved correct – Irene Wilbur hadn't moved in yet. There was still time.

"Let's go in and get warm," Helen said. "I'll light the stove."

"We were happy here once, Edwin and I," Helen said. The stove was well-alight. Soft lamplight threw shadows on the whitewashed walls of the cosy front sitting room. Framed prints, showing images from a Greek bestiary. An orange-and-green Aubusson rug. Books, books everywhere, overflowing the alcove shelving and piled on the floor. A stack of handwritten pages lay fanned across a low wooden table. It was a good room. A room I felt at home in.

I also knew I'd been here before.

"Have you eaten?" Helen asked.

I laughed. "It's been a hundred years at least," I said.

"I can warm up some soup. I made it yesterday."

"That would be lovely." I wasn't hungry – quite the opposite – but I was curious to see how food might taste here. In fact, it tasted like potato soup, thick and nutritious and well-seasoned. We ate, dipping bread into our bowls, and I asked Helen what she was working on.

"I've been helping to edit a collection of essays by women on the subject of war," she said. "I want to include writing by German women as well – letters, memoir, whatever I can get hold of. The publisher was against this at first but I managed to persuade them how important it is, essential even. You don't think it's too soon?"

I shook my head.

"I'm glad. We have to use every weapon we have."

"Weapon?"

"To make people understand what war really is. The madness of it." She fell silent, head bent. "Dora, I know I shouldn't really ask you this, but do we succeed? Do we succeed at all?"

I know I shouldn't answer, and I don't, not then, but the

following week, when I know that Helen will be at her meeting, I return to Milliver Road for one final visit. I have an envelope with me, addressed to Helen. I post it through the front door of the house, hear it fall on to the scuffed brown linoleum of the communal hallway. Inside is a second-hand copy of John Hersey's memoir, *Hiroshima* in the original Pelican edition, its pages faded and brittle but clearly readable, the most concise response to her question that I can think of. What good will it do? None at all. But Helen asked me a question and she deserves an answer.

"That doesn't matter now," I said in 1927. "What I mean is – it matters, but there are more urgent things to think about. Urgent for you, anyway."

"You're frightening me."

"In a month's time, Edwin is going to be murdered. If you stay here you are going to be blamed for it. There will be a trial and –"

"You're telling me I'm going to be hanged. For a crime I had nothing to do with."

I stared at her, horrified.

"I thought it was a dream," she said, more quietly. "That man. He sat on the edge of my bed and told me about it. He was crying. He seemed quite mad. When I told him to go away he did. I wish I'd been kinder."

Arthur Rawlin. So he had used the watch to try and save her, after all.

"None of that is going to happen," I said quickly. "But you must leave London, and Edwin. You need to pack your things and get as far away from here as you can."

She nodded slowly. "I've been planning to go, anyway. To leave Edwin, I mean. Whatever we had – it's over. I could say he's changed but really I think it's me. I see him differently now." She paused. "I see everything differently."

"Can you think of any reason why anyone would want to kill

Edwin?"

She was silent for a long time, lacing and unlacing her fingers. Finally she sighed. "I really don't involve myself with Edwin's business any more, but I do know there are people in the Four Brothers he's fallen out with. Badly. Edwin believes – I don't know, that we should do something to signal the start of the revolution. Something dramatic, something violent even. He says he has people standing by – bomb makers." She shook her head. "I don't know how much of this is true, and how much is just talk. The more he drinks the more he talks, Edwin. That's something I've noticed. Not that half the brethren would see much wrong if Edwin really is planning to blow people up. I think mainly it's about power within the group – who has it and who doesn't. There are some who see Edwin as a threat, who think he's getting above himself. I'm sure they'd be more than happy if he were out of the way. Can you believe that?"

"I can more than believe that."

"They don't like him because he's clever, because he doesn't give two hoots about their old hierarchies. Because he's from Manchester, even." She turned to look at me. "I keep asking myself if it's partly my fault, that things have gone this far. If I could have talked to him more, maybe? But I've come to understand that Edwin never cared about what I thought, not even at the beginning. He wanted an audience, that's all. Now that I no longer listen, he cares even less."

I was tempted to tell her about Ray and me, but decided that would be unfair. Ray's no bomb maker, just another man with an ego who needs it stroking. Now that I no longer have to live with him, I can even enjoy his company from time to time. "Where will you go?" I said instead.

"I have a friend, Elsa Ehrling, in Berlin. She says I can stay with her as long as I need. I can teach English. And there are other things I can do to make myself useful. Elsa says workers for peace need to make their voices heard in Germany, now more than ever."

You'd be right there, I thought, but did not say. I'd interfered enough already. Besides, she would be safe in Berlin, at least for a time.

"I would wait until the new year – but not much longer," I said. "And tell no one what you are planning – not even Daphne. You can write to her from Berlin. She will understand."

"I know she will. And Dora – thank you."

We talked of other things then: the book she dreamed of writing on poetry and war, my love of numbers and the loneliness I'd always felt in having to abandon them.

"But you never did abandon them – your being here is proof. You can see that, surely?"

She was right in a way, I suppose. But I'm no Sophie Germain.

The stove gave out its warmth, and we sat beside it. I understood that this was the moment of change, that if I had indeed met with Helen before, I would not do so again. That I had done what I had come to do, and that this was goodbye.

I felt time tremble in the balance, then come to a standstill. There are moments when time lies in stasis, and this was one of them. But time always moves on.

"I'm pregnant, by the way," Helen said as I was leaving. "Edwin doesn't know, don't worry."

My heart leapt up at her words. I think I knew this was your story, even then.

Edwin Dillon lived. With Helen gone and his plans in ruins, Leonard Bell must have decided that murdering him was too much of a risk. Or perhaps he waited, hoping for a better opportunity and never finding it. A year later, the Four Brothers disbanded. Leonard Bell went to Germany, where he became part of the communist movement dedicated to getting rid of Adolf Hitler. He was arrested and deported back to London in 1934. Edwin Dillon headed a splinter group, also calling itself the Four Brothers, and believed to be one of the main instigators of the notorious plot to assassinate Oswald Mosley in 1936. He served four years for his involvement and, although it is not known whether it was prison that made him lose his appetite for radical politics, he cut loose from all his Four Brothers contacts and after the war returned to working as a freelance journalist. You can find feature articles by Edwin Dillon in the archives of The Times, The Guardian and the Glasgow Herald, among other places. He died in 1971.

He was briefly involved with the Irish writer Eena Mowbray, with whom he had one son. Douglas Mowbray also worked as a journalist, and was known to be a fervent supporter of the IRA. Douglas died aged thirty-one, when he killed himself and his young daughter Gemma by driving off a bridge on the outskirts of Belfast. His son Padraic, who was also in the car at the time, survived. I have been unable to trace his whereabouts. There is every possibility that he is still alive.

Real history is a mass of conflicting stories. According to the official records, Helen Mildred Bostall was tried and found guilty of the murder of Edwin Patrick Dillon and was sentenced to death. The execution was carried out on August 14th, 1928. History seems content with this judgement, though there are many, including myself, who would argue that capital punishment is never justified.

There are also anomalies, if you care to look for them. The Library of the Sorbonne records the publication, in 1941, of a pamphlet by Ellen Tuglas with the title *On War: the imaginary reminiscences of hell's survivor.* The work was originally written in English, although a French translation was provided by Ivan Tuglas, a Russian exile resident in Paris since the 1920s and Ellen's common-law husband until his death in 1952.

On War is a peculiar work. Lodged halfway between fact and fiction, it has aroused some interest among scholars of World War Two literature because it appears to predict the nuclear destruction of Hiroshima. *I remember where I was when they told me,* states the unnamed narrator. *I have never before felt able to speak my feelings aloud, but what I wanted, when I heard, was simply to be there. To be not guilty of this thing, to help one person up from the rubble, even if such an action brought about my own destruction. I yearned to haul myself across bleeding Europe with my coat in tatters and no money in my purse. You will say that these feelings were selfish and I would not blame you for saying so. Some crimes are so huge there can be no recompense.*

On War is dedicated to Ellen's daughter, Isobel Elsa, who was eleven years old at the time of its publication.

I knew Ray's mother was called Isobel, but she was old, and living in Paris, and I never met her. She died three years ago. I know that Ray sent her photos of you when you were born. I imagine they were there beside her bed on the day she died.

Ray was always meaning to take you over there, so she could get to know you. It's too late now, but that's Ray all over. He loses track of time.

Dearest Clio. We can only cheat time for so long, and I knew when I went back to Milliver Street that final time it should be the last.

Your great-grandmother, though: Ellen Tuglas, whose name was once Helen Bostall. I should have guessed she would find a means of letting me know our escape plan succeeded, and that her name would be Clio. Clio, the daughter of memory, the muse of history. I should have known that – through you, Clio – Helen and I would one day meet again.

I carried on writing the book, of course I did, my account of Helen Bostall and how she was hanged for a crime she didn't commit. I'd come so far with my research I didn't feel like giving up – and as a story, as I say, it had everything: bomb plots, political feuding, affairs of the heart, as many double crosses as you might find in *Tinker, Tailor, Soldier, Spy*. My editor at *History Recollected* even thinks she's found a publisher for it. I doubt it'll make me rich but it should do all right.

You can read the book when you're older. Make of it what you will. Godmothers can be boring, can't they, especially godmothers who also happen to be lawyers? At least you can tell yourself that your boring lawyer godmother once changed the world. A little bit, anyway. I don't imagine you'll be telling anyone else.

Front Row Seat to the End of the World

E.J. Swift

Day Ten

The water is up to my neck. Immersed in its warmth, the thought of slipping further down, letting it close over my head and invade my mouth, is almost attractive. As if surrender is something noble. But that would be preemptive. I jam my feet against the end of the bath and gaze at my toes. Chipped red nail polish, the last evidence of Michelle's hastily rescheduled wedding. That, and the headache. I settle back into the bubbles, trying to ignore the uneasy stirring of my stomach and the memories of last night's consumption. I'm repenting now, but what else are you supposed to do when you've got ten days left?

When the water's drained away I swaddle myself in my dressing gown and turn on the TV. Professor Brian Cox is on again, talking about the force and velocity of the asteroid, the asteroid which should have missed us by some millions of kilometres had it not collided with the other asteroid. Cox sounds surprisingly mellow about the asteroid's malignant trajectory, but then he sounds pretty laid back about everything.

The Guardian has already published its 'Greatest Feats of Humanity' and the comments section is in overdrive. I should probably make my own list. I get out my iPad, and then decide paper is more appropriate for one of my final acts, not that it will ever become an artefact. Literature. That was one of the Feats. 'Feats' sounds far too epic for the common homo sapiens. I write

'Achievements' instead. I sit for a while, humming, chewing the pen lid, filtering my memory for evidence of worth. On TV, slow-motion graphics show the asteroid connecting with Earth's atmosphere. I press mute.

I don't suppose when Cox was playing keyboards in D:Ream that he ever imagined he'd be narrating the end of the world. To be fair, in my aspirational teenage years I didn't imagine at age forty-four I'd be living alone in a studio the size of a mouse, earning less than I had in my twenties and facing death by incineration.

Manchester is quieter this morning. With the advent of day ten, the official countdown has begun broadcasting from the Shanghai World Financial Centre. Ten has always been a symbolic number – nothing and everything, the universe encapsulated in two strokes of the pen. I've got the app on my phone. It's frightening how easy it is to become mesmerized by the neon seconds ticking down. To let everything else slip away. The more attuned I am to the quiet, the more aware I become of those digits and the blankness of the paper in front of me.

Finally I write: Katherine.

For God's sake, Mum, how many times –

I cross her name out and write Kat.

I turn the page over and write 'Failures'. Underneath that I write Kat again.

Day Nine

My ex-husband is the last person I expect to call me. I let the phone ring, not inclined to talk to the condescending prick, but no sooner has the phone gone dark than it lights up again.

"What do you want, Oliver?"

"Nice to speak to you too, Nell."

I wait.

"Listen," he says. "I've been thinking about things."

"Yes?"

"I've been reflecting."

"If you've found God, I'm not interested."

"Jesus, Nell, for once will you just hear me out. I mean about us."

"There is no us."

"That's the point. Everything that happened, I keep thinking about it – wondering how we let things get that far. Aren't you?"

"No," I say, which is true. "It was over a decade ago."

There's a long pause. When he speaks again, there's a note in his voice which I've never heard before. Panic.

"I don't know what to say to Kat."

"She's an adult, Oliver. It's not like you can spin her a fairy tale."

The words rush out. "It's all going to shit. I can't face her. I can't – I can't protect her."

So that's what this is about. My suave, charming, self-assured ex-husband has finally come up against something he can't control. When I first met Oliver, he looked like a young Idris Elba – not that anyone knew who Idris Elba was back then – which could have gone on the Achievements list had our marriage endured. These days Oliver runs his own law practice, and still looks like Idris Elba.

"Come to London," he says.

"No."

"Please. Please, Nell, I'm asking you this."

"You know what she said. She never wants to see me again. You backed her up. Besides, it might have escaped your notice but there are no trains and I've got three litres of petrol in the tank, that is if someone doesn't torch the car between now and D-day. The Merc over the road made a hell of a bonfire."

He rallies.

"I know you, Nell. It might be over a decade but I still know when you're taking evasive action. You do care. She's your daughter, for God's sake."

"Oh, don't do that to me, Oliver. Not now. I'm the one who

left, remember? I'm the bad mother! Isn't that how the story goes?"

He goes quiet.

"You should talk to her. Think about it."

"I have."

I cut the call.

My face is hot and when I look at my hands they're trembling.

"You bastard," I mutter.

Two years, a blink in the spectrum of humanity, is a hell of a long time in your own head. Two years erodes things. Memories. Certainty.

Now I've got two hundred and eight hours left.

After the incident, Kat sent me an email detailing the events which I could not remember. My mind had closed around them like a shell. I read what she wrote with a sense of detachment. It wasn't that I couldn't believe what I'd said. I couldn't believe she believed I had meant it.

Kat didn't recount the things she had said, which was probably for the best.

I deleted the email.

A few days later I tried calling, and got her voicemail. Unlike my daughter I have never been afraid of scenes, so eventually I turned up on her doorstep, only to find Oliver there barring the way like an incarnation of Azrael. It's the only time I've ever known Kat to shout. In a strange way, it was a relief – as if we were finally admitting ourselves to each other. This is who we are. Kat, I thought, had been preparing for this moment. She had needed a justifiable reason. She was – is – that kind of girl. Getting so drunk I couldn't remember the terrible things I'd said was an infallible reason. Adults were not supposed to do this. I was an adult. A failed one.

I stand at the sink, stirring a teaspoon in a cup of instant coffee. I've started taking it black – can't get used to the taste of UHT milk. From the window I can see the skeleton of the burnt-out Mercedes in the carpark, and spaces where other cars have disappeared, their windows smashed in and their engines hotwired. My ancient Volvo is so decrepit-looking I don't suppose anyone thinks it worth stealing. For a week or so we had the army in situ, but even they've left now.

I think about writing Kat an email, then discard the idea. What will Kat do with her two hundred and eight hours? She's still in London, that much I know through Oliver. I start another list: Things I Will Do If The Basher Works. Get Kat back. Then I screw it up. What's the point?

The Basher (even journalists have given up on the technical name) is an international effort, but NASA has been quick to remind everyone that it has been developed under American leadership. If the Basher succeeds, they'll have saved the world, and President Trump will become even more intolerable. Yesterday he claimed the asteroid is a Chinese plot. The Chinese retaliated by blaming the Americans' inferior space programme. North Korea blame everyone and are threatening to unleash nuclear weapons. It's possible the end of the world will come even sooner than we expect. Twitter has christened the asteroid Trump, so our planet's greatest cosmic defence has become the Trump-Basher. Oh Twitter, I'll miss you when I'm dead.

My phone vibrates. There's no way I'm speaking to Oliver again, but it's a text from my friend Bee.

HAVING PANIC ATTACKHELP

I tap out a reply.

Deep slow breaths and head between legs remember?
GOING TO DIE
Not necessarily. Basher might work
NOT helping
Prof Cox said so, it must be true
Tosser
Tosser with an astrophysics degree. Or some shit like that

Don't give a shit about ducking degrees it's a ducking asteroid and that's not the point anyway
***FUCKING fucks sake!!!**
Want me to come over?
Yes
No
Better now
Going to watch made in chelsea
Good plan. Love you Bee xxx
Love you too nellie <3 xxxxx

Where Kat isn't involved, the words come so easily.

Day Eight

This morning's eminent physicist is talking about our astronauts in their escape pods. As the footage shows them jettisoning away from Earth, he laments the fact that we have so few women trained for space.

"And that's what you get for the fucking patriarchy," I yell. The pods are a gesture, anyway. What chance do they have against the debris of a planet?

I haven't left the flat since the wedding and my food supplies are running low. I'll have to face Tesco's – an actual, brick-and-mortar Tesco's, as opposed to the nice delivery man who has brought my groceries to the door for the past five years. Is anyone still going to work at Tesco's? Surely not. I may have to commit a raid.

A maudlin mood descending, I flip through social media feeds. Trending on Twitter is #trumpbasher #rapture #prayforearth #greatestregrets and inexplicably, #taylorswift. It transpires that Taylor Swift is doing an end of the world gig. Tickets for 'Apocalypse Now: The Farewell Tour' start at two grand. I picture the scene: Taylor Swift strutting in denim hot pants and a gold fringe top, framed by pyrotechnics whilst the sky turns from amber to incendiary and the meteor showers begin. It's a theatre designer's wet dream.

My inbox is also encouraging me to think about my last living night, with 50% reductions from a dozen retailers – free, *guaranteed* delivery included. Who the hell are they bribing at DPS? I browse dresses idly. That red maxi is perfect for Michelle's and Hayley's would-have-been wedding in three months' time. Poor, hungover Michelle, last seen in a borrowed bridal gown hugging the toilet in a half-staffed Pizza Express. Even the dough balls were disappointing.

My phone lights up. Oliver again.

Call her.

It's tempting to reply with something snide, but I ignore it and hop over to Reddit for the latest in the conspiracy thread.

Conspiracy 1: Scientists have known about the asteroid for over a decade, but have been sworn to secrecy for fear of global panic. Space stations are orbiting distant reaches of the solar system. They carry geneticists and millions of frozen eggs.

Conspiracy 2: A sub-thread of Conspiracy 1. The (evil) United Nations has identified the asteroid as an opportunity to reboot humanity. There's a long list of people who have died ('died') or disappeared ('disappeared') over the last year. High profile scientists, engineers, doctors, writers, even artists. People who have been deemed worth saving. According to the thread, they are all on route to Mars. Michael Jackson is among them. There is debate as to whether Michael Jackson is a) alive and b) worthy.

Conspiracy 3: The asteroid is a fabrication. The real attack will come from our own leaders – entire populations will be nuked. There's too many people on the planet. Something has to be done, and this way, the troublesome countries can be removed.

Conspiracy 4: The asteroid is a fabrication specifically by the Tory Party, in a final endeavour to remove Jeremy Corbyn and reclaim England's green and verdant hills, untarnished by wind turbines, for fox hunting. This seems credible.

Conspiracy 5: The asteroid is aliens.

Please let it be aliens.

Day Seven

Nila's kitchen is a warm haven of enticing aromas. Today Nila has excelled herself. After the initial crack of pastry, her samosas melt in the mouth.

"I really should have learned to make these," I say. (Cooking: one for the Failures list.)

"They're amazing, Nila." Michelle takes another.

"Your best ever!" agrees Bee.

Silence falls. A panicked look creeps into Bee's eyes. She starts breathing heavily. I put my hand on her knee.

"Hey, hey. It's all right. We can talk about it."

"I used up everything in the kitchen," says Nila, ever practical. Nila would never leave a mess for the asteroid. "We're going over to Bradford tonight. Mum's on her own, so…"

Bee gets her inhaler out of her handbag. Inside, I see an owl-print tea towel wrapped around something silver.

"Jesus Christ, Bee, is that a fucking meat cleaver?"

"Language," says Nila hastily. Her kids, thirteen and fifteen, are in the next room on the X-box, but the door is open.

"It's dangerous out there!" Bee, immediately defensive, hefts the cleaver. "Haven't you seen the riots on TV? All the lunatics are coming out! In London there was a prison break, serial killers and rapists, they're all out there!"

Michelle agrees. "We're getting out of town as well. I don't want to be here – I mean – I don't want to be in a city." I have a vision of Michelle, Hayley and their kids crouched in a rustic barn around a picnic basket.

"Are you going to your sister's, Bee?"

"Yeah, what about you?"

"I'll be here."

Bee drops the inhaler.

"Nell, you can't stay in Manchester."

"And where else am I going to go? Mum and Dad are dead, which frankly feels like a mercy. I've lived here over half my life. This is home."

"What about…?" Michelle trails off. My friends watch me warily. Even after two years, even in these circumstances, Kat's name is a mine in an open field. I shrug.

"Oliver called. Wants me to go to London."

"And?"

"And nothing. He got in touch. She didn't."

"She might be scared," says Bee tentatively. "To reach out."

"Fear isn't in Kat's nature."

From next door there's a shriek of delight; one of the kids has triumphed in Call of Duty. Nila checks the clock on the wall. She'll be worrying about the roads.

"So." Michelle looks round. "We'll see each other on the other side, right?"

"Oh God –" Bee starts crying. Nila murmurs a few words of prayer. In this moment I envy her her faith.

"Come here, girls." I hold my arms out, and we fall into a four-way hug. I think of everything we've been through the past twenty-six years. University, hopeless relationships, drugs, marriage and divorce, birth and estrangement, losing parents, jobs, faith, and friends. I know them as well as I know anyone. But as we pull apart, eyes wet, I can see them turning inward, focus redirecting to those they hold most dear, to flesh and blood, to partners and children.

On the way out Michelle takes me aside.

"Come with us. I don't want you to be on your own."

"I'll be fine."

She sighs.

"One of you has to break the silence. You know that, Nell."

I nod mutely. Watch her climb into the Landrover. Across the road, Bee squeezes inside her Smart car, the bag on her elbow hanging heavy with the weight of the meat cleaver. I watch her drive away, wondering if I could, if I would. If I had someone to protect, no question. Even when they cut you out, even when they hate you, there's nothing in the world you won't do for your kids.

Six days left and I'm on my own. I wonder whether I should follow the girls' lead and get out of town. But there really is nowhere to go. Besides, Manchester is what I have left: the familiarity of a place I've lived and loved and fucked up. I can't leave it. I won't.

Day Six

The buildings change, but the figures flailing down their sides look the same all over the world. The Shard. The Eiffel Tower. Pisa. The Empire State. The video's creator had overlaid the footage with R.E.M.'s 'End of the World As We Know It', but was forced to pimp the song with some kind of Europop backing track after the rights police swooped in. The suicide montage has been on YouTube for an hour and it already has eighteen million views.

There's something undeniably compelling about the film. Many of the jumpers are solo, but some are in pairs or groups, gripping each other's hands for as long as they can. I think of the courage required to take that leap. It's not a courage I possess. I've made my preparations: stocked up on vodka and Valium. I'll be unconscious.

The doorbell rings. I check the eyehole and find a smiling, identikit family of husband, wife and young child, each carrying a fat sheaf of leaflets. I swing the door open.

"Yes?"

Their smiles falter at the sight of a black woman in a Kermit-the-Frog nightshirt with unfettered hair. I give them my best arched eyebrow. (Note to self: this brow deserves a place on the Achievements list.)

"Jehovah's Witnesses?" I ask.

The woman looks affronted.

"We are with the one true Church."

"Fuck off."

"The Rapture is coming," squeaks the child.

"Fuck off," I repeat, and shut the door. Ten seconds later, a leaflet slithers through the letterbox and drops onto the floor.

So far I've had the Witnesses, scientologists, infidel bashers, and a few obscure cults I'd never heard of until the asteroid, but their main commandment would appear to be lining their bank accounts with the lifetime savings of pensioners. I should have offered them my overdraft. According to the believers, this is all poetic justice. We were destroying the planet. We had thought ourselves gods. Now God was coming to show us what omnipotent power really looked like.

Online, President Trump has tweeted his delight that the asteroid defence system has been named in his honour. The Guardian should have added irony to its greatest feats.

Leaving the flat takes more courage than it should. The sky is overcast, a fine drizzle beading my coat. I jam on a hat and take a restless walk around town, tracing the empty tramlines down towards Deansgate. A small crowd has gathered on the bridge over the canal. People still remain in the city, though their movements are furtive, wary. In the water I see a body floating, face down. It's not clear how they came to die. I think of the tower montage and an irrational terror seizes me – Kat wouldn't…?

No. Kat wouldn't do that. Kat is not that kind of girl.

Since our estrangement I feel that I know my daughter much better. Perhaps it took the distance for her to come into focus. Our relationship was always fraught, right from the forty-two hours it took to bring her into the world. In birth the hormones are supposed to kick in, activating that nurturing bond, but in my case it didn't happen. I didn't understand. I had thought myself happy; now I cried all the time. No one in my family had ever talked about post-natal depression. I thought I was going mad.

Oliver remained calm and professional. Whilst I unravelled, he seemed immune to the sleepless nights, the baby's crying and the endless cycles of laundry. My depression lifted eventually, but it left me profoundly shaken; no longer sure of myself, my relationship, or my child. The young couple who had picked out buggies and rattles seemed a world away. Now we bickered constantly. I didn't want Kat wearing pink; Oliver loved those saccharine babygrows with 'Daddy's Little Princess'. He was already looking at private schools, I wanted her state educated. Had we had these arguments before? It was true that Oliver had always read The Telegraph. Day by day, I felt myself forced deeper into a mould I didn't fit. I was no longer depressed, but I was suffocating. I was going to lose myself with my Idris Elba husband and my beautiful little girl in her velvet and chiffon party frocks.

And then there was Kat. I assumed she would blossom into the kind of noisy, boisterous brat I had been myself, but my daughter dealt with emotions in a different way to me. If I raised my voice, she stared at me coldly. If I hugged her in public, she stood stiff. She tolerated affection, but never sought it. The one exception was in the aftermath of a nightmare, when she'd crawl into my bed, clammy and trembling, whispering unintelligible words, some private amulet against the dark which only Kat could know.

She was five when I left. Oliver demanded primary custody and even if the circumstances had been in my favour, I didn't want to argue. All I wanted to do was get out. It didn't feel like selfishness, it felt like survival.

I had Kat at weekends. She adapted quickly; kids are resilient, and Kat, even at five, had a core of steel. I kept waiting for the child I knew I should have had to emerge. By the time I accepted that wasn't going to happen it was too late; the rift was unbridgeable. In private, I could make her laugh, but I never met her friends and as she got older the weekends shortened, then dropped away. Eventually I realized I was a part of her life she preferred to keep hidden.

Something broke inside me then.

Over the years I thought I had grown resigned to the situation, accepted my loss, accepted the intractable label of Bad Mother that lurked behind every interaction with a figure of authority or judgemental parent. We can't succeed at everything, I thought. Kat and Oliver moved down to London and I told myself it was for the best.

It's dark by the time I head back to Greengate and I hurry, annoyed with myself for staying out so stupidly late. Across the river from my block there's firelight, music pounding; from my window I can see the impromptu rave that has sprung up the other side of Trinity Way. It's tempting to go down there, but I know it will turn violent later. I login to Facebook, scrolling through the all-encompassing messages of love and desperate optimism. It all feels utterly false.

Oliver calls again but I don't pick up.

I told Kat I didn't remember what happened, and in the immediate aftermath I didn't. But there were chinks in the shell. The night came back in snapshots and sketches.

Her seventeenth birthday. I was surprised to have been invited, but Kat said she wanted me. As an added incentive Oliver wouldn't be there. Once I arrived the reason for my invitation became clear: I was here for the dispensing of some long-awaited punishment.

"Oh, you must meet my mum," Kat introduced me to her friends. She'd relaxed her hair, and although I mourned the natural she looked, in my eyes, more beautiful than Beyoncé. "She left us when I was five. Amazing I'm not a junkie really, isn't it?"

The Bad Mother label floated somewhere to the left and right of my eyes. I remembered then that Kat was taking Psychology as one of her A-levels. Clearly Freud needed removing from the curriculum; people had no idea the damage he was doing. There was red wine on the table. I got stuck in. The evening continued, darts of hostility thrown my way, enough to sting but not quite enough to make me leave. By the time Oliver turned up I was very drunk, and so was Kat.

"Your fucking daughter's learned some really delightful tactics," I said. "I wonder where she could have got those?"

"I'll order you a taxi," said Oliver.

I almost made it out the door. Kat got drunkenly to her feet.

"Oh, look everyone. Mum's leaving. Again!"

I turned. Oliver's hand was on my shoulder. I pushed him away. I felt strangely detached from the scene.

"Come on then, Kat. Why don't you say what you need to say. Get it out, in front of everyone. You'll feel better."

"You think you have a right to tell me what to do? You abandoned us," she said. "You fucked off without a second thought."

"If I'd stayed it would have been miserable for all of us. You would have been miserable."

She wasn't comfortable, I could see that. She wanted the row, but she didn't know how to do rows. She didn't know about yelling until you were hoarse and then crying and laughing and hugging and making up. So she'd got pissed to engineer this confrontation.

"Kat, this isn't you."

"Nell's leaving," said Oliver firmly. His entire body screamed embarrassment. He started making signals to Kat's guests that they should leave. No one moved; I guessed that Kat, a meticulous planner, had briefed them.

"How would you know, Mum? How would you know what is and isn't me?"

"Let's go somewhere and talk about this properly."

"You'd love that, wouldn't you," she sneered. "You'd love to just walk away again."

I gazed at her. My poor conflicted girl, who had hidden so much for so long. What a mess, I thought. What a mess we have made.

I said, "I wish I hadn't had you then."

How do you take back those words? You can't. You can't ever take them back. I couldn't say to Kat, I didn't mean what you thought I meant – that I never wanted you – I meant exactly what I said. I wish I hadn't had you *then.* I wish I'd had you when I was well. When I was happy. When I wasn't halfway through discovering I'd married the wrong man, a man I resented and knew I would eventually hate, if I stayed, and who I was now tethered to irretrievably for the rest of our lives.

I couldn't say any of those things because, unsurprisingly, after that night she said she never wanted to see me again.

Day Five

Alex from Tinder is shorter than advertised with a receding hairline that Instagram filters had managed to obscure. I almost shut the door, but I don't. My cleavage owes some debts to Instagram. We endure the awkward chat phase while I mix up a couple of whisky sours. More whisky than sour.

"So," asks Alex from Tinder. 'What have you been doing, since…?'

"I went to Tesco," I say.

"How was it?"

"No staff, of course, but an old lady with a trolley was using the self-checkout. I felt so guilty I almost paid for this." I lift the whisky bottle. "How about you?"

"Aggressive cycling around town. The buses have all stopped. It's great."

"I daresay I could get used to a pedestrianised Manchester."

This is a lie. I bloody love my car, even if it is a clapped-out old banger. I make a mental note to add *Driving test first time* to 'Achievements'.

Sex with Alex from Tinder is better than expected, which means it's almost good. Afterwards I recoup the whisky and we finish the bottle. We talk drunkenly about the regrets of our lives. The paths we might have taken, probably should have taken. I don't mention Kat. Her name chokes my throat. Sad and weary, I have an abrupt insight into what it must feel like to be old. My mum was sixty-eight when she went, young by today's standards. But she had two decades on me. Mum would have believed the asteroid was the wrath of God. Dad would have replied that if that were the case, God had a terrible sense of perspective. I wish they were here now, though that's a selfish wish. I wish I could ask them how they made it work.

I sleep for a while. When I wake, Alex is sitting on the edge of the bed, hands in his lap, staring out the window. I can hear sirens. There have been more sirens the last few nights. There are people out there who won't abandon their jobs. Better people than me.

"Is it a clear sky?" I ask.

He shakes his head.

"Still clouded."

"In films it's always a clear sky, so you can see it coming."

"I think I prefer it this way."

When Alex has gone I feel a different, smaller tinge of regret. If it wasn't for the asteroid, I might have got in touch again. But perhaps that's just my perspective shifting.

Day Four

The roads are preternaturally quiet as I drive down Oxford Road. Past the Palace Theatre, past the university, through the curry mile and into the student village. Every official media outlet is urging us to stay calm, continue life as normal, but life appears to have already stopped. A blue bus has been abandoned at the crossroads in Fallowfield. I swerve around it and continue south towards Didsbury.

The rescue centre has a closed sign in the window, but I can see someone moving around inside. I tap on the glass. No response. I knock louder. They come to the door. I point to the sign.

"I want to rescue a dog," I mouth.

There's the click of a lock and the door opens cautiously, revealing a thin white girl, younger than Kat, in an oversized hoodie.

"I want to rescue a dog," I say again.

She stares at me for a moment, evaluating, before opening the door wide enough to let me inside. The interior is a pet shop; we go through to the kennels out the back. Barks break out as we enter the yard. I count ten kennels. A couple of Jack Russells, two Staffies. There are always Staffies.

"Have you had a dog before?" asks the girl.

"When I was a kid."

"We only want owners who can offer a forever home."

We look at each other.

"You don't run this centre, do you?" I say.

She shrugs. "Someone has to feed them."

I point to the dog I want, the dog I noticed as soon as we entered the yard. It's a young Husky, male, two or three years old. The kind of dog I have eyed enviously when strolling through parks. The kind of dog you can hug close in a crisis. I crouch down and hold out my hand for the dog to sniff.

"Lovely temperament, that one," says the girl. She's warming up.

"I'll take him. I've got the car outside."

The girl loads up several bags full of dog biscuits and treats, bowls, a leash, and a purple flea collar. The Husky barks and licks my hand enthusiastically.

"I'm amazed you've got petrol," says the girl. "Pumps are dry. Everyone's getting out of town."

"To go where?"

"Fuck knows."

We load up the boot.

"What do I owe you?"

She shakes her head. "His name's Vader, by the way."

"Are you serious?"

"Wasn't me who named him."

Vader takes the passenger seat. Vader is the happiest dog in the world. In my rearview mirror, I watch the girl closing up as we leave, her skinny form hurrying away down the street. The newsagents' door on the corner swings freely on its hinges; glass is scattered over the pavement.

Day Three

Vader loves the car. Vader loves pedestrianized Manchester. In fact, Vader loves everything. In an enthusiasm showdown between Vader and Professor Brian Cox, it's not clear who would win.

My lists have expanded. On the Achievements list, I have added *Travel to five countries not my own*, *Eyebrow*, *Driving test* and *Last minute dog*. After Kat on the Failures list is *Oliver*, obviously, *Cooking*, and *That fucking job at Barclays*.

At two thirty in the afternoon the landline rings. I pick up without thinking.

"Hello?"

"Mum?"

For a few seconds my heart scrunches up, my body freezes. I can only stare at the hundreds of tiny scratches on the parquet floor. Vader's nose comes into my field of vision. He paws at my leg.

"Kat?" It comes out as a croak. I clear my throat. "Kat, is that you?"

There's a few seconds silence, and then her voice comes through, cool and assured.

"Dad said I should speak to you."

"Is that why you're calling? Because your father told you to?"

She hangs up. I curse my inability to self-censor. I distract myself by watching the top 100 gifs of all time. A leopard licks marmite. Its majestic head lifts, eyes and mouth widening in an expression of exhilaration or horror, it's impossible to tell which. Am I a terrible person to be so entertained by a marmite-eating leopard in the final days of Earth?

Half an hour later, we try again. I pace around the flat, phone pressed tight to my ear. Vader translates this as time for a walk and starts barking.

"What's that noise?"

"That's the dog."

"Since when did you have a dog?"

"Since yesterday. His name's Vader."

"Are you serious?"

"I didn't name him."

"Well, that's ridiculous."

I feel immediately defensive on Vader's part.

"He likes it."

"How would you know?"

"Kat, are we going to have a conversation here? Are you okay? I mean, what are you doing, who are you with, where *are* you?"

"I'm with Liam."

"Liam, is that your –?"

"My partner, yes. We live together."

Oliver never mentioned *that*. The bastard.

"Actually, we got married."

"So did Michelle, last week – you remember Michelle?"

"Of course I do."

"I bet there's been a rush on registrars."

"This was last year, Mum."

"Last year. *Last year*."

"Mum –"

"Jesus, Kat. You got *married*? You're nineteen!"

"And I'm not going to make the mistakes you made –"

A chasm of silence opens up. Of course she won't make the same mistakes. She can't. I feel the two years between us then, clear and cold. I feel the rift that stretches beyond the incident, further and further back. It's no good, I think. It's too late.

But when Kat finally speaks her voice is small and scared, and she breaks my heart all over again.

"Mum? It's going to work, isn't it? The Basher?"

"Of course it is," I say firmly. "Professor Cox says so."

"I don't want to die, Mum."

"Kat, no –" The memory tumbles into my head, Kat climbing into my bed after a nightmare, the monsters still present in her frantic beating heart. Clutching her to me, a wrench of that terrible, searing love that feels more akin to fury, at the idea that anyone or anything might hurt my little girl. All these years and everything that's passed between us and that memory is undiminished. There is nothing tender about motherhood; it's open warfare on the heart. And today, I and every other mother on the planet have failed to protect our little girls.

"Dad's a mess," she says. "He came over and just – burst into tears. I've never seen him like that."

"He's scared too, love. He doesn't want to lose you, is all."

Since when have I defended Oliver?

"Everything's so awful."

"I'll drive down to London," I say. "I'll leave right now."

"You won't make it. There's no petrol. The roads are chaos."

"I'll find a way."

"I don't want you to." Her voice trembles. "Don't you see? If you come – it's like there's no hope left."

There's a long pause.

"Okay. But you have to keep in touch. Promise me, Kat."

"Okay. I promise."

I know she'll keep her promise. That's who she is.

Day Two

I watch all of the Star Wars films back to back. Not the prequels, obviously. Vader barks happily, ecstatic to see his namesake up-close and remastered. Whilst Luke Skywalker blows up the death star, Kat and I message back and forth.

Sometimes, the words are easier on a screen.

After you were born, I was depressed for months. I didn't understand what it was then, people didn't talk about post-natal. I thought something inside me had gone wrong. I thought I couldn't be a proper mother…

After you left the nightmares wouldn't stop. I didn't want to tell Dad. It would have upset him or he wouldn't have understood. I was so scared without you there…

What I said that day, it didn't come out right. I've never regretted having you, Kat. What I regret is you never had the family you should have. You never had a family like mine. I wanted that for you so badly.

It was revenge, me getting married. Not that I don't love Liam, I do love him and I always will. But I knew one day you'd find out and I knew it would hurt you. It was stupid.

Not if you love him.

On the day the only person I wanted there was you.

It doesn't matter now. None of it matters.

I hug Vader to me. His fur is so warm against my chest, his canine heart beats twice as fast as another human being. The adoration in his eyes as he gazes up is almost unbearable.

Towards the end of the day, the signal is failing and the texts squeeze out like the final dregs of a toothpaste tube. The networks will be down by morning. I mix coffee and whisky. I don't want to go to sleep. I don't want to let go of my thread to Kat.

Day One

I look at the vodka and strip of Valium on my bedside table. I've got clean sheets, a hot water bottle, a soothing playlist lined up on the laptop. I had it all planned out, but that was before she called. Now the idea of being asleep is abhorrent, impossible. Anyway, I've got Vader to look after. I can't let Vader die alone. I pull on a coat and boots over my pyjamas, grab the vodka and Vader's treats.

The rooftop belongs to the top flat but they cleared out weeks ago. Probably lying on a beach in Barbados. That's one way to go. Somebody's already kicked open the door. I hear voices drifting down, hesitate for a moment, then head up the steps myself, Vader padding behind me, close as a shadow. Does Vader know? Animals have a sixth sense about death.

On the roof there's a small group of people who I recognize as neighbours, although we've never spoken. I don't know their names, but we greet one another. Weirdly, it feels right to be with strangers. It's how we come into the world after all - an unknown quantity.

We sit or stand companionably. The guy from the flat above mine is playing Oasis on a portable speaker. We get chatting, compare gig histories. He agrees that Noel has got more acceptable with age but Liam's still a tosser. It seems absurd now to think I've lived alongside these people for years, but we've never spoken until today. So much mistrust for our fellow human beings. Why didn't we introduce ourselves, make more connections? And even if we survive as a species, can we really do any better, or will it be the same old carousel of shit?

Around now, NASA will be launching the Basher. The sky is very light, very bright, but it might be the pollution, or the residues from thousands of fireworks, or the glow from fires breaking out all over Manchester. The sirens have finally stopped, but even now there are people out there, singing, shouting, fighting. I allow myself to hope. Maybe the asteroid will be destroyed. Maybe we'll all get a second chance, even if we don't deserve it. I text Kat. *I love you.* Message failed. I try WhatsApp. She doesn't reply, but everyone's doing the same thing and the networks must be jammed.

Vader pushes his nose into the palm of my hand. I feed him treats from the rescue centre's collection.

"I should have got Kat a dog," I tell Vader, crouching down

and hugging his shoulders. All at once the fear hits me, vast and impregnable. "I should have –"

My phone vibrates.

love you too mum

I look up. Fierce patches of orange smear the sky. It's beginning. In this moment, I don't care if it's the end. I've got my girl back.

About the Authors

Nina Allan's stories have appeared in numerous magazines and anthologies, including *Best Horror of the Year #6*, *The Year's Best Science Fiction and Fantasy 2013*, and *The Mammoth Book of Ghost Stories by Women*. Her novella *Spin*, a science fictional re-imagining of the Arachne myth, won the BSFA Award in 2014, and her story-cycle The Silver Wind was awarded the Grand Prix de L'Imaginaire in the same year. Her debut novel *The Race*, originally published by NewCon Press, was a finalist for the 2015 BSFA Award, the Kitschies Red Tentacle and the John W. Campbell Memorial Award. Nina lives and works in North Devon.

Rachel Armstrong is Professor of Experimental Architecture at Newcastle University. Her practice is deeply involved in imagining and building new experiences and worlds and interrogating them through a variety of media – from materials to poetry and circus arts. Specifically, she innovates and designs sustainable solutions for the built environment using advanced new technologies such as synthetic biology and smart chemistry. What is passed off by some as 'science fiction' – is to Armstrong a platform for a new civilisation in the making.

Rose Biggin writes stories and plays. Her published fiction includes "A Game Proposition" in *Irregularity*, "The Modjeska Waltz" in *The Adventures of Moriarty* and "The Gunman Who Came In From The Door" in *Defenestration Magazine*. Theatre work includes genderqueer retelling *Victor Frankenstein* and *BADASS GRAMMAR: A Pole/Guitar Composition in Exploded View*. She has a PhD in immersive theatre and tweets at @rosebiggin.

Eric Brown has won the British Science Fiction Award twice for his short stories, and his novel *Helix Wars* was shortlisted for the 2012 Philip K. Dick award. He has published over fifty books, and his latest include the crime novel *Murder at the Loch*, and the SF novel *Jani and the*

Great Pursuit. He writes a monthly science fiction review column for the *Guardian* newspaper and lives in Cockburnspath, Scotland. His website can be found at: www.ericbrown.co.uk.

J.A. Christy's writing career began in infant school when she won best poetry prize with her poem "Winter". Since then she has been writing short stories, screenplays and *SmartYellow*™, her first speculative fiction novel. She holds a PhD in which she explores the stories we use to construct our identities and writes to apply her knowledge to cross the boundaries between science and art, in particular in crime, speculative and science-fiction genres.

Genevieve Cogman is the author of the *Invisible Library* series of novels. She lives in the north of England, and for her day job she works as a clinical classification specialist. Her hobbies include patchwork, knitting, and role-playing games.

Jaine Fenn is a classically trained ballet dancer and author of the Hidden Empire series of far future space opera novels (published by Gollancz), along with numerous short stories, some of which are set in the Hidden Empire universe. You can support her on Patreon (www.patreon.com/jainefenn), follow her on twitter (@jainefenn) or buy her a drink (in the bar, at any time). One in every ten of her bios contains a lie.

Peter F. Hamilton has been writing Space Opera novels for twenty-three years now, so he reckons he's only got another ten years to go and he'll have got away with not having a proper job for most of his adult life. He lives in Rutland with his family, and escapes this Earth every weekday by sitting in his shed at the bottom of the garden to 'write' while listening to playlists of 70s music. Which is what inspired this story.

Nancy Kress is the author of thirty-three books, including twenty-six novels, four collections of short stories, and three books on writing. Her work has won six Nebulas, two Hugos, a Sturgeon, and the John W. Campbell Memorial Award (for *Probability Space*). Most recent works are the Nebula-winning *Yesterday's Kin* (Tachyon, 2014) and *The Best of Nancy Kress* (Subterranean, 2015). Her work has been translated into Swedish, Danish, French, Italian, German, Spanish, Polish, Croatian, Lithuanian, Bulgarian, Romanian, Japanese, Chinese, Korean, Hebrew, Russian, and Klingon, none of which she can read.

Ian McDonald is a science fiction writer living in Holywood Northern Ireland. His first novel *Desolation Road* came out in 1988; his most recent is *Luna: New Moon*, from Gollancz and Tor. Forthcoming is *Luna: Wolf Moon.*

Bryony Pearce lives in the Forest of Dean and is a full-time mum to two children, one husband and various pets. She is vegetarian and loves chocolate, wine and writing. People are often surprised at how dark her writing is, as she is generally pretty nice. When the children let her off taxi duty and out of the house, she enjoys doing school visits, creative writing workshops and other events. Her novels include *Angel's Fury* (a dark thriller centred on reincarnation), *The Weight of Souls* (a thrilling ghost story), *Phoenix Rising* and *Phoenix Burning* (dystopian pirate adventures for teens), *Windrunner's Daughter* (a science-fiction adventure on Mars) and *Wavefunction* (about a boy who can jump between universes). Find out more at: www.bryonypearce.co.uk

Jack Skillingstead is the author of two novels and a collection. He has been a finalist for both the Theodore Sturgeon Award and the Philip K. Dick Award. Since winning Stephen King's "On Writing" contest in 2001, he has sold more than forty short stories to major science fiction magazines and original anthologies. Jack occasionally teaches writing workshops. He lives in Seattle with his wife, writer Nancy Kress.

Tricia Sullivan won the 1999 Arthur C. Clarke Award for *Dreaming in Smoke.* Her other novels include *Maul*, *Lightborn*, and *Occupy Me.* A New Jersey native, she now lives in Shropshire with her family. She is an MSc student at the Astrophysics Research Institute.

E.J. Swift is the author of The Osiris Project trilogy, a speculative fiction series set in a world radically altered by climate change, comprising *Osiris*, *Cataveiro* and *Tamaruq*. Her short fiction has appeared in anthologies including *The Best British Fantasy* (Salt Publishing, 2013

and 2014) and the digital book *Strata* (Penguin Random House, 2016). Swift was shortlisted for a 2013 BSFA Award in the Short Fiction category for her story "Saga's Children" (*The Lowest Heaven*, Jurassic) and was longlisted for the 2015 Sunday Times EFG Short Story Award for "The Spiders of Stockholm" (*Irregularity*, Jurassic).

Adrian Tchaikovsky is the author of the acclaimed ten-book Shadows of the Apt series starting with *Empire in Black and Gold* (Tor UK). His other works include novels *Guns of the Dawn* and *Children of Time* and the new series Echoes of the Fall, starting with *The Tiger and the Wolf* (all Tor UK), short story collection *Feast and Famine* (Newcon Press) and novellas *The Bloody Deluge* and *Even in the Cannon's Mouth*, both for Abaddon. He has also written numerous short stories and been shortlisted for the David Gemmell Legend Award, the British Fantasy Award and the Arthur C. Clarke Award.

Neil Williamson's debut novel, *The Moon King* (NewCon Press), was shortlisted for the BSFA Award and the British Fantasy Society Holdstock Award. His short fiction has been shortlisted for the BSFA and British Fantasy awards and, with Andrew J Wilson, he edited *Nova Scotia: New Scottish Speculative Fiction*, which was shortlisted for the World Fantasy Award. He lives, works, writes and makes music in Glasgow, Scotland.

NewCon Press: The First Ten Years

2006
Time Pieces (anthology)

2007
disLOCATIONS (anthology)
In Storage (collaborative short story chapbook)

2008
Celebration: Commemorating 50 Years of the BSFA (anthology)
Myth-Understandings (anthology)
Subterfuge (anthology)

2009
Beloved of My Beloved – Ian Watson & Roberto Quaglia (collection)
Starship Fall – Eric Brown (novella)
The Gift of Joy – Ian Whates (collection)
And God Created Zombies – Andrew Hook (novel)
The Push – Dave Hutchinson (novella)

2010
The Bitten Word (anthology)
Conflicts (anthology)
The Unlikely World of Faraway Frankie – Keith Brooke (novel)
Orgasmachine – Ian Watson (novel)
Anniversaries: The Write Fantastic (anthology)
Shoes, Ships, and Cadavers: Tales from North Londonshire (anthology)

2011
Further Conflicts (anthology)
Fables from the Fountain (anthology)
A Glass of Shadow – Liz Williams (collection)
Now We Are Five (chapbook anthology)
Cyber Circus – Kim Lakin-Smith (novel)
Diary of a Witchcraft Shop – Trevor Jones & Liz Williams (humour)

2012
Imaginings 1: Cold Grey Stones – Tanith Lee (collection)
Dark Currents (anthology)

Saving for a Sunny Day – Ian Watson (collection)
The Outcast and the Little One – Andy West (novel)
Imaginings 2: Last and First Contacts – Stephen Baxter (collection)
Hauntings (anthology)
Imaginings 3: Stories from the Northern Road – Tony Ballantyne
Imaginings 4: Objects in Dreams – Lisa Tuttle (collection)
2013
Across the Event Horizon – Mercurio D. Rivera (collection)
The Peacock Cloak – Chris Beckett (collection)
Imaginings 5: Microcosmos – Nina Allan (collection)
Diary of a Witchcraft Shop 2 – Trevor Jones & Liz Williams (humour)
Imaginings 6: Feast and Famine – Adrian Tchaikovsky (collection)
Looking Landwards (anthology)
Legends: Stories in Honour of David Gemmell (anthology)
Imaginings 7: Twember – Steve Rasnic Tem (collection)
Shake Me to Wake Me – Stan Nicholls (collection)
Colder Greyer Stones – Tanith Lee (collection, expanded and reissued)

2014
The Moon King – Neil Williamson (novel)
Imaginings 8: Strange Visitors – Eric Brown (collection)
Noir (anthology)
La Femme (anthology)
The Race – Nina Allan (novel)
Marcher – Chris Beckett (novel)
Sibilant Fricative – Adam Roberts (nonfiction)
Paradox: Stories Inspired by the Fermi Paradox (anthology)
The End – Gary McMahon (novel)
Imaginings 9: Saint Rebor – Adam Roberts (collection)

2015
Total Conflict (eBook only compilation anthology)
Pelquin's Comet – Ian Whates (novel)
Imaginings 10: Sleeps with Angels – Dave Hutchinson (collection)
Legends 2: Stories in Honour of David Gemmell (anthology)
A Better Way to Die – Paul Cornell (collection)
Rave and Let Die – Adam Roberts (nonfiction)
Lifelines and Deadlines – James Lovegrove (nonfiction)
Imaginings 11: The Light Warden – Liz Williams (collection)

Orcs: Tales of Maras Dantia – Stan Nicholls (collection)

2016

Digital Dreams: A Decade of SF by Women (eBook anthology)
Obsidian: A Decade of Horror Stories by Women (eBook anthology)
The Dead Trilogy – Paul Kane (eBook collection)
Splinters of Truth – Storm Constantine (collection)
Azanian Bridges – Nick Wood (novel)
The 1000 Year Reich – Ian Watson (collection)
Disturbed Universes – David L. Clements (collection)
Secret Language – Neil Williamson (collection)
The Sign in the Moonlight – David Tallerman (collection)
Now We Are Ten (anthology)
Crises and Conflicts (anthology)
The Spoils of War (Tales of the Apt 1) – Adrian Tchaikovsky (collection)
X Marks the Spot (anthology/nonfiction)
Just Three Words – V.C Linde (poetry)
Ten Tall Tales and Twisted Limericks (anthology)
Tanith By Choice: The Selected Short Fiction of Tanith Lee (collection)
A Time of Grief (Tales of the Apt 2) – Adrian Tchaikovsky (collection)
Imaginings 12: Mementoes – Keith Brooke (collection)
Barcelona (anthology)
The Iron Tactician – Alastair Reynolds (novella)

Lightning Source UK Ltd.
Milton Keynes UK
UKOW02f0350210616

276753UK00003B/53/P